HER MONTANA CHRISTMAS COWBOY

BIG SKY CHRISTMAS BOOK 1

JENNA HENDRICKS

J.L. HENDRICKS

Isla,
Cowgirl up! Love that
you ride horses. Keep it up!
God Bless,
Jenna H

Cover Design by Victoria Cooper

First Edition October 2020

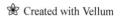 Created with Vellum

BOOKS BY JENNA HENDRICKS

Triple J Ranch –

Book 0 - Finding Love in Montana (Join my newsletter to get this book for free)

Book 1 - Second Chance Ranch – also available on audio

Book 2 – Cowboy Ranch

Book 3 – Runaway Cowgirl Bride

Book 4 – Faith of A Cowboy

Book 5 – TBD

Book 6 – TBD

Big Sky Christmas –

Book 1 – Her Montana Christmas Cowboy

Book 2 – Her Christmas Rodeo Cowboy

See these titles and more: https://JennaHendricks.com

OTHER BOOKS BY J.L. HENDRICKS (MY 1ST PEN NAME)

New Orleans Magic

Book 0.5: Magic's Not Real

Book 1: New Orleans Magic

Book 2: Hurricane of Magic

Book 3: Council of Magic

Worlds Away Series

Book 0: Worlds Revealed (join my Newsletter to get this exclusive freebie)

Book 1: Worlds Away

Book 2: Worlds Collide

Book 2.5: Worlds Explode

Book 3: Worlds Entwined

A Shifter Christmas Romance Series

Book 0: Santa Meets Mrs. Claus

Book 1: Miss Claus and the Secret Santa

Book 2: Miss Claus under the Mistletoe

Book 3: Miss Claus and the Christmas Wedding

Book 4: Miss Claus and Her Polar Opposite

The FBI Dragon Chronicles

Book 1: A Ritual of Fire

Book 2: A Ritual of Death

Book 3: A Ritual of Conquest

See these titles and more at https://www.jlhendricksauthor.com/

TABLE OF CONTENTS

Prologue..1
Chapter 1..17
Chapter 2..25
Chapter 3..31
Chapter 4..39
Chapter 5..49
Chapter 6..63
Chapter 7..77
Chapter 8..85
Chapter 9..95
Chapter 10..107
Chapter 11..111
Chapter 12..121
Chapter 13..131
Chapter 14..141
Chapter 15..147
Chapter 16..157
Chapter 17..167
Chapter 18..175
Chapter 19 185

Chapter 20...193
Chapter 21..201
Chapter 22..205
Chapter 23..213
Chapter 24..221
Chapter 25..231
Chapter 26..237
Chapter 27..247
Chapter 28..257
Epilogue..261
Author's Notes...271

NEWSLETTER SIGN-UP

By signing up for my newsletter, you will get a free copy of the prequel to the Triple J Ranch series, Finding Love in Montana. As well as another free book from J.L. Hendricks.

If you want to make sure you hear about the latest and greatest, sign up for my newsletter at: Subscribe to Jenna Hendricks' newsletter. I will only send out a few e-mails a month. I'll do cover reveals, snippets of new books, and give-aways or promos in the newsletter, some of which will only be available to newsletter subscribers.

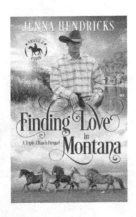

PROLOGUE

"Oh!" Chloe Manning yelled as her foot slipped where the driveway met wet grass. The water pooling on the concrete driveway wasn't something she'd planned on when scheduling her move. Since it had rained early that morning, she could not have foreseen the hazard and rescheduled. But, she also knew that her brothers and sister had scheduled their week to help on this one day. "Great, just what I ne—"

A strong, masculine hand reached down and offered to help her up.

"Thanks," she said without looking up.

"My pleasure." A husky voice that Chloe didn't recognize turned her face up just as she stood, and she yanked her hand out of his. "Ah!" Not looking where she was going, Chloe fell over the headboard she had dropped when she'd fallen the first time. This time she fell on the wooden headboard and smacked her knee good.

"I'm sorry, I shouldn't have let go until you were steady." The stranger furrowed his brow and bent down to help her get back up, again.

"No, no. It was all my fault." Chloe's face heated up, and

she did her best to stand. She inhaled a quick breath when she put pressure on her right leg. While she knew enough medicine to know she hadn't broken anything, she was going to be sore.

In addition, she'd fallen flat on her face not once, but twice, in front of a very handsome cowboy. Her pride had also taken a huge hit. To make matters worse, Chloe hadn't dressed to impress; she was wearing an oversized, faded University of Montana sweatshirt and yoga pants. Her blonde hair was up in a messy ponytail, and she had zero makeup on. The only upside was that she doubted this handsome cowboy would recognize her again.

A bright, white smile greeted her when she stopped wobbling and took a step away from him. "Thank you. I don't know what's gotten into me today."

"Are you the one moving in?" The cowboy looked between her and the house.

Chloe nodded. "Yup."

"Well, welcome to Frenchtown. You must be the new medical billing manager everyone has been talking about." The cute cowboy put his hand out. "I'm Brandon Beck."

Well, there went that thought. He knew exactly who she was. No way was she going to be able to hide her embarrassment behind anonymity.

Standing taller, she straightened her sweatshirt and blew her bangs out of her eyes. When she took his hand, a jolt of electricity swept through her entire being. "Ah, I'm…" She cleared her throat. "I'm Chloe Manning." She shook his hand and noted the calluses, but also the strength in his warm touch.

"Nice to meet you, Miss Manning." When he ended the handshake, he touched the brim of his hat and nodded.

"This is my sister, Elizabeth, and our brothers." Chloe

pointed to them all and introduced her five brothers to Brandon.

Elizabeth looked between Chloe and Brandon and gave her twin sister a sly smile. If Elizabeth didn't know better, she'd think Chloe already had an admirer. But really, who *wouldn't* be attracted to Chloe, even in moving clothes? The men of Beacon Creek had always admired her sister. The only reason Chloe wasn't already married was because she had made it known far and wide that she wanted to move away as soon as possible.

Brandon took a closer look at the newest resident to Frenchtown, and something in his gut told him to watch out for this little filly. She just might cause *him* to fall at *her* feet. He wondered if that would be so bad.

* * *

ONCE BRANDON HAD MOVED ON, the sisters went inside with the headboard and set it up in Chloe's new bedroom.

"Wow, sis. You did good. This is a rental?" Elizabeth Manning walked around the room checking out the wooden floor and blocked wainscoting on all the walls. "There's so much potential with this place."

Chloe Manning agreed. She couldn't wait until the day the owners let her buy it. This was exactly what she wanted. The deal she'd made was to rent for a year, and if everyone was happy then she would buy it. The owners wanted to make sure she stayed there with her job and didn't go home. Mr. and Mrs. Rice, who owned the quaint house, lived next door and felt it was important to like their neighbors. They worried if they sold her the house now, she would leave and sell to someone they may not like.

Chloe knew she was home and wouldn't be going

anywhere. "Yes, I think I'm going to be very happy in this house, and in this town." She beamed at her sister as they unloaded their boxes into a spare room.

Chloe and Elizabeth were twins. While Chloe had always wanted to get out of Beacon Creek, Elizabeth was happy to live there for the rest of her life. When Chloe was offered the chance to move to Frenchtown and manage the local medical clinic's administrative side, she'd jumped at the chance to leave her small hometown. Not that Frenchtown was much bigger, but it did offer her a chance at new experiences and a promotion at work.

The plan was to work in the Frenchtown Clinic and manage it for the next five to seven years, and then she could start applying for jobs in the big cities, like Bozeman or Helena. Then, she would be doing exactly what she had wanted her entire life—get out of Dodge, so to speak.

"What about the men? If they're all as handsome as that cowboy we just met, then I think I won't be the only one getting married next year," Elizabeth teased her sister.

Heat shot up Chloe's neck and face. She deserved the ribbing after everything she'd put Elizabeth through when her now fiancé came back to town last summer.

The man who had helped Chloe up from the ground was gorgeous. Too bad he'd met her when she was at her worst. No makeup, hair a mess, and then to fall flat on her backside? She knew he wouldn't be back.

Just thinking about slipping and falling in front of the handsome Brandon Beck caused her face to heat up again. She wasn't normally a klutz, but today seemed to be her day of making a fool out of herself.

Even after he'd helped her up, she'd still tripped over the headboard because she wasn't looking where she was going. Instead, she was focused on the very good-looking and tall cowboy with chocolate-brown eyes and medium-brown hair that looked as though it needed a cut. His hair curled around his ears and above the back of his collar, which only served to make Chloe even more attracted to the cowboy.

All she could think of was running her fingers through his soft hair. Where that thought came from, she couldn't say. But when she'd realized where her mind was, that was when she'd tripped over the headboard.

C hloe Manning loved Christmas. It was the best time of the year. Not only were people nicer in general, but the scents surrounding Christmas always energized Chloe. She had a habit of heading into the little coffee shop that served the best peppermint mochas she'd ever had.

The peppermint mocha was on their menu from the day after Thanksgiving until New Year's Day, and the previous Christmas season she had spent every day stopping in there before heading in to work.

While it did cost a lot, she needed something to help her feel more grounded. And probably to help her feel better after Brandon had left. While the sweet drink didn't heal her heart, it did comfort her and help her get going every morning. Then, in the afternoon she would make a cup of Joy Christmas tea to get her through the rest of the day.

This year, she was bound and determined to keep her little routine up starting the moment the Frenchtown Roasting Company began serving her favorite beverage. Not because she was still bemoaning the loss of Brandon, but because she was going to need the energy.

"Hi, Lottie." Chloe smiled at her friend when she walked into the Frenchtown Roasting Company. It was mid-November, but the owner of the shop was already beginning to decorate for Christmas.

Some time after Chloe left the previous morning with her mocha, Lottie had put up garland around the windows and doors that was wrapped in red-and-white, candy cane-striped chunky ribbon. Chloe knew that from now until Thanksgiving there would be something new added every day, and she couldn't wait to see as it unfolded each morning.

Music played softly on the overhead speakers. It wasn't Christmas music, yet. Lottie was adamant about waiting for Black Friday before she began the Christmas tunes. Today, it sounded like Lottie had chosen 80s pop. Every day it was a different type of music, or a different era. The electronic notes of a song that sounded faintly familiar played, and then the distinctive voice of Simon Le Bon came over the air and filled her spirit with peace. Chloe would know that voice anywhere.

One of her favorite songs was "Rio," but she was also a huge fan of "Hungry Like the Wolf." Lottie must have put on their album, because the next song was also by Duran Duran.

Chloe chuckled and looked out the window before heading to the line to place her order. The view out the window onto the street was almost like a Christmas card. An inch of snow had fallen overnight, and it hadn't yet melted or turned to goo. It would soon enough, but for now she was going to take in the sight. Chloe loved the snow, especially during the Christmas season. And now that the coffee shop was beginning its decorating, she hoped it snowed a little bit every night just so she could *feel* Christmas surrounding her.

She knew Christmas was much more than decorations and gifts. As a Christian, she had grown up going to church and learning the true meaning of Christmas. But that didn't mean she couldn't enjoy the flavors, scents, and images of the season.

This was what had helped Chloe bond with Lottie last year. That first morning she'd walked past the coffee shop and saw the beginning of the Christmas decorations, and it had put the first smile on her face in a week. She had just learned that Brandon was leaving town to join a rodeo crew. He wasn't going to ride, but he was going to work with the horses and bulls.

Brandon wasn't planning on coming home when the season was over, either. He would be heading to a ranch in South Dakota, where he would stay with the owners of the cattle company he'd be working for. Not even a long-distance relationship could work if he would only be home once a year, if that.

When Brandon broke up with her after only dating a for month, she felt like he'd ripped her heart out of her chest. Logically, she knew it had only been a month and they shouldn't have gotten so serious so quickly, but she had fallen in love with him the moment he'd helped her up from her fall when she was moving into her house.

Since he'd left, she hadn't seen him. Not even once.

That Christmas she drove home for one day, and then came back Christmas night so she could be at work the next morning. As the new person, she wasn't allowed any vacation time yet. Which was a good thing. Being so busy helped her get through the rough time. As did the peppermint mochas and daily chats she had with Lottie.

"Chloe! Good morning, my friend. I have a surprise for you." Charlotte Keith, who went by the nickname of Lottie, walked around the coffee bar to give her friend a hug.

Chloe's eyes widened. "Really? Do you have a new brew for me to try?"

Lottie loved to experiment with different roasts and flavored beans. Usually she had Chloe try the new flavors before deciding if she was going to sell them.

The coffee shop owner shook her head. "Nope, something better." She made her way behind the espresso maker and began crafting a specialty coffee. "No peeking. I want this to be a surprise."

Without being able to see the labels on the ingredients, Chloe had no idea what Lottie was making her.

Her nose lifted and she smelled the air, but with so many different types of coffee and teas being served up, Chloe had no clue what Lottie was doing. "Do you have a new Christmas blend for me to try?" She couldn't stand there waiting without talking, and she really did want to know what Lottie had in mind.

It wasn't Thanksgiving yet, so she knew it wasn't her favorite drink. A month ago, Chloe had tried to talk Lottie into serving up the Christmas drinks early, like a lot of the big city coffee shops did. The proprietor did love Christmas, and she always started decorating early, so it only made sense. But Lottie was adamant about waiting for Thanksgiving.

Lottie only grinned and continued making her drink.

Chloe could tell it was going to be some sort of flavored mocha. She knew the pump for the mocha flavoring, and when Lottie pumped it four times into her large cup, she at least recognized that ingredient. The bottle holding the flavored syrup was covered, so she couldn't read the label.

When Chloe thought her friend was done, Lottie turned around to the cabinet behind her and pulled out a shaker bottle, also covered, and poured something out on top. Then followed it up with something else. Since Lottie had her back turned, she was blocking Chloe's view of the masterpiece in progress.

Excitement rang through Chloe as she wondered what it could be. She had been up to Bozeman at Thanksgiving before and had a fancy cinnamon mocha once. She thought that might be the drink Lottie was making. If it was, she'd be in here every day before work getting one of those until her peppermint mochas were available.

Lottie turned around with the white cup already covered. "Tada!" She extended the drink to Chloe. "Let me know what you think."

When Chloe took a sniff, she was in heaven. She couldn't believe her friend had done this for her. Before she said anything, she took a sip and sighed in utter delight. "Oh, I think this is even better than last year."

"I knew you'd like it." Lottie clapped her hands and her blonde ponytail swished behind her.

After two more very satisfying sips, Chloe licked some of the peppermint-flavored cream off her lips and eyed her friend. "I thought you said the peppermint mocha couldn't come out until *after* Thanksgiving. What's up?"

When Chloe had spent an hour trying to talk her friend into bringing out the drink early and Lottie emphatically declined many times, Chloe had resigned herself to waiting a few more weeks for her favorite drink. Something must have happened to get Lottie to make it early. Granted, it was only about two weeks early, but still.

Something was wrong. Chloe's shoulders stiffened and she set the cup of coffee on the counter in anticipation of bad news.

The smile on Lottie's face faltered, and she looked around the shop. She waved her friend back to the break room.

Chloe picked up her drink and followed her friend.

Once they were both in the room, Lottie took a deep breath. "Alright. I don't know how this is going to affect you, which was why I brought the Christmas drink out early." She bit her lip, hating that she was going to be the bearer of bad news. "You might want to take a seat." Lottie pulled out a chair.

Chloe was really worried. She hoped her friend wasn't going to tell her she was sick or something horrible like that. But that wouldn't cause Lottie to bring out Chloe's favorite drink, would it? "What's going on? You're worrying me." Chloe set her drink on the table and took the offered seat. "Are you alright?"

Lottie laughed. "I'm fine. Sorry, I'm making this out to be more than it really is."

Chloe blinked and waited.

"Well"—Lottie took a deep breath—"Brandon is coming home. For good."

A sharp pain hit Chloe's chest, but she wasn't going to acknowledge it. And she certainly wasn't going to let Lottie know about it. Her fingers flexed and she tried to rub her chest, but as her hand went up to the spot, she redirected it to grab the cup of peppermint mocha.

Before Chloe said a word, she needed some liquid courage. She took a long drink from her cup and winced when the hot liquid burned its way down her throat. "Why?" She couldn't get anything else out before she swallowed…hard.

Lottie sighed. "This isn't known yet, but you know how gossip goes. Plus, where you work." She winced. She was actually surprised that Chloe didn't know this yet. "Brandon's mom is sick."

Chloe's brows furrowed, and she thought back to the last time she'd seen Mrs. Beck. She had seen her in the clinic a few times over the last few months. She also knew, but could not say, that several referrals to doctors in Helena had been ordered. However, she had never heard the diagnosis. She wasn't going to ask Lottie if she knew, but when she got into the clinic she would look it up. She probably had some forms on her desk waiting for her in regards to the billing for Mrs. Beck's latest visits, which would say something about her diagnosis.

Since Chloe was the medical billing manager, she would have access to anything in a patient's file. But, she would have to be very careful with the information when she looked it up. Normally she didn't bother with reading a patient's diagnosis—she only managed the files and submitted the billing for insurance or Medicare payments.

With a heavy heart, she sighed and nodded. "So, he's moving home? When?" Most people who got sick usually had cancer or heart disease, if it wasn't an accident. Had Mrs. Beck been injured in an accident, she would have known that for sure. So, it was most likely cancer or heart disease. She felt awful for the nice, quiet rancher.

"Soon. I don't have an exact date. But he's needed back here on the ranch to help his mom. She's not doing well." Lottie winced, knowing this was going to hurt her friend more than anything else going on at the moment.

Mrs. Beck had always been very nice to Chloe. Even after Brandon left, she always had a smile and nice things to say. In small towns most single ladies gossiped, but not Mrs. Beck. Since her husband had died five years earlier, she had been too busy to worry about gossiping. And with Brandon gone for the past year, there certainly wasn't any time for the lady to sit around drinking tea, or whatever those gossipmongers drank, and talk about other people's lives.

Chloe saw her every Sunday at church, and while the

woman did talk to a few of the parishioners and attended most events, she wasn't a talker. Mrs. Beck seemed to listen more than she spoke.

When they first met, Chloe got the feeling that the woman was a bit shy. Over the past year, Mrs. Beck had been seen at some of the local events, and at least once a month she would help out with various charities. In fact, she was usually the person who headed up the Christmas festival. Her illness must be the reason Chloe hadn't seen her at the last planning meeting.

"That's horrible. I hope she'll be alright. I'll keep her in my prayers." Chloe sighed and sat back in her chair.

Brandon coming home was going to be tough, but poor Mrs. Beck. If Brandon was coming home before the planned time, then it must be serious. He'd had to leave for at least three years to learn the business and make the contacts needed so his ranch could raise and provide more bulls for the rodeo.

When Brandon had first told her about his plans to leave, she'd asked him if he would be home soon, but when he told her it would take three to five years to learn the ropes, she was torn up. While they hadn't been together very long, there was something about Brandon that made her think he was the *one*.

Her sister told her to take it slow when she spoke about her feelings for the cowboy, and now she wished she would have listened. While Chloe was glad that Brandon would be coming home to help take care of his mother, she hoped she wouldn't have to see him too often. At least, not until she got used to the idea of him being back.

She would have to be very careful around town. The last thing she needed was the handsome cowboy breaking her heart again. No way was she going to give him a chance to hurt her. Not after what she'd gone through last year.

Right after he left, Chloe had taken it hard. But eventually she'd gotten past him. Although, she had only been on one date in the past year, and it wasn't good. She did think that she could see Brandon and not be affected by their past…too much.

No matter what, he couldn't see that he still had any claim to her heart. For he did not. Did he?

CHAPTER 1

"Mom, are you here?" Brandon Beck called out as he entered his family ranch. He put his hat on the peg near the door and took off his jacket and hung it on the peg under his hat. Right where he had always put his outer gear.

He hadn't been back since last Christmas, when he was only here for two days. That was the plan: he was supposed to be gone for three years minimum, only coming home for Christmas. This year he was supposed to come home for two weeks for Christmas and New Year's, and have a real vacation with his mother, sister, and her family.

But sometimes the best-laid plans, and all that…

Now, he was home for good. It felt right, but also wrong.

It wouldn't have bothered him to be home—he loved his ranch and Frenchtown. It was the reason he had to come home that had him upset. If he was a better son he would have noticed the signs sooner, and his mom could have gotten the help she needed earlier. Who knew how much damage had been done in the past year while he was gone? And she'd ignored most of her issues only because she had too much to handle at the ranch.

Yes, they had help. But not nearly enough. Not when his mother needed to take it easy now and go to the doctor so much for testing. Soon, hopefully, things would get better and she would improve. If only he knew more about her condition, then he could do more to help her. He wasn't going to let his mother go through this all alone. Brandon was going to be by her side the entire time.

Nothing, not even the ranch, would take precedence over his mother and her health.

"In the kitchen, dear," Melanie Beck called out.

Brandon dropped his bag in the entryway and headed back to the large kitchen to greet his mother. "Mom, it's been too long. I'm sorry I wasn't here sooner." He leaned down and kissed his mom on the top of her head.

Patch, their old Australian Kelpie, stood up and came to him. Brandon leaned down to pet the old dog. "Hey, Patch. I see you're keeping a close eye on Mom. Good boy."

Melanie sat at the kitchen table, too achy to stand up. But she wasn't about to complain to her son. Instead, she put as much as she could behind her smile and patted her son's arm when he stood back up. "Why don't you get a cup of coffee and take a seat with me?"

"Of course. How about I bring over the rest of the pot?" Brandon walked to the cupboard and pulled out his favorite coffee mug. It was black with the words, *The 2nd Amendment is my God-given right* in white. And on the other side of the mug was a cowboy holding a shotgun in his left hand. He'd always thought it was funny that a left-handed, gun-toting cowboy was taking about "right" when he held his gun in his left hand. No one else got the joke but him.

A smile crossed his face as he filled the mug. He was home. Something inside him settled and he sighed.

Then he pulled out the dark-green coffee carafe, filled it

with the remaining coffee from the pot, and went and joined his mother. He knew from experience they would sit there for a few hours discussing the business of the ranch before she ever answered a single question about her health.

Brandon would let her do it her way. As much as he wanted to talk about her treatments and what was next for her, he also knew she had to do it her way. His mother was tough as nails, but cried whenever they had to put an animal down. It didn't matter if it was a pet, a cow, or a bull. Her tough exterior only covered up her soft heart.

Patch was back on his old doggie bed, watching his mom. In the past the dog always stuck close to Melanie, but there seemed to be something more going on here. It was almost as though Patch was keeping watch over his mother. The dog even whimpered a little when Brandon noticed his mother wince.

They finished off the coffee and started another pot by the time Melanie got Brandon all up to speed on the ranch and its comings and goings since he'd left. Thankfully, it being winter, there wasn't a lot going on now.

The ranch hands had harvested the last of the fall crops, and the animals had all been inspected and were healthy. Come the new year, they would have a few new cattle. Hopefully they would even have a bull or two that could be raised and trained for the rodeo. He couldn't choose the sex of the cattle—only God could do that.

Brandon mentally made plans to ride out the next morning and check on the cattle himself. He never liked to have cows delivering during the dead of winter, but it did make for tougher cattle when they were born during a massive snowstorm. Surviving hard winters only served to force the cattle to be strong.

For the next two to three months, it would be all about

ensuring the cattle stayed healthy and doing indoor improvements to the barn and house. They always saved inside work for the winter if they could.

"Mom"—Brandon put his hand on his mother's—"tell me about you. What does the doctor say? Is there anything we should be doing to help you?" He had looked up her condition online, but sometimes you just could not trust the internet.

Melanie winced, not wanting to talk about her condition. It was all still new to her, and she wasn't sure yet how to feel about it. Both of her children wanted to take care of her, but her daughter was married with four children of her own and lived several hours away. Bayley could not be expected to help care for her.

When she'd told Brandon about her sickness, he quit right away and came home. The rancher her son worked for understood and supported Brandon's decision to leave, but she felt rotten for being so weak. Her son wanted to do that work and learn about what it took to raise championship bulls. If they could get their own stock of bulls going, they wouldn't have to depend so much on the price of beef.

With how the government had treated cattle ranchers these past years, diversifying was more important than ever. She had seen ranchers driven out of business by the government that was supposed to protect them. More and more of the American beef supply was coming from outside the United States. Not because they couldn't produce enough, but because the government was on a kick to outsource everything they possibly could to foreign countries. It made no sense.

She sighed. "Well, I have to take it easy. I just started a new medicine. It should help me to feel better in a few weeks if it's the right one for me to take. Thankfully there are many options these days for multiple sclerosis treatments."

"Is there a cure?" Brandon had read that a lot of researchers were working on a cure, but to his knowledge there was not one yet.

His mother shook her head. "No, only medicine to help slow the progression of the disease. And some say a paleo diet is best."

Brandon's brows furrowed. "Paleo? You mean all meat and no carbs?"

She smiled. Her son knew her well. "Yes, well. I guess I can have some carbs, but not many."

Not sure what that meant, Brandon thought about what he had read. "I think I did read something about an anti-inflammatory diet being the best way to go for MS patients. I ordered a cookbook online, and it should be here any day now."

Melanie stood up with shaky legs. "Yes, a package arrived for you this morning." She left the kitchen, doing her best to not let her son see how weak she was. Her primary care doctor wanted to give her a walker to use when she felt the weakness in her legs, but she refused to look like an old woman. She could walk without any help, thank you very much. She just needed to go slower.

By the time she made it back to the kitchen, she needed to sit down before her legs gave out on her. It was one of her worst days in weeks. If this new medicine didn't help her, she might have to bite the bullet and get a walker. Maybe a cane would work? There were some very interesting canes. One of her neighbors had a cane with a sword inside it.

Maybe if she got one, she could tell herself it was a tool for self-defense. They had been dealing with coyote issues lately. Anything would be better than a walker. Only old people used them. And by George, she was *not* old.

Brandon took the package from his mother and eyed her. There was something wrong with her gait. "Mom, are you having trouble walking?" He scratched his head and narrowed his eyes.

She refused to look at him. "I'm just tired. No need to worry about me." In an effort to take the focus off her, she asked, "So, have you had a chance to talk with Chloe yet?" Melanie had always liked the girl and hoped that Brandon would open his eyes and see they were a perfect match. But her son was a typical male.

"Changing the subject?" Brandon did not want to talk about his ex. It had taken forever for him to get over her when he left. The last thing he needed was Chloe Manning taking up all his waking—and sleeping—thoughts. No, he needed to focus on his mom and their ranch. He didn't have time to date the beautiful blonde.

Besides, he doubted she would still be interested in him. Most likely she was dating someone else now. It had been a year since he'd left her.

Melanie knew when to leave well enough alone. She would have to find a way to get the two together now that he was back home. But for now, dinner was needed. "How about pizza for dinner tonight? I didn't have a chance to get into town for supplies this week, so I'm afraid I don't have anything prepared yet."

Brandon knew something was very wrong. His mother would never choose to heat up pizza for her family, even if it was just the two of them. When he was growing up, he would have to beg her to let them have pizza a few times a year. Eventually when he was a teenager and could drive, he would drive into town for pizza most every Friday. But his mother would always make a proper meal.

"How about I go into town and get supplies and stop by the diner for something healthier?" He raised a brow at his mother, who smiled in return.

She put a hand on his forearm. "Thank you, dear. I would like that very much. What did you have in mind?"

"I think we should have the diner's famous chef salad." Brandon knew that salads full of meat and colorful veggies would be better for his mother than a pizza full of carbs and fat. "How about I look through my new cookbook and pick out a few recipes, and then you can put together a shopping list for me? I can help cook tomorrow."

Melanie raised a brow. "You, cook? Since when has my son ever cooked a meal?"

He chuckled. "Since I moved out of my momma's house." While he lived on a prosperous ranch, he did not live in the main house. He had a small trailer with a tiny kitchen. Over the past year he had gotten tired of microwave dinners and taught himself how to cook some basic meals. Turned out he was a fairly decent cook. He wouldn't go so far as to call himself a chef, but he knew his mother would be pleasantly surprised when he made his favorite beef stew.

The crockpot was his friend. It was difficult to mess up a meal in the slow cooker as long as he kept it on low all day long.

CHAPTER 2

The next morning was Saturday, and Chloe didn't have to go into work. As an administrator, she only had to work Monday through Friday. She loved lazy Saturdays, when she could take her time getting up and walking over to the coffee shop her best friend owned and operated. She would have breakfast, sit by the window, and watch as the inhabitants of her little town busied themselves down Main Street.

Today was a real treat. It was chocolate chip pancake day, and since Lottie had started serving the peppermint mochas, she was about to be in heaven. During the week, breakfast at the Frenchtown Roasting Company was all about quick and easy. But every Saturday was a different special. Once a month it was pancakes.

Chloe only ever had breakfast at the coffee shop on pancake day. The rest of the month she made healthy breakfasts for herself.

And she wasn't the only one who enjoyed the monthly treat.

After Brandon had checked on the cattle, he came back to

find his mother sitting at the table drinking coffee. Normally, she would have had breakfast all prepared for him. But not that day.

"It's pancake day at the Roasting Company." She waggled her brows and jangled her keys. "Take a quick shower and let's head out."

The huge smile crossing his mother's face prevented him from telling her it was too unhealthy for her. He would have to go with her and then talk to her later about ensuring she ate better. When he remembered Lottie's special pancakes, though, he couldn't help but grin as well. "I'll be quick."

Brandon couldn't remember a time when he'd showered so quickly. The thought of his favorite treat lit a fire under his feet. He hadn't had them in over a year.

When he and his mother were off, his smile diminished when he remembered the last time he had the Frenchtown Roasting Company's honey-kissed pancakes. When he left for his new job, he hadn't realized how difficult it would be to leave a certain cowgirl. He had thought of her often since leaving last Thanksgiving.

At first, he had to continually remind himself to put his phone away and not call her. It wasn't fair to keep her hoping for something that couldn't happen for at least three years, maybe more. But now that he was back home, he would have to keep his distance still.

With his mother so sick, he knew it wouldn't be fair to her or Chloe. There wouldn't be enough time in the day to have a girlfriend. And if he did try, then it would take time away from his mother, who needed him right then. Or his ranch who also needed him. Without the ranch, they wouldn't survive.

The drive into town was quiet. Brandon wasn't sure what his mother was thinking about, but he knew he had to put

Chloe out of his thoughts and focus on his mother. She needed him now more than ever.

He wasn't surprised when they had to park two blocks away; the coffee shop was a popular place for breakfast on Saturdays. He knew he wouldn't be the only rancher in there after feeding his stock. Especially since it was pancake Saturday.

What did surprise him, however, was the rush of emotions and loss of breath when he saw the beautiful blonde sitting in the back of the room with Lottie's little girl, eating a late breakfast.

He should have known she would be there. This was where they'd met. Well, the *second* time they met, but it was where he'd first asked her for her phone number, and then the next month where they had their last date. He'd broken up with her later in the day after they had shared a pancake breakfast.

Brandon didn't know enough about Chloe to know that she had breakfast at Frenchtown Roasting Company every time they served pancakes, but he should have known. She did tell him that chocolate chip pancakes were her favorite breakfast meal.

Chloe hadn't yet seen him, so he stood there waiting for a table and taking in her features. It seemed her blonde hair was longer than the last time he'd seen her. She smiled and laughed with Quinn, Lottie's eight-year-old little girl, and his heart stopped. She was going to make a great mother.

Where that thought came from, Brandon had no clue. But he was going to have to expel it. There was no way he was going to torture himself with thoughts of a woman he couldn't have.

The bell over the door rang, and Brandon watched as Chloe looked up to see who'd come in. At first a radiant smile crossed her face, and then when she noticed him it left just as quickly. His heart sank, and he wished he could have hidden before she saw him.

The sound announcing a new customer caused Chloe to look up, and she was excited to see Christopher Lambton and his wife, Jessica, come in. The elderly man had a jolly countenance as evidenced by his belly full of jelly, a huge smile that could be seen through his perfectly groomed white beard, and the little red cheeks he sported on cold days. Normally the man had a very short-trimmed beard, but as Christmas grew closer he let it grow out.

Chris was the perfect Santa Claus. Last year, when she'd met him for the first time, he was in his red suit with his wife next to him at the town's Christmas party. Even though the children of Frenchtown knew Chris all year long, it seemed as though they forgot he used to own and run the general store. During Christmas, he was Santa. And Jessica was Mrs. Claus. The entire town called them by their Christmas names, which they loved.

The day after Thanksgiving, Mr. and Mrs. Claus would debut wearing their various Christmas sweaters that made them hard to miss. Any time someone had a Christmas party, they were invited, and attended. The town loved their Christmas royalty, and it showed. It was also well deserved. From what Chloe had heard, they'd played their roles beautifully for the past thirty years. And would most likely do so until their last Christmas here on Earth.

But the moment she caught a familiar sight to the left of the door, her smile vanished. Her heart sank. She knew she would see him soon, but didn't realize it would be on her favorite Saturday of the month. Seeing him there, inside the Roasting Company, brought up the bad memory of the last time she saw him—right there in that shop. Thankfully, he had waited until they left before breaking her heart. At least he didn't do it publicly.

When the bell rang again, she gratefully turned her attention to the new person walking in and was surprised to see the town superstar, Cove Hamilton.

Quinn Keith, Lottie's eight-year-old daughter who had been having breakfast with her, noticed Cove and squealed when she jumped up. "Uncle Cove, Uncle Cove! You're back in town!" She ran straight into his legs and hugged his waist.

Cove was a rodeo star and close family friend to the Keiths. He and Quinn's daddy had been high school friends and then joined the rodeo circuit together right out of high school. When Lottie's husband died bull riding, Cove had been there for them. Even though they weren't related, Cove was a sort of godparent to Quinn, and she loved the cute rodeo star.

Every time he came home, he had something for Quinn. And sometimes he even had gifts for Lottie.

Seeing the little girl so happy caused Chloe to forget about her heartache, and she could not help but smile at the cute pair hugging and greeting one another.

She turned back to her plate and ate the last bite of the gooey chocolatey pancake before downing the rest of her peppermint mocha. Chloe knew the place was crowded, and she should give up her table so others could sit down and eat. She told herself that it had nothing to do with Brandon being there.

After repeatedly saying it in her mind, she was half convinced it was the truth. When she stood up to go pay for her meal, Brandon walked toward her. This was the last thing she wanted to do on her lazy Saturday.

"Chloe, it's good to see you again." Brandon's hands were

damp, and he wiped them down the sides of his Wranglers before putting out a hand to shake.

With a deep breath in her mouth and out her nose, she decided she needed to be polite and not let him know he had any hold on her emotions whatsoever. Their history was too long ago, and so short in duration, that he would think her a fool if she still had feelings for him, which she did *not*.

She took his outstretched hand and shook it with a small smile. "Brandon, I'd heard you were coming home." She looked at his mother and noted the smile on her face. But there were also rings around her eyes. Mrs. Beck looked as though she hadn't been sleeping well lately. "Mrs. Beck, it's so good to see you again." And it was. Chloe was truly happy to see the woman who had always been so very nice to her.

When she leaned in for a hug, the motherly woman returned her hug and held her just a moment longer than necessary.

"It's good to see you too, Chloe. How are you today?" Melanie smiled at the woman who had captured her son's heart a year ago. She was surprised when Brandon broke up with her and didn't even try to have a long-distance relationship with her. They could have made it work. She knew her son cared deeply for the pretty blonde. And if the way he looked at her now was any indication, his feelings never changed.

All she could do now was try to get them back together again. Even if it was the last thing she did, she would see her son happily married to Chloe Manning.

CHAPTER 3

This year was different from all the rest. There was a special note in the air, or was it a special assignment this year? The town's Mrs. Claus had felt that there was something important she would be accomplishing this year, but she couldn't quite put her finger on it. Something in her spirit told her that today was an important day, and she needed to get going.

"Chris, hurry up or we'll be late," Jessica Lambton called to her husband as she put her red velvet cape on. She loved this time of year and could not wait to get out and start playing their roles as Mr. and Mrs. Claus. Plus, she didn't want to miss the coming cue to what her special assignment was this year. She hadn't had one in almost a decade, and the excitement was beginning to spill over.

The entire town seemed to brighten during the Christmas season. While it wasn't technically the Christmas season yet, it was close enough that she and Chris had decided to wear their Christmas coats and red sweaters when they went to the Frenchtown Roasting Company for pancake Saturday. It was there that she knew her assignment would present itself.

Most of the town had breakfast there on pancake Saturday, and Jessica could not wait to see everyone, especially the little kids. The joy on their faces when they saw Santa lit up the entire town. No one could be sad when Santa was around. It didn't matter that everyone knew who they were, they all still *believed* in the magic of Christmas, even the older kids.

"Yes, dear." Chris came out to the front room and kissed his wife's cheek. He knew life wasn't perfect, but there was something about this time of year that erased any ill will he sensed in the world, or even in his own town. Everyone was on their best behavior, and people in general were nicer to everyone around them.

"Would you like to walk today? Or should I bring the car around?" Chris preferred walking the five blocks to the coffee shop whenever possible, but with winter coming he wasn't sure if his wife wanted to be out in the cold and biting wind.

Jessica pulled the hood up over her head and smiled. "It's not too bad, yet. I think we should walk." She loved the leisurely walk and hated when the weather didn't permit it. She knew that come December they would have to drive. But the closer it got to Christmas, the better the chance they'd have of using their sleigh. She did enjoy that means of conveyance.

Her husband smiled into the face of the woman he had loved for longer than he could remember and dropped a quick kiss on her lips. "Mrs. Claus, I think you are more beautiful every year."

Jessica could feel the warmth on her cheeks and grabbed her husband's arm. "Oh, Chris. You're such a sweetheart. I love you more every year." She reached up and kissed his cheek before they opened the door.

As they made their way down the sidewalk toward the Roasting Company, others on the streets waved and called out, "Good morning, Santa and Mrs. Claus." Both Jessica and Chris loved how the entire town got in on the Christmas fun, even though it was not yet Thanksgiving.

They waved back and returned the well wishes with huge smiles on their faces. Since their children had grown up and moved away, the townsfolk had become their family. The Lambton children would come back at Christmas for a few days, but Chris and Jessica understood that they had their own homes now and couldn't spend too much time in Frenchtown.

When they entered the doors of the coffee shop, everyone stopped their conversation and looked to the cute elderly couple who looked just like the iconic Normal Rockwell painting of Santa and his wife. Jessica had braided her long silver hair and pinned it up like Angela Lansbury had done in *Mrs. Santa Claus*.

She also had a cloak very similar to the iconic one in all of the stock photos of the popular actress posing as Mrs. Claus, but she never wore it until after Thanksgiving. It was rather warm with the white faux-fur trim and lining, and was perfect on the cold winter days when she and Chris were outside in the Christmas parade, or attending the town square tree lighting or other official Christmas events. Today, she wore a simple red jacket with a hood to help keep out the winter wind.

Chris had on a red coat over a red Santa sweater. Only his jeans and brown boots reminded anyone looking at him that he wasn't the real Santa. The kids never minded; they'd all grown up thinking it made sense for Santa to wear jeans and boots, especially since he had to work long days in his workshop making toys.

As the children grew up, they recognized that Chris Lambton was a man just like any other, but he had a calling to bring joy to the Christmas season for all of Frenchtown and anyone who came to visit.

The bell above the door jingled when they entered the Frenchtown Roasting Company. Chris held the door for his wife as she passed him and entered the little coffee shop. She inhaled the wonderful aromas of roasted beans, sweet syrups, tangy teas, and the unmistakable scent of pancakes and maple syrup.

"Santa!" Multiple little voices squealed as the little kids ran straight into Chris's legs and all vied for their spots around him, hugging his legs. Those who were tall enough hugged him around his waist, while a smaller child held on below.

Even a few of the little girls ran to Mrs. Claus and hugged her while waiting for their turn with Santa.

Lottie came up and smiled at the town's favorite couple, no matter the time of year. "Chris and Jessica, it's so good to have you here today. I started the Christmas drinks early this year, so if you want a peppermint hot cocoa just let me know." She winked at Chris before moving on to clean off a table for the elderly couple.

Brandon looked to the door when the Clauses walked in. "Mom, I want to say hi to Chris and Jessica before we sit down. Are you alright with that?" Like the rest of the town, Brandon loved the town's royal couple and he hadn't gotten a chance to see them last Christmas. He had missed celebrating with the town last year. One good thing about being home so early was getting to enjoy all the Christmas events this year with his mother.

"I'll join you, son." Melanie stood up from the chair where she sat by the door and joined her son when he went to say hi to the Lambton family.

Brandon smiled and held a hand out for the jolly old man.

"Santa, it's good to see you again." He nodded at Jessica. "Mrs. Claus, I've missed you both."

Jessica beamed at him. "We've missed you as well. But I hear you're back home for good now." She looked from her husband to Melanie and back to Brandon again. A sly smile crossed her features. "Was that Chloe who just walked outside?"

A light-pink hue tinged Brandon's cheeks. "Ah, as a matter of fact, yes." He rubbed the back of his neck. Since he and Chloe had only dated for a month, he didn't think anyone would remember. After all, it had been a year since they'd broken up.

But the memories of some people were too clear.

"She's such a sweetheart, isn't she?" Mrs. Claus winked and smiled at Brandon, causing his cheeks to grow warmer.

This was it. Mrs. Claus had that feeling in her heart that her mission was standing right in front of her. Was it possible that, for the first time ever, she was to help a young couple find their way to each other? Or was there something else going on with Brandon? Either way, Jessica was going to spend some time in prayer asking the good Lord to guide her ways this season.

Brandon looked to his mother and mentally asked for help.

Melanie Beck knew her son well. "Chris and Jessica, it's always so wonderful to see you don your Christmas clothes. This is my favorite time of the year." She leaned in and kissed Jessica's cheek. "I look forward to the tree lighting ceremony after Thanksgiving. I can't believe we're already talking about Christmas." She looked around the coffee shop and smiled. "And seeing decorations as well."

Lottie walked over to the group and put an arm around

Melanie. "But you know you love it when I start decorating early."

Melanie chortled. "Yes, I do. Your decorations and Christmas drinks always put a smile on my face."

"And everyone else's as well," Cove Hamilton said as he walked over to greet the town's royal family. "Santa, Mrs. Claus. It's always so good to see you two." The cowboy smiled and nodded at the elderly couple holding court.

"Cove, how long are you home this time?" Brandon and Cove had always been friendly. They grew up together but didn't spend a lot of time together. However, while Brandon was away on the rodeo circuit learning about raising bulls for pro-rodeo they had become closer friends.

With a pat on Brandon's back, Cove winked at Lottie and looked back to Brandon. "I'm not sure. My season is over."

"I'm sorry to hear that. But I guess your family will be happy to have you here for the Christmas festivities." Brandon knew he was glad to be home for the entire season. No one did Christmas like Frenchtown. Part of the reason was that no one had Santa and Mrs. Claus living in their town.

Cove looked at Lottie, and then over to where Quinn was sitting and smiled. "I think I'm going to enjoy spending the entire season at home."

Lottie's brows furrowed, but she said nothing.

Mrs. Claus watched the coffee shop owner and eyed the rodeo star. She wondered if there were possibly two assignments for her this year.

When the smile faded from his mother's face, Brandon went into protective mode. He put a hand over his stomach and smiled at Lottie. "I think we already know what we want."

Lottie laughed and nodded. "Take a seat and I'll get your regular orders put in."

Since his mother had looked like she was ready to sit, Brandon led her to a table that had just been vacated but still needed cleaning. Once his mother was seated, he got to work cleaning off the table before Lottie or one of her helpers could do it.

Something about the setting and the decorations started to work on him, and memories began making their way through his head. He was glad to be home.

Last Christmas Brandon had worked on the pro-rodeo circuit with the team who handled some of the best bulls in the business until the finals in Vegas, which were in early December. Then he went back to the Dusty Rose Ranch in South Dakota. He was only able to come home for a quick visit with his family, then he had to high-tail it back to the ranch for more training before the season began again in January.

Brandon knew it was mostly the same for Cove. Although, the rodeo star had been able to stay in town for a little bit longer since he didn't have to go train elsewhere during their off-weeks.

Brandon had spent the entire year working, other than the two days he spent at home last Christmas with his mom, his sister, and her family. Now that he was back home, he really didn't know what to do with himself. Although, since his mother had been sick, she had been a bit lax with some work needed around the ranch. He would probably spend the next two months just getting things back in shape before he could begin on any larger projects, like adding a new supply shack.

Though with their winters, he most likely wouldn't have time to get the foundation set before winter fully set in. Spring would be crazy busy with ranch business, but he would find a way to get that new supply shack started before the weather forced him back indoors.

He did have his work cut out for him this winter. And he was right glad there was plenty of work to keep him busy.

Anything to keep his mind off the pretty blonde he most certainly had not missed this past year. Nope, he did not miss her or think of her at all.

Yeah, right. If he believed that he had a bridge to sell himself...

CHAPTER 4

M ore snow had dropped over the weekend, and the town looked like a cozy winter wonderland set in a Hallmark movie. Chloe smiled as she stepped onto Main Street and headed toward her favorite coffee shop. Today would be the first day of many early-morning stops into her favorite store for her peppermint mocha.

Yesterday she had prepared herself for seeing Brandon at church, but when neither he or his mother showed up, she worried that Melanie might be having a bad day. First up on her list when she got into the office was to check the files to see what Melanie had been diagnosed with.

Chloe had battled with herself all weekend about whether she should be nosy and find out what was wrong with Brandon's mom. As of this morning, she had decided it was better to know. Maybe she would even have some ideas to help with her condition. Even if it was only a pamphlet on diet, she wanted to do something to help the nice woman get through whatever the situation was. Chloe had no plans to tell anyone anything about Melanie's case, but she couldn't help thinking there might be something she could do.

Melanie wasn't the most social person in town; she only had a couple of good friends. Maybe Chloe could be a good friend to her? No matter the diagnosis, Melanie would need at least one friend who understood what she was going through.

Chloe was stuck in her memories and never even noticed the sounds of shouts coming from the general store as she neared the front door. When the door opened and a young man wearing rags ran out, he plowed right into Chloe and she fell over and landed on her backside.

With stars dancing above her, she lay there wondering what was going on.

"Sorry, ma'am." The sound of a young man was heard as he ran away.

A hand showed up in her vision, and she grabbed for it. "Thanks..." She stopped talking when she realized who owned the strong and rugged hand that had been offered to her.

"Are you alright?" Brandon looked into her eyes and held her by the shoulders until she had her bearings. A lot like the first day they'd met.

"Um. Yeah." Chloe couldn't take her eyes off the man who seemed to show up whenever she fell on her backside and rescue her. "Thank you." She looked around and noticed several of the townsfolks looking at them and whispering. "Do you know what just happened?"

"I think the general store had its first thief in years." Brandon chuckled and watched as the clerk stopped running and bent over at the waist, huffing and puffing to catch his breath.

"Thief? Are you saying the store was just robbed?" Chloe put a hand to her chest and took in a deep breath. It couldn't have been the robber who mowed her down. That was just a teen who needed some new clothes. Realization dawned on her. "Was he stealing food?"

Brandon rubbed the back of his neck. "I think so. He had a loaf of bread in one hand and a can of soup in another."

Chloe rubbed her shoulder. "That explains it."

"Explains what?" He furrowed his brow and looked at where she was rubbing.

"Something very hard hit my shoulder. It must have been the can of soup." She chuckled and dropped her hand. A bruise would develop, but it wouldn't be the worst thing she'd had to deal with since moving to Frenchtown.

His hands lingered on her shoulders, and she wondered when it had gotten so hot.

Brandon looked down into her eyes and kept his hands on her and he felt his heart beat strong against his chest. He wanted to say something, but words would not form. He just kept looking at her.

When the store clerk came back, still panting, and asked if she was alright, Brandon's mind cleared the fog away and he jerked away from the pretty cowgirl.

* * *

WHEN CHLOE WALKED into the Frenchtown Roasting Company, she took in a deep breath and sighed. The smell of fresh-brewed coffee and sweet pastries in the air relaxed her shoulders. She hadn't realized how stressed she was feeling until that moment. Thinking about Melanie, and then seeing Brandon the way she did, must have upset her more than she realized. If she was going to be a friend to Brandon's mom during this time, Chloe was going to have to let go of her worries and give it all to God.

A stressed-out or worried friend would do Melanie no good. And she'd have to get his scent of cinnamon and leather out of her mind. It didn't matter that he smelled like a cup of Joy tea—she was over him and had moved on.

Well, at least *he* had moved on.

"Chloe!" Lottie waved and smiled as Chloe entered the store.

The last time Chloe was here had only been two days ago, but the store had changed even more since Saturday morning. Christmas lights were up all over the store. Some twinkled and some did not. The metamorphosis of the shop was going to be fun to watch over the coming weeks.

"Good morning, Lottie. How about my Christmas usual?" Chloe grinned and stepped in line behind three other women who were on their way to work as well. This would take her mind off the crazy encounter with the cute cowboy.

Lisa Hamilton was in line when Chloe stepped inside the shop. "Hey, Chloe. Are you ready for Christmas yet?" The curly red hair that barely fell past her shoulders bounced when she turned her head toward her friend.

Chloe laughed. "Not quite yet. I think this week I'll start decorating after work so I don't have to worry about it over Thanksgiving."

"Oh, that's right. You're going home for the long week-end, aren't you?" Lisa's smile faltered a tad bit.

"Ah, yes I am. I can't wait to see my family again. It's been too long." Chloe longed to go home for a visit. Especially now that Matthew, her brother, was engaged. His wedding was coming up fast, and she didn't want to miss any of the fun surrounding the preparations. Plus, she really liked her new soon-to-be sister-in-law. Claire was so sweet, and her love of Whiskers, Chloe's horse, really helped the two of them bond when Chloe first met her.

"What are your plans for Thanksgiving?" Chloe knew Lisa had family here, but she would also have to work that weekend. Thankfully, the Sip 'n' Go was closed on Thanksgiving Day. Most stores in town were closed. But Black Friday would see all shops open very early to accommodate the sale shoppers.

They may not be a large city, or even have a department store, but the local shops still participated in Black Friday sales to help keep shoppers in town for at least part of the day. Online shopping had stolen some of their business the past few years, but the smart shop owners had good online stores as well.

Lisa sighed. "I have to open the store on Black Friday." She shook her head. "You'd think being the manager would mean I could choose the shifts I want to work. But, nope. The owners want me opening all weekend."

"Well, at least you'll have the evenings to spend doing all of the town's Christmas events, right?" Chloe tried to keep a positive attitude whenever someone seemed down. But she also understood why Lisa wasn't too keen on opening all weekend.

Her red curls bounced with her nod. "True, but I was hoping to get in some Black Friday shopping myself." She laughed, but it wasn't a happy laugh. It sounded more sardonic than anything else.

"Can you do online shopping?" While Chloe didn't mind online shopping, she knew her friend well enough to know she was the type who liked to touch something before she bought it. The feel of the fabric or the roughness of the leather always spoke to Lisa more than it did Chloe.

Lisa shrugged. "I suppose I can if I get up about one a.m., then shop online before I have to be at the store."

"But what I don't get is that your store is a convenience

store and gas station. It's not like you have a lot of items for Black Friday shoppers." Chloe's brow furrowed as she imagined hordes of people ramming down the doors to the Sip 'n' Go for discounted sodas and chips.

This time when Lisa laughed, it did sound happy. There was a depth to it her first laugh didn't hold. "Actually, we do bring in some items just for the weekend sales, like electronics that everyone always wants. But most of the customers are there for gas and snacks to get them through the day. It's one of our busiest days of the year as well."

"Huh, I guess I never thought about gas stations and convenience stores doing much business the day after Thanksgiving." She would have to pay attention if she was out on Black Friday shopping back home or in Bozeman to see what the gas stations were doing.

"At least I have Thanksgiving Day off. That's really the best part. I get to spend the entire day with my family stuffing my face with all the good stuff." Lisa's grin spread from ear to ear, and Chloe couldn't help but mimic the other girl's enthusiasm.

"Very true. I can't wait for our traditional Thanksgiving meal. The entire family and the in-laws will all be at the Triple J Ranch this year. It's sure to be a hoot." When Chloe arrived at the counter, she waved to Lisa as the convenience store manager took her cup of coffee and walked away.

Lottie handed the peppermint mocha cup to Chloe and winked. "Here ya go. I hope you enjoy it as much today as you did on Saturday."

Chloe practically snorted her disapproval. "Knock it off. Nothing's going on."

"Oh, come on, Chloe. You gotta give a girl a chance to live vicariously and all that." Lottie still wasn't ready to move on since the death of her husband. She had loved him with everything she was. The entire town doubted Lottie would move on until after her daughter was grown up and married herself.

Chloe looked around. "What about you? I saw Cove here this weekend and I heard rumor that he's home until at least January." She raised her brows and laughed when Lottie's face went red.

She put her hand up. "Hold up there, sister. You know I'm never getting involved with anyone who's a part of the rodeo." Lottie stared her friend down.

With peppermint mocha in hand, Chloe winked and walked away. That should teach Lottie to tease her about Brandon.

As Chloe walked down the street to her office, she smiled after each delicious sip of her rich, chocolatey, and pepper-mint-y mocha. This was the start of Christmas. And if she wasn't mistaken, there was romance in the air.

Not for her, but for her friend who deserved to be happy.

When Chloe entered her office, she shut the door and began going through the records she still had to upload for billing. When she found Melanie Beck's file, she stopped and looked around. Even though it was normal for her to look at a patient file before submitting the codes to get payment, she still felt *weird*.

Never before had she looked at a file and purposely sought the condition of the patient. Sure, Chloe had read many patient files in order to ensure she was submitting the proper medical codes into the Medicare system, but she had never looked for a diagnosis for personal reasons. As long as she kept the information to herself, she wasn't violating any HIPAA laws.

She took a long drink from her now-warm peppermint mocha and sighed. When she opened the folder, the diagnosis was right on top, along with the medication the doctor had prescribed. Multiple sclerosis. Chloe closed the folder and began to pray immediately. There wasn't a cure for MS. And if a patient were to progress very far in the disease, she would suffer greatly before a slow and painful death.

Dear Heavenly Father. I want to lift up Melanie to you. Only you know exactly what is going on with her and how this will all end for her. I ask that you comfort her and her family during this difficult time.

Chloe sighed and wiped a tear from her eye.

And Father, I would also ask that you heal her. I know you still do miraculous healings, and I pray right now that you would wrap your loving arms around Melanie and take this disease from her. But if that isn't your plan, then still wrap your loving arms around your daughter and give her and her family peace. In Jesus' holy name I pray, amen.

Thankfully there were a lot of treatments available, especially if it was caught early enough. A feeling of peace settled over Chloe, and she closed the file. Once she had gone through all her e-mails, she would then begin to input codes for payment. And she would start with Melanie Beck's file.

By the end of the day, Chloe was bone-tired. She stood up from her desk with both hands on her lower back and stretched her torso. First she leaned back and then she leaned forward, then side to side. Sitting in a chair all day long, no matter how comfortable or ergonomic the chair, still wasn't good for anyone's back.

When she glanced at the clock, she almost jumped. It was close to seven at night. She knew she had put in a long day. With Thanksgiving weekend coming, she needed to get ahead of the files so she didn't come back to chaos on her desk. Chloe figured maybe two more days of this and she would be all caught up.

So far, November had been a very busy month. With the cold front that had come through there were a lot of sick people getting check-ups, making sure they didn't have that new super-virus that had done a number on the world last year. Thankfully, it seemed that most people just had normal colds and flu. There were also a lot of people getting the flu shot this year, more than normal.

If they had a CVS or Walgreens in town, most of the patients could have just gone there for a free flu shot and their insurance would have covered the cost with the drugstore. But their small drugstore didn't have a setup yet with the insurance companies to get paid for the flu shots. So most people still came into the office for their vaccinations. Which in turn created a lot of extra billing for Chloe.

Not that it was difficult, just time-consuming data entry.

Since it was so late, Chloe decided to stop by the local diner for a quick meal. She wasn't in the mood to cook anything for herself after such a long day in the office. Plus, it would give her a chance to say hi to a few of the locals, and maybe she would even be able to see a friend or two. Sitting in her office working hard all day got to be a little lonely.

Normally, water-cooler talk was something she partici-pated in when she took her short breaks, but this week she was on a mission to get everything done. And if what she saw when she went into the breakroom earlier to fill her water bottle was any indication, she wasn't alone. Hardly anyone had taken a break, from what she could tell.

The little bell above the door that normally sounded when she entered the diner was different. Something about it caught her ear, and she stopped to look up. The sound had been a tad bit muffled, but it was also deeper than normal. When she realized what it was, she couldn't help but smile. Dixie, the diner's owner, had replaced her regular bell with a sleigh bell and a ball of mistletoe. Chloe was going to have to be very careful about walking through that door for the rest of the year.

Especially when a man like Jake Johnson was coming her way.

CHAPTER 5

J ake Johnson had been nice to Chloe when she first arrived, and when Brandon broke her heart he had been there to sweep up the pieces. Or so he thought.

In actuality, Jake was a preener. Some might even call him a dandy. Sure, he was good looking and nice, but he seemed more interested in himself than anything—or anyone —else. The one date Chloe had with Jake was a flop. When he came to pick her up, he complained that her yellow blouse clashed with his red-and-white shirt. When she changed it to a blue blouse, he only sighed and shook his head.

The night just went downhill from there, as just about everything he spoke about had to do with him. He didn't ask a single question about her unless it was what she thought about him or what he'd said. Chloe had never been so happy to go home early from a date.

Since then, Jake had been cordial but a bit distant. His flirtatious attitude changed, and he was only polite when they crossed paths. If he had been anyone else, she probably would have been hurt by the change in attitude. In this case, she could not be happier.

Chloe had no desire to be anywhere near the mistletoe when Jake entered, so she hurried along to an open booth and sat down before Jake could enter the diner. She reached over to grab a menu from the end where they were kept and opened it up to help hide her face from the cowboy before he noticed her.

"Jake!" an annoying voice called out, and a petite hand shot up in the air, waving him over.

Chloe had her eyes just above the top of her menu and watched as Jake sauntered over to May Preston's table. She and May had never gotten along. It probably had something to do with how possessive May was over Jake, even though they weren't dating. Well, as far as Chloe knew they weren't.

"Hi, Chloe. What can I get ya?" Lulu Devin, Dixie's granddaughter, asked while chewing gum. The teenager had a thing for movies made or set in the fifties, and she seemed to want to be like Sandy from *Grease*. She went so far as to wear the same clothes as her favorite movie character before Sandy went all biker-chick to catch Danny's attention at the end during the school fair. It was cute.

"Hi, Lulu. I think I'll take the chef salad and a sweet tea tonight, thanks." Chloe put the menu down on the table and turned her eyes back to the unlikely pairing of Jake and May. Or maybe it was a good pairing? Chloe wasn't sure how a relationship between a man who was too self-involved to pay attention to a pretty girl would do with a woman who fawned all over him.

Lulu chuckled. "Yeah, they've met here the past few nights for dinner. I guess they'll both get what they want." The teen shook her head and walked away.

Not that Chloe wanted the gossip, but Jiminy Christmas, those two would end in fireworks for sure. In this case, she wanted to make sure she was a mile away when May realized that Jake did not make for a good boyfriend after all.

The bell above the door jingled again, and Chloe's eyes drifted from the crazy couple destined for an avalanche to the door, and her eyes widened. She knew she would see him again, but she wasn't prepared to see him now. The hope she had of getting some time to get used to him being back in town waned, and she prepared herself to have to say hi as he walked by.

Instead, the Wrangler-clad legs of the cowboy stopped at her table and she looked up into his smiling face.

Chloe's heart skipped a beat, but thankfully only one beat before she smiled and said, "Howdy."

The cowboy standing in front of her was tall, at least six feet two inches, if not more. And his brown hair with matching chocolate-brown eyes always caused Chloe to lick her lips and think of the luscious sweetness of that first kiss she'd shared with him. Now she was mentally berating herself for looking into his eyes and letting herself remember their kiss.

Brandon tipped his hat, and a million-watt smile covered his face. "Hey there." He looked to the empty seat across from her and then back to her again. "Are you waiting for someone?"

She shook her head and sighed. "Nope. I was working late, so decided at the last minute to stop by for a quick meal." Chloe bit her lower lip. "What about you? Are you meeting anyone?"

He chuckled. "Nah, the same here. I was in town on business and realized how late it was, so I thought I'd stop in for a burger." He hesitated before asking, "May I join you?"

Her head popped back, and she knew she had done a rotten job of hiding her surprise when he held up a hand.

Chloe's heart rate rose so much, she feared she was about to end up with a massive coronary.

"Oh, sorry. I shouldn't have asked, should I?" His smile disappeared, and lines developed between his brows.

"Um. No, not at all." She shook her head. "I mean, please." She waved a hand at the empty seat across from her. Then took a few deep breaths in an effort to still her beating heart.

Brandon gave her a tentative smile. When he slid on the seat, she heard the squeaking of the pleather diner seats and smiled.

The sound reminded her of the diner back home in Beacon Creek—Rosie's. They had the same red pleather seats and they made the same sounds. It seemed all diner booths had the same distributor and they all made strange sounds.

He grabbed a menu to hide his embarrassment. It wasn't like he'd actually made a bodily noise; it was the seat that made the noise. But he still felt awkward. "So, have you ordered yet?"

Chloe couldn't help but giggle. She knew he was embarrassed. In fact, that same thing happened when they went on their first date. Most jeans when scraped across the fake leather seats of the booths made that noise. He seemed just as nervous tonight as he did that first time they went out.

When she realized what she had done, she chided herself for comparing this situation to a date. It certainly was no date. They were just two old friends who happened to be at the same place at the same time for a meal. That was all.

"Yeah, I got the chef salad. It's pretty good here. You should try it." She wanted to add, *for your mother*. But she knew she shouldn't say anything about his mom and her condition unless he brought it up.

Brandon nodded. "Yeah, I picked up a couple of them the other night for Mom and me. It was really good."

Chloe opened her mouth and then shut it. While he did mention his mom and a salad, he hadn't mentioned anything about her health. Even though she was itching to tell him about some of the ideas she had for his mom's health, she knew she needed to stay mum on the subject.

She nodded. "I've been trying to eat healthier lately. For a while I wasn't very good, but now"—she shrugged—"I think it's important to put food into my body that will help it and not hurt it."

He looked up from the menu in front of him. His lips pursed into a straight line and he watched the cowgirl in front of him. "You know, don't you." It wasn't a question; it was a statement.

Here was the opening Chloe wanted. Instead of being ready to delve into the topic, she was hesitant. The look of pain and maybe even anger on Brandon's face stopped her. Was he mad at her or the situation? She couldn't be sure, and now she wasn't sure if she wanted to say what was on her mind.

Turned out, she didn't need to.

Lulu walked up to her booth with a glass of ice-cold sweet tea. Condensation rippled down the sides of the drink and a small splash hit the table when the waitress put it down. "Hey, Brandon. Good to have you home. What can I get ya?"

The girl smacked her gum, and it was all Chloe could do to keep from laughing.

Brandon looked to Chloe, then down at his menu and back up to Lulu. "How about the barbecue chicken salad?" If he was going to get his mother to eat healthier, then he would have to lead by example. It didn't matter that she most likely wouldn't know what he had to eat—he would eat the way he wanted his mother to. Hopefully his example would set the right tone for her.

"And to drink?" Lulu asked.

"Sweet tea, please." Brandon closed the menu and put it back in its place in the holder on the far end of the table.

Lulu smiled and wrote down the order, then looked back at Jack and to Brandon. She nodded at Brandon and leaned down to whisper next to Chloe's ear, "He's much cuter."

"Lulu!" Chloe gasped, knowing that the cowboy in question had to have heard. The girl did not know how to whisper properly.

Brandon smirked, but when he looked back and saw it was Jack that Lulu had compared him to, he almost growled. His mother had told him that not long after he left, Chloe went out with the dandy. But she never said anything again about Jack and Chloe.

When he looked back at Chloe, he noticed her blush and relaxed his features. While he wasn't ready to smile, he did like how the cowgirl across from him looked when her cheeks were rosy.

Lulu giggled nervously and walked off to place the order.

"Did you know that Jack and May dated in high school?" Brandon casually asked.

Chloe blinked. "Ah, no. I didn't know that." She wondered why he was telling her about Jack.

"Yeah, they actually make a perfect couple. I don't know why they didn't make it work before. Hopefully they can this time." Brandon chuckled.

Chloe furrowed her brow. "Really? You think they'd be good together?" With a man so self-involved, she had no idea how any woman would pair well with him.

Brandon looked back over his shoulder and noticed that May was draped all over Jack, and he was happily lapping up her attention. "Yup. He's so into himself, and she's so into him, it seems like a perfect match." He chuckled.

Chloe snorted and put a hand in front of her mouth. She was embarrassed and had to look away.

Her cowboy laughed and leaned forward. "Come on, think about it. Who else would do well for him but a woman who loves him just as much as he loves himself?"

She wanted to slap him, but he was too far away. However, he made a good point. "Alright, I see what you mean. At first I didn't think they would be good together. How could any woman be with a man who loves himself more than her? But since she seems to feel the same for him"—she shrugged—"it might be the perfect combination."

Brandon was quiet for a moment, then looked around. When no one was close, he asked, "What about you? What kind of man are you looking for?"

Chloe cleared her throat before she could answer, *Someone like you.* Their time was past, and she knew it. But Jiminy Christmas if there wasn't still chemistry between them.

The way he looked at her, she felt his intense eyes on her and she wanted nothing more than for him to come over and sit next to her on the booth, like they had several times when they were dating. She loved how he would put his arm on the booth behind her and scoot closer to her. His warmth would seep into her body and her heart would pick up and...

She had to stop. Thinking about those times and the way things were between them would do nothing but hurt her, again. She could not do that to herself.

Instead of answering his question, she asked him one. "Did you learn everything you hoped to at the Dusty Rose?" There, she had changed the topic and put it all back on him.

In her experience, most men would take the bait and talk about themselves when given a chance.

He sat back and smirked. "Nice change of subject. But, no. I came home early." Brandon had not planned on talking about his mother. So he stopped short of saying *why* he'd come home early.

"Do you think you learned enough in the past year to help your business out?" Chloe really did wonder if the past year was enough for Brandon and his mom to move their business to the next level. She sure hoped he had.

While she was originally upset over his move, she also knew it was good for his family. It was an opportunity of a lifetime. She doubted she would have turned down something like that for her career. Not after only dating a guy for a month. It would have been stupid to turn it down.

It would have been simpler for her and her heart if he had stayed away for the three years he'd planned. But she couldn't be upset with him for coming home to take care of his mother. Not when she had MS. Again, he had made the best decision for his family.

Lulu came back with Brandon's drink. When she set it down in front of him, she turned her head toward Chloe. "Should I hold off on your salad until Brandon's is ready?"

"Uh, sure. That'd be fine." Chloe smiled at the thoughtful girl.

It would have been rude of her to eat her dinner before Brandon's was served. Her mother had drilled into her the importance of manners, especially table manners. Her brothers, well, they had a lot to learn. But she and her twin sister Elizabeth understood the importance of being a lady. Even if Lulu had served her the salad before his was ready, she would have pushed it to the side and waited for his to arrive before eating hers.

After Lulu nodded, she turned and walked back to the kitchen.

"Where were we?" Chloe asked.

"I think you wanted to know more about what I learned while I was away," Brandon answered.

She nodded and waited for Brandon to talk about his experience and what he learned. They spent the next five minutes discussing his business and who he met and what he learned. When both of their salads arrived at the same time, he stopped talking about himself.

"Would you mind if I prayed?"

Brandon had never asked to pray before their meals. It was a pleasant surprise to have him ask. In the past when they went out to eat together, she had to pray.

"Of course."

They both bent their heads, and Brandon began to give thanks to God for the bounty before them. Before he closed the prayer, he asked God to heal his mother. Brandon didn't go into details; it was a quick request, but one that hit Chloe to the core.

If he was praying without being asked, and even asking for the Lord to heal his mother, she was curious to learn more about the changes in him.

They ate and chatted about nothing important, mostly talking about the events coming up for the Christmas season. Before they finished their meal, Jack and May walked toward them. Chloe put her fork down and wiped her mouth by the time they arrived at her table.

May was draped over Jack's side, and she gave a condescending smirk to Chloe. "Oh, it's so nice to see you finally going out with someone. But don't expect too much, dear."

Jack laughed, and they walked away.

Chloe furrowed her brow and wondered what the crazy girl was talking about.

Brandon rolled his eyes. "Wow, I think they really do make a good couple, but I'm not sure a mean couple is what this town needs."

A giggle escaped Chloe's mouth, and she put her hand over her lips and tried to keep her laugh inside. While she agreed with Brandon's assessment, she didn't want to start talking about Jack and May. They weren't worth her energy.

After the jingle sounded from the strange couple's exit, Chloe heard the bells ring again and looked up to see who was entering. A huge smile crossed her features, and she relaxed. "Santa and Mrs. Claus, it's so good to see you both out tonight."

Christopher and Jessica Lambton smiled and greeted the pair eating salads.

"Santa, are you out for a late dinner?" Brandon asked.

"Ho, ho, ho. No, Mrs. Claus and I are out for dessert." Santa put his hands on his thick black belt. He wasn't wearing a Santa costume, not yet. But he did have on black jeans, boots, and a red Christmas sweater.

Mrs. Claus had on a red wool coat with red boots and a dark-blue denim skirt. As she began to undo the buttons on her coat, Chloe noticed she was wearing a red matching Christmas sweater. The couple looked so cute, dressed alike for Christmas.

They may have only been out for dessert, but everyone in the diner perked up, and when Chloe looked around there was not a sour face in the joint. Only big smiles all around.

"Dixie makes a fantastic hot cocoa and pecan pie." Mrs. Claus took her coat off and put it on the coat tree next to the booth where Chloe and Brandon sat.

Chloe, ever the polite hostess, asked, "Would you like to

join us? We just started on our supper, but I'm sure Lulu will be happy to serve your cocoa and pie here." She started to scooch further into the booth.

Mrs. Claus took Santa's arm. "Thank you, sweetie, but I think we should sit at our own table." She looked pointedly around. A line was starting to form close to them.

Chloe and Brandon both chuckled.

"It looks like a simple night out isn't so simple for the Claus family, is it?" Chloe knew they were a very popular couple, and this time last year they always had children around them. But she hadn't realized they couldn't even go out for dessert without being inundated with children wanting to tell Santa what they wanted.

Santa winked. "I happen to love this part—hearing what the kids want for Christmas, and then working with their parents to ensure they get it if they were good the past year. It's very satisfying."

The popular couple walked to a table that must have been their regular table, since that was where the kids had lined up with their parents.

All hopes of a serious conversation were squashed as Chloe watched parents bring their children into the diner to tell Santa what they wanted. Since he and Mrs. Claus sat at a booth, they weren't able to sit on his lap; instead they stood politely at the end of the table and spoke to Santa.

Some of the kids whispered so that Chloe couldn't hear what they asked for. But some were loud enough that she could hear their requests. The more outlandish ones, like an Xbox or PlayStation, were shot down by Santa in a nice way.

One boy who looked to be about eleven or twelve asked for a PlayStation with all sorts of bells and whistles.

Santa's response was fantastic. "Joey, don't you already have an Xbox One?"

"But Santa, that's my brother's console. Not mine," Joey pouted.

"Does he let you play it with him?" Santa asked.

The boy's lower lip protruded in a pout. "Yes, but I want my own."

The mother standing behind the boy lightly shook her head and looked sad.

"How about a new game for the machine? What if you had your own game for Christmas? Maybe the new Fortnite?"

The mother winked, and Chloe smiled. A feeling of Christmas joy entered her, and she remembered when she was a kid and would visit the Santa in the Bozeman mall. When she was young she usually got what she wanted. But when she was about nine, Santa did try to steer her in a different direction. Just like with this boy. That was her last year sitting on Santa's lap. The following year a mean kid at school ruined the magic of the season for her, and she refused to see Santa.

This would probably be Joey's last year seeing Santa, too.

Joey's mom smiled and gave a quick nod.

Santa smiled, patted Joey on the head, and pulled a candy cane from his pocket. It was the tiny kind, but really, that was all that a kid needed so late at night.

When a thirteen-year-old walked up next, Chloe was shocked. She turned back to Brandon, who chuckled.

"Yeah, the kids here believe in Santa all through high school. Chris told them a long time ago that as long as they believed, they would get Christmas gifts. Only a few kids act tough and refuse to believe. Those kids get presents from their parents, but they don't get the special gift from Santa." Brandon took a bite of his chicken salad.

One of Chloe's brows raised. "You mean Chris gives every kid who talks to him a gift?"

He put his fork down and thought a minute. "No, not every kid. He usually works with the parents. If they can't afford it, then Chris does see to it the kids get the gift, if the parents approve."

"Wow, that's got to be very expensive. How does he do it?" Chloe could not imagine how one small-town Santa could ensure all the kids who still believed got the one present they wanted each year.

Brandon chuckled. "The town pitches in every year. We have a Christmas tree in the town square with gift-request ornaments on it. Someone comes by and picks a paper ornament off the tree and signs up to buy that gift. They buy and wrap the gift with the ornament taped to the top and bring it to Santa by the twentieth of December. Then Santa and Mrs. Claus deliver the gifts to the parents before Christmas Eve and they secretly put the present out after the kids go to bed."

"Wow, that's fantastic. And all the ornaments are picked each year and the gifts purchased and delivered?" She loved this tradition. It was one she could get behind. Especially when a kid wearing a jacket two sizes too small for him came inside with his mother.

Brandon saw the sadness enter Chloe's eyes, and he turned to look at the Miller kid and his mom. Once they were in line for Santa, he leaned forward. "The Miller family. That's Stacy and Buddy. He's nine. He has a sister who's only five. Times are tough for that family. I'll bet Santa sends them a little something extra this year."

"Where's the dad?" Chloe whispered back.

"He died two years ago in a car accident. Stacy runs the farm, but I don't know how much longer they're going to be able to keep it. She needs help. My mom brings them food a couple times a month, as do some of the other women in the church."

"The Miller family." Chloe nodded and began to think of how she could help them have a nice Christmas. She may not be able to do anything about their farm, but she could ensure that each child had proper winter clothes and a couple of toys. "Are there any other families in the area that need help?"

Brandon nodded. "This past year was tough on a few families. Most ranches and farms around here go through tough seasons. And this year, rain was light so the crops weren't as good."

Chloe pursed her lips. "That's so sad. I didn't see anything last year for a toy drive besides the giving tree, or a food drive. Does the town do something like that?"

He shrugged. "Sometimes they do. But since I've only been home a few days, I don't know much about what's going on this year. Thanksgiving weekend we'll see a list of the various ways helping hands can help."

Thinking to herself, Chloe knew exactly what she was going to do. Frenchtown was going to have a magical Christmas this year.

And Chloe would need to remind herself on a regular basis why she had to stay clear of Brandon. The way he'd affected her last year when he left was enough to keep her resolve in place.

This impromptu dinner with him had her heart beating way too fast. She promised herself she would not let him, or any other cute cowboy, hurt her again. Even if Brandon was still interested in her, which she doubted, he did not have the time for her. And she did not have the time for him.

Especially now that she was starting to see her reason for being in this town.

CHAPTER 6

Two days later when Chloe entered the doors of the Dixie Diner, she remembered the unexpected dinner with Brandon. They'd parted ways after they finished their meal and Chloe thought that she just might be able to be friends with the cowboy. As long as she never looked into his delicious eyes again.

When Lottie first told her he was coming home for good, she was nervous and afraid of what she might say or do in front of him. But now that they had seen each other and even shared a meal together as friends, her thoughts were different. She had to remind herself that the meal was strictly two old acquaintances who just happened to show up at the same diner at the same time, alone. No one wanted to eat alone when they could share a meal with an old friend and catch up.

However, she was confident they could be friends with no awkwardness between them...at least, she hoped.

"Hi, Chloe. Take a seat wherever you want," Dixie greeted her.

It was lunchtime, and normally Chloe would have brought lunch, but last night she was up late planning for Christmas.

She overslept that morning and did not have time to make her lunch like normal. So, she went to the diner for a salad. This diner was not anything like Roxy's back home. Roxy had plenty of healthy options on her menu, besides salad.

Dixie's menu had salad. At least she had three different types of salad. Once in a while if her son had a successful day at the lake, then she might have a fish special. During the summer they had fantastic barbecue meals, which was much better than fried food or greasy burgers. Not that Chloe only ate healthy meals, but she did try to steer clear of fried or greasy food whenever possible.

Chloe turned to head to her favorite booth when a welcomed voice called out, "Chloe!"

She turned to see the smiling face of Melanie Beck, Brandon's mom. "Mrs. Beck. It's so good to see you again." She walked over to the woman, who sat alone with a cup of coffee in front of her.

"Please, join me. That is, if you aren't meeting anyone." The hopeful look on the woman's face would have been enough to get Chloe to cancel if she had planned on meeting anyone that day for lunch.

"Thank you, I'd be happy to join you." Chloe took off her coat and scarf. At the end of each booth was a tall pole with hooks that acted as a coat rack. She hung up her coat and scarf on the rack before scooting in the booth.

Chloe noticed the other jacket on the rack was red. Melanie always wore something red. Today it seemed she was wearing a red snow parka. But she also peeked beneath the table and saw that instead of the woman's normal cowboy boots, she had on red snow boots.

Chloe couldn't help but smile. Melanie's little quirk of always having something red on was sweet.

It had snowed overnight again, and the day was cloudy

and cold. The snow was starting to stick, and she doubted they would have to worry about it melting any time soon. "Have you eaten already?"

Melanie took a sip of her coffee and set it down. "I just ordered the chef salad."

Chloe smiled and waved for Dixie to come take her order. "I'm very happy to hear you're eating healthy. It will help you feel better."

Melanie's brows furrowed. "Did Brandon tell you?"

Chloe froze. She should have kept her mouth shut. She was just so happy to hear that the woman had made a healthy choice. And she had wanted to talk to her about her diet. Not all doctors believed that diet made a huge difference in MS patients' lives.

While Chloe didn't personally know anyone with MS, she did know a lot of people with health issues that always felt better when they ate right.

"Uh, no." While she had hoped Brandon would have said something the other night, he didn't say anything specific about his mom's health to her.

Melanie's head tilted to the left. "Is gossip already spreading?"

Chloe shook her head. "No, nothing like that. I just submitted the records to your health insurance for payment." She gave a pointed look at the woman sitting across from her in the back booth.

"Oh, that's right." Melanie rubbed her temple. "I forgot that you do the medical billing. Of course, you would know all about it."

"Don't worry, HIPAA laws don't allow me to talk to anyone about your files." She tried to give a sympathetic smile, but was sure she'd failed when Melanie didn't return her smile.

Before Chloe could try and let Melanie know her secret was safe, Dixie came over to take her order. "What can I get for ya, Chloe?"

"I'd like a cup of hot tea. Do you have peppermint?" Chloe looked up to the grandmotherly owner of the diner.

"Of course, anything else?"

"Yes, I'll have the chicken salad." Chloe smiled at Dixie as she walked away to fill the order. "Melanie, really, you have nothing to worry about. I haven't said a thing to anyone." She wasn't about to tell her that Lottie was the one who originally told her that Mrs. Beck was sick. Melanie did not need to know that part. And Chloe doubted that Lottie was going around telling the entire town why Brandon was home.

Chloe made a mental note to remind Lottie to keep quiet about Melanie. But she would have to call her, as that night after work she was leaving and heading straight home for Thanksgiving with her family.

"Thank you, I would appreciate it if you would keep it to yourself." Melanie took another sip of her hot coffee.

Dixie came over with Chloe's hot water and peppermint tea bag. She also had a fresh pot of coffee in her hand. "Would you like a top-off?"

Melanie put her cup out, and Dixie filled it. Chloe watched as Melanie put one sugar and two creamers in before stirring it.

After Chloe fixed her tea, she hesitated, but then went ahead with her questions. "Melanie, is there anything I can do to help you?"

The woman shook her head. "No, I just have to finish the testing and get through the first month of my new medicine."

"Are you taking a daily pill?" Chloe had researched the latest medicines and hoped the pill would work for Melanie.

The idea of having injections gave her the creeps. She had never liked needles. Which was why she'd gone into medical billing instead of nursing.

"Yes, but it's making me feel sick to my stomach at times." She looked around before continuing, "And I've lost a lot of hair."

Chloe's heart dropped. Melanie was not an old woman; she was about the same age as her mother, mid-fifties. She should not have to deal with hair loss at her age. "I've read that some of those pills are very strong, but your body will adjust and after a time the hair will come back. And your upset stomach can be treated with another pill if it continues for very long. Have you spoken to your doctor about this?"

She nodded. "He said the same thing. He wants to wait another month before adding any more pills. But I can take Tums or Pepto if it bothers me too much."

When their meals arrived, they turned their conversation to a better topic: Christmas.

Last Thanksgiving, Chloe had gone home for two days and then came back to finish organizing her house. She knew she wouldn't have a lot of time to work on it during December. Not that she went to all the Christmas activities; she worked late a lot. The person whose role Chloe had taken ended up leaving a lot of work to be done, and Chloe had to get it all submitted before the end of the year.

This year, while she was going home for four days during Thanksgiving, she would come back and enjoy as much of the Christmas season as she could. And after her revelation the other night when Santa held court for a few local kids, she was also preparing a large toy and kids' clothes drive. She wanted to make sure that all the kids of Frenchtown had a least one toy and proper-fitting winter wear.

Melanie had shared several of the more popular events in

town with Chloe, like the Christmas Craft Faire, and the town's Thanksgiving dinner. She would miss the dinner; it was always the Saturday after Thanksgiving and it was potluck style. Everyone in the area was invited, and no one was turned away. The practice had started almost one hundred years earlier when many families didn't have enough for their own Thanksgiving dinner. The mayor and sheriff that year had organized it.

Now, the local churches worked together with a lot of the nearby ranches and farms. The turkeys were always donated, along with several bushels of potatoes and some vegetables. The local churches took turns cooking the turkeys and potatoes. The rest of the town signed up for various sides and desserts.

Next year, Chloe was going to try to be back in town for the event. It sounded like it might be the event of the year.

"And after we've cleared away the desserts, Santa sits on his chair and the kids get to go and sit on his lap and tell them what they want for Christmas." Melanie sighed. It was one of her favorite events of the year.

Chloe could see the happiness bubbling up in Melanie's heart as she told her the stories from years past.

"You know, that's where my Stan proposed to me." Melanie looked off into the distance, trapped in her memories of the past.

Chloe smiled and hoped she would one day find a man who engendered such love in her heart.

But it would not be Brandon. No way, no how. That cowboy was not going to get another chance to hurt her.

After they each paid for their lunches, they walked out together and Chloe stopped short on the sidewalk when a pair of brown cowboy boots stopped in front of her. She was looking where she was walking to make sure she didn't step on any ice, so she hadn't seen him approach.

"Brandon, thank you for coming to get me." Melanie smiled at her son and stepped closer to him.

Chloe's head popped up and she pasted on a smile. "Brandon, good to see you again."

He tipped his hat toward Chloe. "Nice to see you too, Chloe. Aren't you leaving today to head home for Thanksgiving?"

She chuckled. "You remembered."

He shrugged. "It was only two days ago you told me your plans for this weekend. I hope my memory isn't so bad as to forget already."

"Well, I better get back to work if I want to get out of here on time." Chloe looked up at the sky. "It looks like the snow isn't done yet for today, and I'd like to get home before it gets too bad."

Melanie put a hand on her arm. "Please don't drive if it's snowing hard when you leave. Pay close attention to the weather report. I don't want you to get into an accident."

"Thank you. I'll be careful." She smiled at the woman. "I plan on making sure that I'm healthy enough to enjoy this Christmas season."

After saying her goodbyes, she headed back to the office and tried hard not to appreciate the good-looking cowboy whose smile could light up an entire town. How anyone could have such straight, white teeth always baffled her. That was one more place on the cute cowboy she had to avoid looking at. Maybe she should just avoid him moving forward?

Her thoughts went back to work. When she got back to her desk after lunch, a brand-new pile of files that needed inputting had shown up. Chloe sighed. "Great. I better not miss my window of opportunity to drive home tonight."

Just past three in the afternoon, her boss walked into her office. "Chloe, what are you still doing here? The snow will be coming soon. You better get going if you want to make it home to Beacon Creek before they close the highway." Jillian Stewart was a great boss. She was the head nurse, and while Chloe was technically the office manager, she still had to report to someone. So she reported to the head nurse.

"Jillian, did you see the stack of files that mysteriously appeared on my desk while I was out to lunch?" Chloe sighed and sat back in her chair. She had almost finished the files before she left for lunch. Now, she doubted she would be going home.

The nurse waved her hand. "Oh, they can wait. You need to get home for the weekend. I don't want to hear that you had to turn around due to the storm." She raised a brow and put her hands on her hips.

Chloe couldn't help but chuckle. 'Yes, ma'am." She closed the file she was working on and put the stack in her bottom drawer. "I hope you have a wonderful Thanksgiving, too."

"Thank you, dear. Now go on, scoot." She waved her hands in a shooing motion for Chloe to leave.

Chloe grabbed her purse and outer gear while she laughed. "I'm going. Geesh, one would think you were trying to get rid of me or something."

"Or something." Jillian put her hands on her hips and followed Chloe out of the billing manager's office. She stayed in the hallway and watched as Chloe locked her door.

"Have a happy Thanksgiving," Chloe said over her shoulder as she put on her coat and walked toward the front door.

"You too, dear." Jillian waved and walked in the opposite direction, toward the nurse's station.

"Whoa." Chloe looked around and watched as snow fell and stuck on the ground. She bit her lip and wondered if she was even going to be able to get out of town. Her bags were packed and in her truck. All she had to do was leave. But first, she checked the weather app on her phone.

"Do I, or don't I?" she whispered as she read the storm report and wondered if she could even make it home.

Beacon Creek was east of Frenchtown. The storm would be hitting her town first. When she got into her truck and turned on the engine, she called her dad via the integrated Bluetooth. If she was lucky, the storm would just stay on her tail the entire way home.

"Chloe, please tell me you're almost here?" Her dad's gruff voice warmed her heart.

"I'm just now leaving work. How bad is the storm?" Chloe turned up the heat and clicked the button for her heated seats. She didn't always use them, but on a day as cold as this one, it would be nice. Then she turned the switch for the heated side mirrors.

"Weather Channel says the worst of it isn't here yet. Maybe two hours until it hits us. It's going to be bad. I don't know if you should come tonight. Maybe wait until tomorrow after they plow the highway?" Her dad did not sound convinced it was the best option. He sounded unsure and maybe a bit sad.

"Is everything alright?" She put the truck in reverse and headed out. The moment she heard her dad's voice, she decided she would get as close as she could. If the storm was too much, or the highway was closed, there were a few places along the way she could stop and wait it out. Then she would be that much closer for when the highway opened up again.

"Of course. I'm just worried about you, that's all. I don't

think it's a good idea to drive in this weather." His deep voice came through just fine over the phone.

"At least the cell service is still working." Chloe knew that once the cell sites started going down, it was bad. "I'm already on the road heading toward the highway. I'll see you soon."

"We'll pray for you to have a safe trip." He hesitated. "But Chloe, if it gets bad, please promise me you'll stop and wait out the storm?" His anxiety came through the clear cell reception.

"Of course, Daddy. You know I'm the one with a good head on her shoulders."

He guffawed. "Yeah, right. I know exactly who I'm talking to. You were always the little diva, not your sister."

Chloe laughed and said goodbye before clicking the off button on her steering wheel. It was probably smarter to pay attention to the road than to be chatting on her cell, even if she used the Bluetooth.

Once she had been on the road for about an hour, she began to relax. The storm was on her tail, but she felt as though she was going to make it.

Not twenty minutes later she chided herself for jinxing her trip. Then she prayed for safety. She was between towns, and since she was only going about forty miles an hour, she might not make it to the next one before the worst of the storm hit her.

While the sun technically hadn't set yet, it looked dark enough with the thick clouds to be night. Chloe had turned her lights on the moment she'd left town earlier, and her wipers were already moving as quickly as the truck allowed. Visibility was low, and her body began to tense up as her wheels started to slip in the snow.

Cutting her speed even more, she inched along the white

highway and wondered how the road wasn't already closed. When she'd thought she was going to make it, she had turned on a CD and listened to Christmas music. Now she realized she should have been listening to local radio so she could get the weather and highway reports.

With a click of a button, the version of "The Fruitcake Song" by Mannheim Steamroller switched off and the local radio station kicked in. And she wanted to kick herself for not paying more attention.

The highway was closed. She must have just missed the highway patrol closing it off when she passed Clinton. The next town was about another thirty minutes at her current speed, maybe more. Chloe worried her bottom lip and tried to decide what to do.

She decreased her speed slowly, and when she stopped she put her truck into four-wheel drive. It might be a little late, but at least she'd figured it out before the snow was too thick. Then she pulled out her cell phone and looked to see how far away she was from the next exit with services. It wouldn't help her to get off the road if there was nothing there to help keep her warm while she waited for the storm to pass.

Just when she realized she had at least twenty-five minutes to drive, her phone rang. Thinking it was her dad or mom, she answered, "I know, I know. It's bad out here."

"Chloe? Are you alright?"

Confused by the voice coming through her truck's speakers, she looked at the caller ID. "Brandon? Is that you?"

"Yes, where are you? I heard you left work a little later than you should have, and the storm is really bad. Please tell me you've pulled off at a gas station or diner to wait it out?" He sounded more worried than her father had earlier.

Which made her wonder how bad the storm was going to be.

"Actually, I'm stopped on the highway. I just put my truck in four-wheel drive and was checking Google Maps to see how long before the next exit with services." She looked up and around, hoping to see some lights from the highway patrol, or possibly a snowplow.

"That doesn't sound good. How far away are you?" Brandon asked.

"Ah, at a safe speed, about twenty-five minutes away. Maybe longer if I need to crawl along." She told him exactly where she was, and he told her about the storm.

"You're right in the middle of it. It's supposed to dump at least another foot in the next thirty minutes. Do you have gear for spending the night in your truck? I doubt the snowplows will be out until just before sunrise." He took a deep breath and released it slowly.

"Ah, I think I can make it to the next town. If I go now I can get there, and I'll just wait at the gas station. I'm sure they'll be open. If not them, I can find somewhere to wait." She did not want to sit on the side of the highway all night. She might have a blanket and her big coat, but sitting along the side of the road would not be safe, especially once the snowplows came out.

Brandon cleared his throat. "Alright, but please be careful."

"I will."

"And, Chloe?"

"Yeah?"

"Call me when you get off the highway to a safe place. I need to know you're going to be safe for the night."

She felt her cheeks warm, and something inside her chest fluttered. "I will. And thanks."

She hung up and began her slow and scary drive to the next town.

When she was only a mile or two away her tires began to slide, and she took her foot off the gas and let her truck slow on its own. Once the vehicle was stopped, she gave it a little bit of gas and inched along at a snail's pace.

She just about broke out in cheers when she saw the exit sign. Again, she took her foot off the gas and let the truck's momentum take her down the offramp. Instead of stopping at the stop sign, she rolled through and prayed a cop wasn't watching.

Chloe wasn't sure if she could have gotten her truck over the mound of snow in front of her if she came to a full and complete stop. As it was, she had to give it more gas and prayed she wouldn't spin out or get stuck a few hundred yards away from the local diner and gas station.

CHAPTER 7

When she finally made it into the parking lot, she stopped her truck right in front of the main doors to the diner, which was open. Several truckers were parked in the lot, along with a few other vehicles. Chloe guessed she wasn't the only one who had hoped to wait out the storm in the Roadside Café and Gas Station. The name of the place was a bit on the nose, but she guessed no one would really care about a fancy name in a small roadside town like this one.

Chloe bundled up against the wind and snow pelting down on her truck and stepped out. It looked more like buckets of hail than snow. But when she put her gloved hand out, the large snowflakes landed on her hand before being blown away by the biting wind.

"Well, I guess it had to happen on at least one of my trips home." She wrapped her arms around herself after closing and locking the truck and trudged to the doors.

The short walk to the café was not easy. She had to walk against the wind until she was in the entryway of the café, which thankfully blocked the worst of the wind. But the cold.

Brrr. It was not stopped by the protection of the building. She still felt the below-freezing temperature on her cheeks.

"How I enjoyed playing in this type of weather as a kid will forever elude me. No way do I want to build a snowman right now." As she continued to talk to herself, she made her way to the door and abruptly stopped in front of the double doors made of glass and steel.

A trucker had watched her get out of her truck, and he came to the door and held it open for her when she stopped.

"Thank you," she said before looking at the burly man who smiled down at her. "It's really blowing out there, isn't it?" Her nerves flamed, and she stepped away from him and toward the waitress at the counter.

"Burl, leave the poor girl alone, why dontcha. She must be colder than a popsicle." The twang in the waitress's voice and her stern look at the man behind her relaxed her nerves.

Chloe looked at the man who towered over her and noticed how he cowed under the remonstration of the tiny woman who had put her fists on her hips.

"Come on, darlin', I'll get you set up in a warm spot and bring ya coffee." The waitress waved her hand, and Chloe followed.

When she brought her to a warmer corner of the place, she noticed two families sitting in booths next to hers and she smiled at them. They all smiled back, and Chloe relaxed in her booth seat.

When the waitress handed her a menu, Chloe noticed the nametag and smirked. How many roadside cafes had hard-nosed waitresses named Flo? She would bet most of them did. Was it a fake name, or a prerequisite to get the job? "Thanks, Flo. I appreciate it."

"Huh?" The woman scrunched her face. "I'm not Flo."

Chloe pointed. "But your nametag says you are."

Flo's eyes widened, and she laughed. "Well, I'll be tarred and feathered. You're the first one to point out my mistake." She chuckled again and shook her head. "Flo is my older sister. I'm Reba."

Chloe laughed. "I take it your sister works here as well?"

Flo—well, Reba—scratched her head and then shook it. "Nah, she works at the Gas 'n' Go next door. I must have picked up the wrong nametag earlier when gettin' ready. We be roommates."

"Ah, that explains a lot." Not really, but Chloe didn't want to get into the woman's whole story. Instead, she asked, "Are you still making breakfast? Or is it only the dinner menu?" She looked down at the picture of the chocolate chip pancakes with whipped cream and strawberries and sighed.

"We serve breakfast twenty-four seven 'round these parts." Flo smiled and walked away to get a mug of steaming-hot coffee.

Chloe pulled her phone out of her pocket and realized she no longer had cell service. She held her phone up and moved it around, hoping to find at least one bar. Maybe she could get a text message through to her father, and Brandon. She didn't want them to worry about her.

"No cell service here," the man in the booth with a woman and two kids next to hers informed her.

"Really? Is it because of the storm?" Chloe hoped they normally had cell service here and it would come back on once the worst of the storm passed.

"Yes, ma'am. When we first arrived, we had one bar. Then it went away about an hour ago." He shrugged.

Chloe tried to smile, but sighed instead. "Thank you." She bit her lower lip. "Have you heard anything about the storm? Like how long it will take to pass us by?"

He shook his head. "Not really. Without cell service, I can't get anything on my phone."

Chloe looked around for some TVs but noticed there were none. Her spirits continued to deflate. She was stuck in a very small roadside stop. She wouldn't even call this place a town. And to make matters worse, there wasn't a TV or a working cell phone in sight.

When Reba came back with a steaming mug of coffee and a small carafe so she could keep her coffee topped off, she asked if the restaurant had a phone.

"We do, but it's down due to the storm. Sorry, dear." Reba pulled out her pad. "Are you ready to order?"

Before she fixed her coffee—blonde and sweet—she placed her order. "I'll take the chocolate chip pancakes with strawberries and whipped cream. Oh, and add some bacon, too. Please"

Reba beamed at her. "Perfect choice for a night like this." Then she turned to go and place her order.

Right after she took her first sip of coffee, her shoulders relaxed. The place was deathly quiet as people drank coffee or ate their food. Chloe had noticed two of the guys who looked to be truckers were sleeping in their chairs.

"Cal!" Reba yelled. "Order fer ya. Red-and-white sweet cakes with a side of oinkers."

Chloe reached for her napkin, as she'd just about spit out her coffee. She turned her head and looked to the family next to her, who were laughing. She mouthed, *Oinkers?*

The mom nodded. "Yup, gotta love the roadside slang."

Chloe chuckled. "I guess so." She thought she might want to stop here next time when the weather was better and see what all happened on a normal day. It might make for some fun people-watching.

Well, watching Reba would be fun.

.   .   .

BRANDON LOOKED at the clock above the stove. It had been almost two hours since he'd last spoken with Chloe. He hadn't wanted to distract her while she was driving, but after looking at the latest weather report, he knew she couldn't have continued much farther on the highway. "Why hasn't she called me yet?"

He paced the floor in front of his fireplace and wondered if he should call her or text her. If she was still driving for some crazy reason, he didn't want to take her attention from the road. So he decided to send a text.

Chloe, is everything alright? Did you find a safe place to stop and wait out the storm? He hit send and waited for her response.

The storm had already passed them by. Well, the worst of it had. Then he remembered that even he had lost cell service for at least an hour. And he hoped that was why he hadn't heard from Chloe yet.

One hour later, he still hadn't heard from her and was worried. Without knowing how to reach her family, he did the next best thing. He called her best friend.

"Hey, Brandon. What's up?" Lottie's cheerful—but a bit distracted—response gave him hope that nothing bad had happened, yet.

"Have you heard from Chloe?" He leaned over to put another log on the fire and continued his pacing.

"No, should I?" Lottie's voice was still cheerful, but it did sound like she had turned her attention back to the phone.

He heard her voice better now.

Brandon stopped and ran a hand through his messy brown hair, making it even worse than it was before he'd called the local coffee brewer. "I spoke to her a few hours ago and the storm was really bad. She was going to try and find a place to wait out the storm. I had asked her to call me, but she hasn't. I tried reaching her but haven't heard anything yet." He sighed. "I'm worried about her, Lottie."

"She's probably right in the middle of that storm and has no cell service. But I'll try calling her, too. How about I let you know if I hear anything, and you'll let me know?" Lottie's voice took on notes of worry now, and Brandon was sure she would do everything she could to get in touch with Chloe.

"Thanks, Lottie." He hung up with his old friend and continued pacing.

Maybe Chloe just didn't want to speak with him? That was probably why she hadn't responded yet. Who was he to demand she report in to him? The more he thought about it, the more he realized that had to be it. While he didn't know her all that well, he did know enough to know that she was a very independent woman.

It probably rankled her nerves to have him going all possessive on her after all this time. But *frostbite* if it didn't bother him to have her out there all alone in the middle of a giant storm. Those blasted weathermen had done a rotten job at forecasting the strength of the front that came through.

If only his sister had come for Thanksgiving, then he could have offered to take Chloe home for Thanksgiving. It would have given him more time with the beautiful cowgirl, and ensured she stayed safe.

Then again, he realized it would also have put them together in a truck for several hours during a snowstorm. If he wasn't careful he'd fall for her all over again, and he couldn't do that to her, his mom, or the ranch.

Running a ranch was more than a full-time job. It was a man's entire life. Add on a sick mother, and he had zero time to court a woman. Having a wife would make the job of running the ranch easier, but what about his mom? Once she was better, she could take up her old responsibilities and then he could think about possibly, maybe courting a woman. And if God blessed him, maybe he could even still have a chance with Chloe.

Turned out to be more of a blizzard than a storm. Those crackpots at the Weather Channel needed to go back to school, or spend a winter in Montana.

After what felt like hours, but was only a few minutes, Brandon realized he needed to go out and check on the horses and cattle. After a storm like what they'd just had, he might have an issue with the barn, or any of his cattle could be stuck.

"Mom!" Brandon yelled up the stairs. "I'm heading out back to check on the stock."

When he didn't hear a response, he figured his mother was resting. She had looked tired earlier when they ate dinner. He hoped she would get a good night's rest and feel much better in the morning. If not, he'd be calling the doc to find out what they could do to help her sleep.

As Brandon dressed for the cold, he decided to put his cell phone in his front pocket. Normally he left it in the house when it was this cold outside. Nothing drained a cell phone battery like the cold weather.

Between his mother not feeling well and needing to make sure he got word about Chloe, he wasn't going to leave his phone behind. In fact, he would go to sleep with it on his nightstand, ringer on high, if he didn't hear from Chloe before heading to bed.

CHAPTER 8

After a very long three hours, Chloe finally had one bar on her cell phone. She had spent the past hours checking her phone every few seconds. Well, to her it felt like it was every few seconds. However, it was more like every ten minutes or so.

She had multiple text messages coming in while she watched her phone flash that she only had four percent battery left.

Chloe knew that her phone was going to die before she could get a call through to anyone. So she sent a text to her dad to let him know she was fine, just stuck at a roadside dinner and her phone was dying.

When she hit the send button, her phone's screen went black and the little tiny white circle showed her phone shutting off before it died. She prayed that her text made it through to her dad.

A tiny niggle in the back of her mind told her she needed to let Brandon know she was fine, but with her phone officially dead, she couldn't.

Once her mini coffee carafe was empty, she flagged down Reba.

"Hey, darlin' what can I getcha?" The waitress pulled a pen from behind her ear and her notepad from the pocket of her black apron.

"My cell phone died. You don't happen to have a charger for an iPhone, do you?" Chloe winced as she waited for a reply.

Reba smacked her gum and frowned. "I'm sorry, I only have a Samsung."

Chloe sighed and sat back. "That's fine. Do you know if your landline is working yet? I really need to call my parents and let them know I'm fine."

"I'm not supposed to let customers use it"—Reba looked around—"but sure. Sweetheart, I'm sure your pa is worried. That was some storm, wasn't it?"

A bright smile lit Chloe's face. "Thank you, I really appreciate it." As she got out of the booth, Chloe decided she'd be leaving an extra-large tip for the waitress considering how well she had taken care of her.

After calling her father, she went back to her booth to wait for the highway to be cleared. She figured she should keep an eye on the truckers. They would most likely be the first ones to know if the roads were passable yet.

When she got back to her booth, a fresh mini-carafe of coffee was waiting for her, along with more sugar and creamer. As she stirred her coffee she wondered what Brandon was up to, then admonished herself for thinking of the cowboy. If she kept thinking about him he would steal her heart again, and then where would she be?

Right back where she was last Christmas. She had zero desire to ruin this Christmas, too. So she forced her thoughts away from the cute guy who had stolen her heart when he rescued her from her clumsiness last year and looked around her.

The mom in the booth next to hers looked at her and smiled. "That waitress is really good, isn't she?"

Keeping her voice low like the mother's, Chloe answered, "Yes, she really is." She looked fondly on the two kids lying in the booth, snoozing. "I wish I could sleep that easily," Chloe muttered.

IT WAS another five hours before the roads were clear. It was still dark and a few hours from sunrise, but Chloe was ready to get on the road. After she paid for her meal and left a huge tip, she got on the road again and headed home.

She plugged her cell phone into the USB charger and prayed she would have a phone to use soon.

The radio was playing Christmas tunes already, and she tuned it to hear a Christmas song by Dolly Parton and Kenny Rogers. The song was exactly what she needed to hear.

Chloe sang along with the radio. "*I'll be home with bells on.*" Then she began to hum the melody. The choir in the background also clapped, and she strummed her fingers on the steering wheel, remembering seeing this video on YouTube before. It was an older song by the singing duo, but she didn't care. Kenny and Dolly always sang so well together.

The radio station continued to play country Christmas songs and the time went by rather quickly, even though she had to keep her speed much lower than normal.

When she finally pulled into her parents' driveway, the sky was beginning to lighten and the stars had already gone to sleep for the day. The tips of what looked to be a glorious sunrise full of oranges and yellows with white, puffy clouds and the slightest hints of purples and blues were in the distance above the mountains she had driven through.

The distant edges of the storm were all that remained. Someone had come after the snow stopped and plowed the driveway, probably Matthew. It made it easier for her to get all the way up to the house. She parked and took her overnight bag out of the truck and headed to the front door.

"It's about time. What'd ya do, drive to Seattle and back?" Matthew laughed and walked toward Chloe with his arms out for a hug.

Chloe hugged him tight and sighed into his strong arms. "It's so good to see you. I thought that storm would never let up." She chuckled and let him go. "Where is everyone else?"

"Pa and our brothers are out back checkin' on the stock. I just finished plowin' the drive fer ya. How was the drive in?" Matthew took her bag and walked her back to her room so she could put her things away.

"It was fine. I listened to the country Christmas station and it helped." Chloe laughed when she saw the frown on her big brother's face. "I know, you don't like Christmas music."

"Nah, it's not that. It's just that it's too soon. Ya gotta wait for Thanksgivin' to be over first." Matthew shook his head and mussed his little sister's hair.

They both laughed when Chloe knocked his hand away.

"You do know that I'm no longer a little kid, right?" Chloe chuckled. She had missed her family, but she was happy where she was.

"Really? Aren't you just a little snot-nosed rug rat?" Matthew laughed and stepped back out of his sister's way.

Chloe had a habit of hitting him hard when they messed around. Matthew was glad his ma wasn't nearby; she always made them take their wresting outside. And it was way too cold to go outside just to mess with his little sister.

"Alright, alright. I need to lay down for a short nap. Tell Ma I'll be up soon to help with breakfast." Chloe pushed her brother out of her room and closed the door behind him before he could say a word.

"Only little kids need morning naps." Matthew chuckled as he walked away, happy to have his sister home safely for the Thanksgiving weekend. He wished she lived closer, but he was happy for her. She had the job she wanted, and he would not wish that away from her.

Before Chloe went to sleep, she texted Brandon that she'd made it safely home and she would tell him all about her adventure when she saw him next. As she lay down to sleep, she covered her yawn and mused over what she had texted to Brandon. Would she see him again? Or would they just be two old acquaintances passing in the night?

LATER THAT EVENING, once they had eaten their traditional Thanksgiving dinner of a fresh turkey—which their mother had plucked only the day before—and all the trimmings, Chloe sat at the card table with Matthew, his fiancée Claire, and her twin, Elizabeth. They were playing spades. Chloe and Elizabeth had always partnered when playing card games. With their twin connection, they could easily read each other's non-verbal cues. And they almost always won. But this time, Matthew and Claire were giving them a run for their money. They always bet with pennies from a giant mason jar that kept everyone's discarded pennies just for their card games.

Once the evening was over, all the money would go back into the jar for the next time anyone wanted to play some cards.

Chloe looked across the table at her sister and partner.

Knowing what she needed to put down for her sister to take the trick and give them the points they needed to win, she discarded an ace of hearts.

Elizabeth tried to hide her smile, but Chloe saw it.

When Chloe looked out of the corner of her eye, she saw Matthew focusing and looking at Claire. He opened his mouth to say something, and Chloe was ready to chide him if he engaged in table talk. They weren't allowed to talk about the game, or anything resembling cards. They could talk about anything else if they wanted. Normally they all wanted to stay focused, so most talk was centered around the weather or barbecue.

Her family was known all over the state for having the best barbecue sauce, and the best beef. They were an organic ranch, and only the best for their cows would do.

Matthew put down a king of diamonds, hoping his Claire had a higher spade than Elizabeth did.

Before Elizabeth even pulled the card out of her hand, she smiled. Then she slapped the ace of spades down on the pile. When it was Claire's turn, she put her last spade, a king, down.

"Ahh, no. I thought you had that ace, not Elizabeth." Matthew sighed and folded his cards. He was out of spades, as was Chloe. She hadn't had any spades the past two hands. The remaining trump cards were between Elizabeth and Claire.

Elizabeth looked to Claire. "Are you all out of spades?"

Claire nodded.

"That's what I thought. I've only got spades left," she announced triumphantly.

Matthew moaned. "Nooo. Not again. I thought for sure this time we would win. I'm sorry, honey." He put his hand across the table, and Claire put hers in his.

"It's alright. That was a good game. Very close right up until the end." Claire smiled and laughed good-naturedly. Even though she was very competitive, all she cared about this weekend was spending time with her soon-to-be in-laws and enjoying some good food before the craziness of a Christmas wedding—and, a few days later, the actual Christmas Day—took over.

"I think you're going to make a great sister." Chloe smiled and took the cards to begin counting.

"Don't bother—you know you and Elizabeth won." Matthew furrowed a brow and looked between his little sisters.

Elizabeth smirked and stood up. "Well, if that's game I better get my husband and get going home. Tomorrow is going to be a very early day at the general store, and I offered to help with the Black Friday sales." She shivered.

Chloe laughed. "That's what you get for marrying the guy who runs the general store." In the past, the two sisters and their mother would drive into Bozeman super early and start their shopping there. Then they would come home to Beacon Creek and finish up at their town's general store.

This year, Chloe wasn't really sure what they were going to do for shopping the next day.

When she went to her room to ready for bed, she realized she had left her phone charging on her nightstand all day long. She checked it for any missed messages and was surprised to see a text and a call from Brandon, as well as two texts from Lottie.

She was about to call her friend when the phone rang. She smiled at the caller ID. "Lottie, Happy Thanksgiving!"

"Figgy pudding, Chloe. What happened? Why didn't you call me and let me know you were safe?" The worry and something else—maybe frustration—came through very clearly.

"I'm sorry, Lottie. I didn't mean to worry you. I left my phone charging on the dresser all day long. It was practically dead when I got here, and then I just forgot about it. The entire family was here today. It's been a bit crazy." Chloe laughed and shook her head at everything they did that day.

"But you were thinking enough to text Brandon this morning?" Now Lottie's voice took on a teasing lilt, and Chloe knew she was in trouble.

"Now stop that right now," Chloe ordered sternly.

"Stop what?" Lottie giggled. "Seriously, I had to hear from Brandon that you finally made it home safely."

"And why were you discussing me with Brandon?"

"He called me when he couldn't reach you last night. Brandon was really worried about you. Besides, that storm was awful. Where did you end up finding shelter?" All teasing left Lottie's voice as she asked for details about Chloe's trip home.

Chloe explained her night and how she finally got home, and the girls chatted about their Thanksgiving Day and family.

Right before Lottie was going to hang up, she asked, "So, Brandon's looking pretty good these days, isn't he?"

Chloe had a feeling she wasn't sure she understood what her friend meant. A pain shot through her chest, and she felt her shoulders tense. "Does this mean you've got a new crush?" That didn't feel right to Chloe. Nor did she like the idea of her best friend and Brandon together.

Lottie laughed. "Would you be alright with it if I did?"

Chloe saw red and was about to yell out *no*, but she decided against it. "I don't know. I always thought you and Cove had something special going."

"No, absolutely no way will I ever date a rodeo cowboy again. You know that." Lottie's voice sounded pained.

Chloe smacked her head and mentally chided herself. She knew better, but she just could not help trying to get her friend's mind away from Brandon. "I'm sorry. I know you and Cove are only so close because he promised your husband to look after you and Quinn."

"That's right. Besides, he's more like my brother than anything else." The young widow's voice was starting to get back to normal, which made Chloe feel better.

She hated that her friend was still so torn up about the loss of her husband seven years ago. She knew it meant that Lottie loved Samuel so much, but she did think it was time for Lottie to move on. Cove would make for a great husband and father... if he ever retired from bull-riding. "All right, well, I've got to get some sleep. Black Friday comes really early around here."

Both of them giggled as though they were teenagers again and said goodnight before hanging up. Chloe was glad that she and Lottie could laugh as they did even after discussing something as serious as Lottie's husband.

Chloe went to sleep thinking about Brandon and how he worried so much about her, completely forgetting to return his messages.

CHAPTER 9

Brandon knew he shouldn't have expected Chloe to respond to his messages on Thanksgiving Day. She was with her family, and he knew it was a large one. They probably had activities from sun-up to sun-down, and he was sure she went to bed early so she could get up extra early on Friday morning for some crazy shopping.

He had never wanted to do Black Friday shopping before. So what was he doing up before the crack of dawn, taking care of their cattle the morning after Thanksgiving? He had a ton of work to do around the ranch if he wanted it all done before spring calving began. Winter was normally an easier time, but since he had been gone for the past year his mother had neglected a lot of the more complex maintenance.

Working the ranch always got his mind off his troubles, and he had plenty to ponder these days. Sundays were always a day of rest, but Thursdays were only a restful day when it was Thanksgiving. Today, Friday, was supposed to be a day full of work on the ranch. Work he *wanted* to do.

His mother had been tired yesterday and not feeling well, which was why he helped her cook their turkey dinner. His sister had invited them to come to her house for Thanksgiving, but his mother didn't feel like going anywhere. He wished they would have. Then she probably would have slept in the car and gotten some of the rest she needed.

However, today was another story. She came into his room before four a.m. and woke him up, telling him he needed to go take care of the stock so they could go shopping. He was surprised by how much she had bounced back. He didn't have the heart to tell her to go by herself.

The sparkle in her eyes was his first clue as to how well she was doing that morning. More would come throughout the day—more that he wasn't prepared for.

He knew he had to go with her. Not for the shopping, but so he could ensure she didn't overdo it and end up in worse shape than she was the day before.

When he met her inside after feeding the cattle, his mother had a thermos of hot coffee waiting for him. "Thanks, Ma." He leaned over and kissed the top of her head. "Are you sure you want to go shopping today? We could do that online shopping everyone's been talking about."

"Honey, it's just not the same. I love the hustle and bustle. All the Christmas decorations. But most especially, I love to touch the items and make sure they're exactly what I want, and good quality, too." She pointed at the door and arched a brow.

If Brandon didn't know any better, he would say she was healthy as an ox. This version of his mother was what he remembered from before he left. If going shopping and having to deal with all those crazy women fighting over one-dollar towels, or whatever the super-extra-special-priced items were that day, he would deal with it. For his mom.

Lord, please give me the strength to keep up with my mom today. Something tells me I'm going to need help to make it through the day, he silently prayed as he went to take a quick shower before they left.

* * *

"MA, HOW CAN YOU STAND THIS?" Brandon's face pinched and he put his hands in front of him to keep a woman from falling into him. The ladies all around him were pushing and shoving to get to the pile of movies that were priced at only three dollars.

They had started out in a nice and orderly line while they waited for the Wal-Mart outside of Missoula to open. Well, for *their* line to open. The store had opened up at five that morning, but not all lines for the different goods on sale were open.

It was the strangest thing Brandon had ever seen. Why in the world would some lines be open and some closed, even though the store was open? He found out the hard way.

Turned out the store needed multiple employees to man each line, so they took turns opening up different lines. It was a madhouse. His mother wanted to get some Disney DVDs that were on special that morning for his sister's kids. Brandon had wanted to go get in line for the power tools that were on sale, but his mother insisted they would still be there after they finished this line. Now he understood why she needed his help.

Brandon pushed and shoved, as politely as he could, to get through to the Disney bin the moment the red tape had been taken down. He couldn't believe the workers wanted the shoppers to swarm the bins this way, but there weren't enough of them to stop the crazy ladies with dollar signs in their eyes instead of any sense.

"That's mine!" one lady in an ugly Christmas sweater

with a reindeer ice skating yelled at a woman who held onto the other end of the latest Disney animated movie.

"No, it's mine! Let go! I had it first!" The other lady wore a red sweater with the face of a snowman on it. The carrot nose stood out so far, it almost touched the woman she was fighting with. He doubted her sweater would survive the day.

Shaking his head, he led his mother to another bin where more copies of that same movie were sitting to the side, and his mother picked up one copy. She looked to the fighting duo and picked up another copy.

"Come on, we need to help." Melanie took her son's hand and walked to the fighting ladies. "Excuse me, but I think you need this." She held out the movie to the closest woman.

The two ladies looked at her with evil intent in their eyes, then down at the movie she held in her hand. Both of them dropped the movie they were holding and tried to yank the one in Melanie's hands away from her.

"Hold up, ladies. There's plenty to go around. One of you pick up the movie you were fighting over, and the other can take this one." Brandon took the movie from his mother's hands and held it up above the two crazy Christmas ladies.

They eyed each other before the one with the ice-skating reindeer bent down to grab the one off the floor. "This one's better anyways," she called before she moved on to the next bin.

"For Christmas's sake, there's no need to fight over the movies. There's plenty here." Melanie tsk'd, and walked away once Brandon gave the movie to the lady with Frosty on her sweater.

Two of the Wal-Mart employees manning other bins shook their heads. One chortled while the other laughed so hard Brandon thought he saw spit flying out of the guy's mouth. He took two steps away from that guy before moving on.

Brandon couldn't help but laugh. His deep, throaty laugh caught the attention of a few other women wearing ugly Christmas sweaters. One of them checked him out while the others growled and pushed past him. "Ma, you really enjoy this?" He waved a hand to encompass the chaos surrounding them.

"Yes, I do. It's invigorating, isn't it?" Melanie beamed and picked up a few more movies and handed them to Brandon to hold.

All the shopping carts had been gone when they'd arrived. They only had a small handheld basket, which Brandon held close to his chest after one woman eyed the movies in his basket. He was afraid she would try and grab them. She might have if he hadn't wrapped an arm around it and moved out of her way.

"Can we go and check out the power tools now? I need a few new ones to get those outbuildings done this spring." He figured if he had to be there, he was going to get one of those good deals, too.

Melanie chuckled. "Of course, right after we check out the four-dollar pajamas. I want to get your sister's entire family matching Christmas pajamas for Christmas Eve." She headed toward the clothing department, and Brandon followed.

As they walked toward the clothes, he noticed another man who looked afraid to move away from the shopping cart he guarded. He stood beside an aisle that didn't seem to have any sale merchandise along it. Behind him were two more men. It looked like Brandon had found the smart husbands' hiding spot. Or, maybe they weren't so smart if their wives had talked them into going Black Friday shopping.

As he walked by, he nodded and chuckled. The men returned the nod, but none of them were laughing. They all kept turning their heads as if they were looking out for an ambush. Brandon wouldn't be surprised to find a crazy woman climbing over one of the racks to steal an item from one of the carts.

He wanted nothing to do with that.

His mom had gotten a few feet in front of him, so he rushed to catch up to her. Losing his mother in Wal-Mart on Black Friday scared him to death. All he could think of was finding her body on the floor, trampled by a stampede of psycho ladies wearing Christmas sweaters looking for the next line to open so they could rush it.

"Mom, don't get too far from me," he called out as he finally caught up to her.

Melanie laughed. "Son, you aren't a small child anymore. I think you can handle being on your own."

"Not in a store full of scary ladies who aren't afraid to knock anyone down. I can't believe I let you talk me into this. Next year, it's all online shopping." He moved his basket to his other side as a scary lady with a Santa hat and a blinking red nose tried to stick her head in his basket.

OVER IN BOZEMAN, Chloe and the women in her family were all wearing matching red Christmas sweaters with a Santa and his reindeer applique sewn on the front. They were also in a Wal-Mart, but they were experienced Black Friday shoppers. They had gotten there at three a.m. that morning and were among the first in line. They had two shopping carts between them and a map of the store that listed everything on sale and what aisle each item was down.

While they waited in line, they worked out their plan of

attack. Each one of them picked a line to run to once the doors opened. Thankfully, it hadn't snowed that night. But since it was cold enough to snow, they were all bundled up and each had a thermos of their favorite coffee.

"Alright, I'll hit up the DVD line," Chloe offered. From the ad, she could see a lot of movies she wanted for her own collection. Not to mention a few for her mother's collection.

"And I'll get in the line for the towels." Elizabeth knew that Chloe needed new bath towels, as did her mother. With the plan to have more homeless women move into their ranch, they were going to need more plain bath towels. But they did want them to be of decent quality. Just because the women were used to living on the streets and not getting a regular shower didn't mean they deserved sub-standard bath towels.

Part of their program was to show them what life was like in a home that was full of love, and essential items they didn't see much of out on the streets of Bozeman.

Elizabeth had started an outreach program not that long ago for the homeless population in Bozeman. It had taken them a long time to get in good with the women, but they were finally making inroads, no thanks to the good-for-nothing sheriff of Bozeman.

Judith Manning, Chloe's mom, closed her ad. "I think I'll get in the line for the dishes. We're going to need a lot more plates and bowls if everything works as planned this next year."

"Perfect, and I'll get in line for the TVs. Who needs a new TV?" Claire didn't watch much television, but since she'd moved to the Triple J Ranch she didn't have one in her room. Given that the one she wanted was only $150, she thought it would be a great buy and it would make it easier for her to watch the dressage competitions and even some horse races so she could keep up with her clients and their horses.

"We could probably use a couple of those cheap ones as well. The cottages the boys have planned for this spring could use a TV in each one. Is there a limit?" Judith opened up her ad once again to look at the electronics section.

"With five of us, we could each get one and then there should be enough if the limit is only one per person." Elizabeth scanned her ad for the TVs her mother wanted.

Everyone discussed what they needed and how many they could buy. Once the doors opened, they were all armed with their lists and a good plan of action. However, Callie, being a sheriff's deputy, had a backup plan in case anything went wrong.

With smiles on their faces and excited chatter, they all made their way inside and each woman peeled away to head to their line as quickly—and safely—as possible. Every one of them had made it to their line and ended up being at least one of the first five, if not the first one.

Judith was blessed to be the first in line. Claire ended up being fifth in line for the TVs, and Chloe was second in line for the DVDs, while Elizabeth was also first for the towels. Only Elizabeth didn't have to wait. The towels were open for her to take what she needed. Since she didn't see any signs about limits, she picked up fifteen bath towels, fifteen hand towels, and thirty washcloths.

The only problems they had were with the electronics. Once Elizabeth was done with the towels, she went to join Claire in line for the TVs. The lady behind Claire was not happy that Elizabeth cut the line to join her future sister-in-law. When Claire offered to let that lady cut in front of her, the woman's attitude changed and everyone was happy.

After a long morning of shopping, they headed back to

Beacon Creek to finish up with the general store. Elizabeth was needed to help at the Beacon Creek general store, so she'd left Wal-Mart as soon as they had completed their purchases and didn't get to keep shopping with the rest of the women in her family.

When Judith, Chloe, Claire, and Callie all walked into the general store, Elizabeth smiled and waved them over to where she was helping a customer. When she was done, they all went to the local diner for lunch and coffee—lots of coffee.

While Chloe loved her family and her hometown, she realized she missed Frenchtown. Especially Lottie's coffee shop. When she felt her phone buzz in her pocket, she pulled it out and a smile spread across her face.

The text message she received sent flitters of excitement through her belly. She unlocked her phone and read the entire message from Brandon. The laugh that escaped her caught the attention of everyone at her table.

Elizabeth eyed her and the phone in her hand. "What's so funny?"

Without looking up, she began to respond to Brandon. *I can't believe you went Black Friday shopping. We just finished up and are having lunch.* She hit send and looked up at the expectant faces. "What?" Chloe hadn't heard her sister, or anyone, as she was so absorbed in Brandon's message.

"Hmm, me thinks that was a text from a cowboy." Callie raised her eyebrows suggestively, and everyone at the table laughed.

"Do you have a new man? Why didn't you tell me?" Elizabeth's round eyes homed in on her twin.

"I don't have a new man." And Chloe did not. Brandon was just a friend. "Brandon just texted me that he went shopping with his mom this morning. Can you believe it?" She giggled.

Judith raised a brow. "Since when did Brandon come home?"

"I thought you two weren't even talking since he left," Elizabeth stated.

Chloe felt cornered and wished she hadn't opened that text message. Now, all the women in her family were going to drill her for answers to the types of questions she did not want running through her head.

"We weren't. At least, not until a couple days ago." She hoped if she was nonchalant they would drop it. Chloe shrugged and put her phone in her pocket, even though her fingers were itching to see his response. The phone buzzed again with a text message she was sure was from him. Not wanting to give her family any reason to think there was more going on, she ignored the buzz in her pocket and smiled at her family.

"So, he's home for Thanksgiving and you saw him?" Judith asked.

"Ah, not exactly."

Elizabeth narrowed her eyes and put her hands on the table in front of her. "Give me your phone. I want to see what's going on."

"No." Chloe's eyes bulged. "It's none of your business." Chloe couldn't believe her sister wanted to read her personal text messages. If she wasn't careful, her sister would find a way to steal her phone. She double-checked that the phone was still in her pocket and left her hand over it.

"What's going on? Who's Brandon?" Callie asked.

Once Elizabeth had explained the situation, all the women at the table waited for Chloe to tell them what was going on.

She blew a breath out. "Fine." After she told them what

little she knew about Brandon, Elizabeth and Callie squealed with excitement.

"You have to see if he's responded." Claire just about jumped out of her chair to move closer to Chloe.

"Geeze, sit down Claire." Chloe chuckled. "I'll see." She pulled her phone out of her pocket and laughed again as a long text message popped up telling her about the Christmas Crazy Ladies he'd come across while shopping. She read it out loud to her family and everyone laughed with her.

"You have to respond. He totally wants to keep a conversation going with you." Claire smiled and clapped her hands. Then she jumped a little in her seat.

Chloe laughed and shook her head. "I think you guys are more excited about this than I am."

"You're my last single daughter. Of course I'm excited when a handsome cowboy shows attention." Judith smiled at her daughter.

With a sister married and two brothers about to get married, Chloe felt like she was about to be considered a spinster. She really needed to stop reading Regency romance novels.

In this day and age, twenty-eight and single did not put her on the shelf. Plenty of women waited to get married until they were in their thirties. She still had plenty of time. Besides, Brandon had made it very clear when he left that there wasn't a future for them. For all she knew, he had a girl back in Wyoming who would be coming out there for Christmas or something.

"Are you going to text him back?" Callie asked.

She had almost forgotten about his message. "Oh, right."

She looked down at the screen and wrote, *You need a team and a game plan to survive shopping on days like today. I had my mom, sister, & 2 future sisters with me. We got everything on our lists without fighting.* She hit send and sat back.

Chloe watched as the little "delivered" message turned to "read." Then the three flashing dots showed up indicating he was writing her back.

She felt a hand on her shoulder as Elizabeth leaned over to read what was on her screen.

"Hey, now!" Chloe exclaimed, and put the phone to her chest to hide the incoming message.

"Oh, come on. You gotta share, sis." Elizabeth laughed and stood up.

"You guys do realize he isn't interested in me romantically, right?" Chloe needed her family to understand this was just a friend texting her. There was not anything going on, nor would there be. When Brandon broke her heart last year, she promised herself that she would move on from him, and she did.

No way would she go backwards. Not even for a cowboy as cute as Brandon.

CHAPTER 10

Sitting in the Frenchtown Roasting Company with a heavenly cup of freshly roasted Christmas coffee, Brandon smiled at his phone. Chloe was taunting him over his lack of preparation for shopping that morning, and he was enjoying the back and forth.

When will you be home? Will you be here for the tree lighting ceremony? He hit send and sat back and waited for her answer.

The sight of a pair of very worn cowboy boots next to his table caused him to look up.

"So, what's got ya so happy?" Cove pulled a chair out and joined his friend at the table.

"It's nothing. Just texting a friend about this morning." Brandon took a sip of his coffee and smiled at his friend. "Have you ever been Black Friday shopping?"

Cove put both of his hands up and sat back against his chair. "Whoa now, them's fightin' words."

Both men chuckled amicably.

"Did some woman try roping you into shopping this morning?" Cove asked.

He nodded. "Sure did."

Cove's eyebrow shot above his hairline. "She must be someone special. Who is it? Anyone I know?" He gave his friend the smile that caused woman all over the country to swoon for the rodeo star.

Brandon pointed a finger at his friend. "Hey now, you get ahold of yourself. This woman isn't for you."

Cove leaned forward and his grin turned almost feral. "Oh really? Wanna bet?"

If Cove wanted to go after his mother, Brandon just might enjoy watching the show. "You think you're man enough for her?" He tried with all his might to keep from laughing.

"I'm more man than you are." Cove chuckled. "What's the matter? Are you afraid of a little competition?"

Brandon laughed and put his hands in the air. "Oh, that's not it at all." Out of the corner of his eye he saw his mother enter the coffee shop. "Wanna place a little wager on who she'll choose for dinner?"

Clove slapped his thigh and laughed. "You know it! Come on, tell me who she is."

"Coffee for the first week in December?" Brandon put his hand out.

Cove shook it. "You're on." His cocky smile was about to be wiped clear.

"She's heading to our table now." Brandon turned to smile at his mother.

Cove looked over his shoulder and tried to see who was coming, but the only person he saw was Mrs. Beck. "Where? All I see is your momma." He whipped his head back around and glared at Brandon. "You didn't!"

Brandon laughed so hard he snorted. "You should have seen your face. That was priceless. Still wanna try for the woman who got me to go shopping today?"

The rodeo star glared daggers at his friend and stood up. He put a nice smile on his face before he turned to look at Brandon's mom. "Mrs. Beck, it's so good to see you again. Did you drag your son out this morning for those pesky Christmas deals?"

Melanie patted Cove's cheek. "How many times do I have to tell you to call me Melanie? And yes, my son took me shopping all morning." She sat down in the chair to Brandon's right.

"Hey, Ma. Did you get everything you wanted at the Sip 'n' Go?" Brandon had come to the coffee shop to wait for his mom to get a few items from the store before they headed home for a quiet evening.

"I did. I thought we might want to try that new gluten-free pizza they have in the freezer. I picked up a pepperoni just for you and veggie for me." Melanie smiled at her son and turned to look at Cove. "Do you have dinner plans? Perhaps with a special barista?" She turned her gaze to Lottie and waved at the woman, who looked her way.

Cove's cheeks tinged with pink, and he coughed. "No, ma'am. No plans for tonight."

"Well, if you like you could join us for frozen pizza," Melanie offered.

Brandon laughed and waited for Cove to answer. If he wanted, he could hold Cove to their bet. His mom did offer him dinner first and Cove second.

Cove glared at Brandon. "That doesn't count."

"Oh, really? A dinner invitation from my mom doesn't count as dinner with a woman?" Brandon arched a brow and waited for Cove to dig himself further in the hole.

Cove spluttered and made an incoherent reply before turning tail and practically running out of the store.

Melanie turned a confused gaze on her son. "What was that all about?"

Brandon chuckled and watched his friend leave faster than a bull bucking out of a chute. "Nothing, Ma. Cove had been teasing me about going shopping today."

Still confused, she looked back at the door and didn't see Cove anywhere.

BRANDON AND CHLOE texted a few more times that weekend, sharing what they had done with their family and how each one marked the official start of their Christmas season.

Before Chloe returned home at the end of the weekend, Brandon thought it was nice to have a female friend. Maybe they could do some of the Christmas events together—strictly as friends—and enjoy the season.

A niggling feeling in the back of his mind told him he was kidding himself if he thought men and women could be just friends. Especially with a woman as beautiful, intelligent, and giving as Chloe Manning. A man would have to be certifiable if he thought he could be friends with her and not want more.

Brandon shook his head and wondered if his heart would get the memo and stay out of the picture.

CHAPTER 11

A fter a great night of sleep back in her own bed, Chloe
stretched before getting up Monday morning. Today
she would head to Lottie's for her peppermint mocha before
heading in to work. She dreaded the stack of billing waiting
for her in her desk drawer, but she was so very grateful to
Jillian for insisting she leave early on Wednesday. If she had
not, she wouldn't have made it out of town until Thursday
morning. And she never would have had her adventure in the
snowstorm.

Now she could laugh at what happened, but on
Wednesday night she was nervous. Plus, the blizzard
prompted Brandon to call and text her. She doubted they
would be planning to meet up later that night at the town
square to get their ornaments for the children's toy drive if
they hadn't had so many conversations over the long holiday
weekend.

Chloe's lips stretched into a huge smile when she saw all
the new decorations on Lottie's coffee shop. Outside, there
was a real tree with homemade ornaments. Most of them
looked to be handmade wooden ornaments, the type of thing

that would survive the winter weather of Montana. Although, the silver star on the tree looked to be a cardboard star covered with aluminum foil. She guessed Lottie threw that away each year.

It was very smart. There were lights and even some red ribbons draped around, as well as a few bows put into the spots that seemed a bit bare. The tree wasn't very large, maybe a four-foot spruce. But it was in a pot, so Lottie must have kept it year-round and reused it each year as it grew.

When Chloe walked inside, she immediately felt wrapped in Christmas cheer. All around her were real green boughs with red velvet ribbons tied to them. Of course, the bell above the door was a jingle bell from Santa's sleigh. On the middle of each table sat a battery-operated red candle with greenery surrounding it. An ornament adorned each of the boughs, making it look like part of an old-fashioned tree. The two larger tables also had lengths of red and green beads woven in and around the boughs.

Lottie also had a tree inside. This one wasn't real, only because of fire code standards. So she had a beautiful fake tree, but it looked really close to real. The lights were white with green wires. The decorations looked like items one would find in a Hallmark store. She had also put silver strands of beads and silver bows all over the tree. The topper was a silver angel with lights in its wings. The tree was gorgeous. It was so beautiful and classy that it could have easily come from the pages of a *Better Homes & Garden* Christmas edition magazine.

Then the scents of the place. Oh my, did Chloe love it. She smelled vanilla, chocolate, orange spices, cinnamon, and something she couldn't quite make out. It must have been the coffee beans, because it was a rich, strong scent that without all the other scents would have overpowered the place. But everything together made it feel like Christmas.

A feeling of warmth, peace, and joy enveloped Chloe, and she sighed. This place was home and Christmas all mixed up in one pretty package. She knew that moving to Frenchtown was the right decision. But texting back and forth all weekend with Brandon, and agreeing to meet him in town later that night? She wasn't too sure of that.

"Chloe! Good to see you made it home safely. No snowstorms to battle last night?" Lottie laughed and came over to hug her friend.

Chloe laughed along with the barista. "Thank goodness, it was an easy drive home. I kept the heater on as well as my heated seats, and it was a fantastic drive as I listened to Christmas music the entire way home." She was really and truly ready for Christmas to start.

Joy filled Chloe's entire being. If she could, she would take the month of December off and do everything she possibly could to help others enjoy the reason for the season. Christmas was her favorite time of the year.

People were generally happier, and more apt to help those in need, than any other time of year. Her new town was really great at doing outreach and showing God's love to not only children, but also to anyone who needed a little extra help.

Her church's fall festival raised money every year to help with Christmas outreach. They sent food baskets to families and singles who needed it, as well as provided Christmas presents for the children who wouldn't normally get anything. Some of the farms and ranches were barely making it. And the past few years had been extra tough with the crazy weather patterns. Some crops failed, and more cattle than usual had been lost to disease.

"I have a new treat for you to try."

Lottie's excited look got Chloe wondering what the baking goddess had created this year. She looked over at the enclosed case with the pastries and tried to see what might be new. "I don't see anything new. What did you make today?"

"Oh, it's not available for sale yet. I whipped it up this morning and want you to try it before I offer it up." Lottie rubbed her hands on her apron and hurried back behind the counter. With a twinkle in her eyes, Lottie pulled out a small box and handed it to Chloe. "Wait until you have your peppermint mocha, then open it and eat it as you drink your mocha. The new item was designed with the Christmas drinks in mind."

Chloe went to the counter to pay for her drink, as it was already done and waiting for her. "Thank you." She put a dollar in the tip jar and smiled at the teen who worked in the mornings before school.

"You're welcome, Miss Chloe. I hope you enjoy it." Tessa handed her the cup and smiled.

"What are we going to do next fall when you go off to college?" Chloe had come to really like the young girl who worked every weekday morning before going into school. She had a work/study program and didn't go in until second period. Then she had all afternoon to get her homework done. Plus, she was on the girls' volleyball team in the spring.

Chloe didn't know how the girl had so much energy. And she maintained a 4.0 GPA. She was hoping to get a scholarship to the University of Montana. Chloe doubted the girl would be able to attend if she didn't get at least a partial scholarship.

Which gave her a great idea for her special Gift to God this year. Every year Chloe chose someone who needed a little extra help. Sometimes it was money, sometimes it was the gift of her time. Last year she helped her neighbors Mr. and Mrs. Rice, who also owned the house she lived in.

Mrs. Rice had fallen and broken her hip right after Chloe moved into her house. Since the Rices lived next door, she noticed how much difficulty Mr. Rice had with taking care of his wife, as well as his numerous properties. Every Saturday during the month of December, Chloe went over and helped Mrs. Rice for the day. She would clean the house and cook up a few meals that could be easily microwaved during the week for lunch or dinner.

This helped Mr. Rice to keep taking care of his tenants when they needed his help, and he didn't feel bad leaving his wife home alone on Saturdays, when he did most of his work. They had a part-time caregiver who was with Mrs. Rice during the week for four hours a day, but it wasn't enough time for Mr. Rice to get all of his work done. So, Chloe went over there and helped out wherever she saw need.

She continued to give them her Saturdays until Mrs. Rice was back up on her feet. Thankfully, Mrs. Rice was in great shape before her injury. It only took her four months before she was healed enough to do her own cooking. They did end up hiring a house cleaner last February, and the woman from their church continued to come and clean once a week. It turned out to be a win-win. The elderly lady needed a job to help supplement her retirement, so a few of the families who could afford it hired her. And this helped Mrs. Rice to continue healing without the need to clean her house and slow down her healing.

Chloe was amazed at how much the local church did for their members, and even those who didn't attend their church. Most of the kids who would benefit from the Christmas presents this year didn't attend their church.

She loved giving back to her community, which was

partly why she became a medical billing manager. She wanted to be a nurse, but she didn't have the stomach for needles. She could handle blood, but bring a needle near her and she'd get so lightheaded she would have to sit down before she fainted.

With Tessa in mind, she went and sat at a table farther from the counter.

Lottie brought the little box over to her with a question in her eyes.

Chloe smiled and asked Lottie to sit with her. "I was wondering if you know much about Tessa's school situation."

Lottie beamed. She loved the young lady who worked for her and was going to be very sad to see her leave. But, she was also very proud of her for getting accepted to UM. "She's working on getting the funding together. But I don't know how much she's going to get in federal aid or scholarships. And even if she does get what she needs, the living expenses are going to be really tough on her and her family."

Chloe nodded. "Yeah, that's what I was afraid of. It's too far for her to drive every day. What if we got a bunch of people to help with some sort of fundraiser? Maybe we could raise enough to help with her living expenses? I know I have a small amount I put away from each of my checks to help someone out every year. I didn't use it last year, and I haven't figured out who to help this year. It could be Tessa."

The tears that developed in Lottie's eyes were enough to cause Chloe to sniff back tears herself. "I've already offered to keep her on for the weekends. She'll come home every Friday night and work a full day on Saturday, then come over before church on Sunday and come back after church."

Lottie closed the coffee shop during church, but she had so many customers who wanted to come by before and after church that she had started opening up for a few hours in the morning and then again in the afternoon a few years back. It helped her make enough to hire someone to help on Sundays. Lottie didn't want to work on the Lord's day. It was the one day of the week she took off and spent with her daughter.

She had staff that took turns working on Sundays, but only as long as they attended church between their shifts. It was always very important to Lottie that her employees never chose work over church.

Chloe respected that choice. In this day and age, it was rare to see a business closed on Sunday. Even in their small town, most shops were open on Sundays. However, several did close during morning services so everyone could attend.

"Do you think we could raise enough funds to help her cover whatever she's short?" Chloe hated the idea of the poor girl coming out in debt to her ears with student loans. The money Tessa could make working at the coffee shop each weekend should be enough for her gas and pocket money.

"It's nine thousand a year for room and board. That's an awful lot of money to raise. But, every dollar would help lower how much she had to take out in loans." Lottie took hold of Chloe's hand and squeezed it. "What did you have in mind?"

Chloe thought about it. She had saved over one thousand dollars for her special fund. She believed the Spirit was guiding her in this, and she would pray for more direction and ideas to help the sweet girl. "Give me a couple days, and I'll pray about it."

"I'll pray, too. Maybe between the both of us we can come up with something." Lottie wiped a stray tear away and then pushed the little box toward her friend. "Alright, now you must try this."

A giddy feeling spread down to Chloe's stomach, and she quickly opened the little box to see a beautiful pastry covered in crushed candy canes and pink whipped cream. "*Oh,* I think I'm going to love it."

Lottie clapped, and her smile stretched from ear to ear as she waited for her friend to try the new idea.

Cream oozed out of the pastry as Chloe took a large bite, and she just about moaned. It was a puff pastry filled with more pink whipped cream, crushed candy canes, and a little bit of chocolate. Once she'd swallowed and licked her lips along with her fingers of all the gooey goodness, she smiled. "Lottie, I think you have the makings of legal crack here."

Both women laughed.

"If you warmed it up just a tad bit, made the chocolate a little bit gooier, you would have lines out the door for this every day." Chloe thought she would probably stop by on her breaks for this most days. But then she considered the weight she would most likely gain and thought better of it.

"I put a hazelnut spread inside, so it's already a bit gooey. Do you think it needs more? If I did that, the whipped cream would melt too fast." Lottie had already considered the idea of warming the pastry before putting the whipped cream on top, but then decided not to do it.

"Hmm, yeah. You're right. That's why you're the successful pastry chef and I'm not." Chloe took another bite and did allow herself to moan over how good it was after she closed her eyes.

Lottie cleared her throat.

Without opening her eyes, Chloe took another bite and moaned even louder this time. "*Oh,* Lottie. You are going to be the death of me. This is to die…" When Chloe opened her eyes, the sight in front of her caused her to choke down what she was about to say.

She dropped what was left of the pastry into the box and quickly picked up a napkin to try and wipe away the mess she had made. Chloe knew her cheeks were pink, and most likely the heat crawling up her neck meant she was red all over.

"Chloe. Nice to see you." He chuckled. "I take it that's one of Lottie's newest creations? Was it as good as it looked?" Brandon licked his lips in anticipation of trying the same treat.

"Well, I better get back to work," Lottie said as she stood up, trying not to laugh.

"Do you have another one of those pastries? I'd like to try it." Brandon smiled at Lottie. "I mean, it looks—and sounds —like it might be your best yet." He winked at Chloe.

Chloe wanted to crawl into a hole and die from embarrassment. How could she have moaned in public while eating? Her mother had taught her better manners than that. But that pastry, oh my. Her stomach was all aflutter in anticipation of taking another bite.

Or was it because Brandon was near?

No, it was the Christmas pastry that had Chloe all excited. She was sure that was all it was. She and Brandon were only friends. And besides, he was laughing at her. There was no way he wanted anything to do with a woman he couldn't eat a meal with in public. If her mom saw her, she would be appalled at her behavior.

"Excuse me, I should clean up before heading into work." Chloe stood up and made a beeline for the restroom.

"Will I still see you later tonight?" Brandon called after her.

Chloe stopped and turned around, face hotter than the coals in Santa's fireplace. The entire shop had quieted and was staring at them. Back home, the Diner Divas would have it spread all over town that she and Brandon were dating again before she even got to work. But here in Frenchtown, the gossip mill was a tad bit slower. By lunch, the entire town would know it.

Brandon opened his mouth to say something, then when he noticed all eyes were on them, he closed it. Even his cheeks took on a pink hue. "I meant, at the Christmas tree. With the rest of the town." He cringed when the couple sitting at the table next to him laughed. He did not need the town to start gossiping about him and Chloe. Their friendship was too fragile to survive the pressure gossip would put on them. He mouthed, *Sorry*, and turned to leave.

When he got outside, he headed back toward his truck. The pitstop for coffee and a Danish would have to be skipped today. He chided himself for what he did. Brandon knew better, but the sight of Chloe moaning over a pastry had his mind all discombobulated. He could not think straight. All he wanted to do was kiss the cream off her lips.

He had to get that image out of his mind. Figgy pudding! What was he going to do?

CHAPTER 12

I t was time for him to leave if Brandon wanted to meet Chloe at the Christmas tree. But he was still feeling like a fool for how he'd reacted that morning. The gossip had made the rounds so thoroughly, even his mother knew about it. Of course, by the time it got to his mom it had changed. Brandon had called out a dinner invitation before the event at the Christmas tree that night, according to what his mother had heard.

He wondered how people got the story so messed up so quickly. The only thing he could think of to cause that change in the real story was because Chloe had been eating a pastry and they were in a coffee shop. But still, he hated gossip.

"Brandon, if you don't get a move on you'll be late for your date." Melanie laughed and shook her head.

"Ma, not you too." Brandon sighed and ran a hand down his face. He hadn't had time to shave. The stubble was actually something he liked. His mother would scowl when he skipped shaving. She told him it looked like he was trying to be a sexy cowboy.

He liked that. But, he did normally shave before going out

at night. Today just got away from him, and he decided it wouldn't hurt to go out with a five o'clock shadow. Besides, most men in the county wore beards all winter. The facial hair helped to keep them warm while working outside in the frozen winter.

At least he didn't let his scruff grow into a full blown ZZ Top beard. Only die-hard beard lovers did that. It would take a long time for any beard to get that long. And Brandon had no desire to look like those rockers from the eighties.

When Brandon walked out of his room, his mother was waiting by the entryway. Her smile followed by a giggle told him all he needed to know. He should have shaved.

"See, you've even decided to go with the sexy cowboy look," she joked.

"Ew, Ma. Don't even go there." Brandon put a hand up. He could not handle his mom calling him a sexy cowboy. He knew she was completely joking, but still. Those words, *sexy cowboy*, should never come out of a guy's mother's mouth.

"Have fun, and tell Chloe I said hi!" She waved at him when he left the house and kept a huge smile on her face the entire time he could see her.

Well, he thought, *at least she was still in a good mood.* Brandon had worried about her on Thanksgiving Day. Then the next day things seemed to do a total one-eighty, and she was her old self again. He didn't understand what was going on with his mom. Maybe she just needed him home again and everything would be alright. She had lived alone for the past year for the first time in her life. It had to be lonely.

Now that he was home, he would have to make sure he did more things with her. Maybe the next Christmas event he would bring her along with him. That would most likely make her feel good. When he got to the tree that night, he would have to check out the list of events and see what was next.

Since it was *not* a date, Brandon hadn't offered to pick Chloe up. So when he arrived at the tree, he had to search for her. He should have known she would be close to the coffee table. At all the town events, Lottie had a table to sell her coffee drinks and treats.

Chloe was laughing and eating a small ball that she ran through some white powder before popping it into her mouth. When she closed her eyes and looked as though she was in heaven, like she did earlier that morning, he wondered what it was she was eating. He might have to try it if it made women go gaga over it.

"Chloe." He waited until she had opened her eyes again before he approached her. He didn't want to embarrass her again. Not when he hoped to spend some time with her that night. And maybe even end the evening with a request for a date.

No, scratch that idea. He couldn't ask her out. His mom needed him. Just the quick change in her energy and demeanor told him that spending time with her was important for her health. Maybe down the road when he had been home for a while and her medicine began doing whatever it was supposed to, he could think about dating. But not now.

But jingle bells, did Chloe ever get his heart pumping. Especially when she ate sweets. Or dressed up nice. Or, shoot, any time he saw her lately he felt his heart rate skyrocket. It was a good thing he didn't have a heart condition, or she'd give him a heart attack with just a smile.

"Hi there, cowboy. How's your mom doing?" Chloe gave him a heart attack-inducing smile.

What was he doing? Every instinct in him screamed at him to move in close for a hug. And maybe to even wipe the small amount of powdered sugar off the side of her lips. Possibly even with his own lips.

CHLOE HADN'T SEEN Melanie since before Thanksgiving, and she really wanted to hear the nice rancher was improving. Just that day she'd seen a request for an infusion treatment that she had to send to the insurance company. If Melanie needed an infusion of steroids, she must be having some pretty serious problems.

He smiled at her and appreciated that she had asked after his mom. "She's actually doing much better since Thursday. I think all the preparations going into Thanksgiving zapped her energy. But what really surprised me was how much energy she's had ever since we went shopping." Brandon shook his head. He was completely drained after their shopping trip and hoped he never had to experience that madhouse again.

"It's amazing what our bodies can do for us when we're happy. I'm guessing your mom normally loves the hustle and bustle of the Christmas season. And Black Friday is the official start of the season. Plus, having you along with her must have been a lot of fun for her." Chloe leaned in for a hug, then stiffened when she realized what she had done.

She did normally hug her friends, but she and Brandon had history.

He hesitated a moment, which only made her feel awkward. Just as she was about to pull away and apologize, he wrapped her in a warm bear hug.

Chloe's heart pitter-pattered when she smelled his delicious scent. He smelled of cinnamon, leather, and something that was all male. With his arms around her, she felt like she was being held in a warm embrace with a cup of Joy tea and her favorite Christmas quilt her mother made her when she was a teen.

She felt as though she was home.

Which only served to cause her heart to beat faster. When she pulled out of his embrace, her cheeks rubbed against his stubble and it was all she could do to keep upright. A handsome cowboy with a little bit of scruff and who smelled so enticing was her dream. The fact that it was Brandon who checked off all those boxes and then some made it so much worse.

She looked down at her hands and noticed they were shaking. If she didn't get a grip on herself, everyone—including Brandon—would see how much he affected her. Chloe could not have that happen.

Brandon couldn't look her in the eyes, so he looked away and agreed with what she'd said. He had to put his hands in his pockets to keep from pulling her back into his arms and kissing her until the sun rose.

The awkward tension between them was only broken when Lottie walked up. "Hey there. How y'all enjoying the event?"

Taking in a deep, cleansing breath, Chloe responded, "Great. How about you? Are you selling tons of hot coffee?" She knew she was being stupid, but her head was like a cotton ball, full of fluffy nothing at the moment.

The barista laughed and looked between the two. "I'm doing alright tonight. Have you had a chance to tell Brandon about your idea for helping Tessa?"

Chloe could have hugged her best friend. "Not yet, we just met up." Now, she would have something to bring up that could help take the focus off her and put it on someone else.

"Tessa? She's the high school kid who works for you, right?" Brandon turned his focus on Lottie and relaxed his shoulders. He needed to get a grip and not think about how good Chloe felt in his arms. That was the last thing he needed going through his head.

"Why don't we get some coffee and I can tell you all about it?" Chloe offered.

They spent the next thirty minutes discussing different ways to help Tessa with school and raising money. Brandon liked the idea of helping her to pay for college. Except, that left out everyone else. "What about the rest of the seniors?"

When Chloe bit her lip, Brandon's eyes wandered to her lips and he took in a sharp breath.

"Ah, how many graduating this year are going to college?" Chloe had no idea how big the high school was. She hadn't attended any of their games or plays. The only high schooler she knew was Tessa.

"We have about a dozen kids planning to go to college. However, two of them already have full rides for football." Brandon attended every home football game—at least, before he'd left he had. He loved to support the boys, and he enjoyed the sport. He played in high school, but was never good enough to get a scholarship. The coach was a friend of his, so he had kept up on the team while he was away.

"So, that leaves ten kids who need help?" Chloe tapped her chin with a fingernail painted red for the Christmas season and thought about it. "I don't know if we could raise enough money to pay for everyone's room and board. How many are going locally?"

"We don't have to raise the funds for all of them. But maybe we could help each out with a small amount?" Brandon wasn't sure how best to help the kids, but he did want to help.

"Do they all need financial help?" Chloe hoped that maybe only two or three were in desperate need.

"Yeah, I doubt the families of all ten kids can afford to send their kids off to college, but maybe one or two can." Brandon nodded his agreement of where Chloe was going with this line of questioning. It made sense to only help those who needed the most help. While all kids did need some help, there were a few who needed it more than the rest.

"Why don't we table this until after we get our helping hands ornaments? Looks like there's not much left to choose from." Chloe pointed to the tree; it was almost empty already.

"Wow, we usually have trouble getting all the ornaments picked up. This looks to be a good year for our kids." He led the way to the tree, where they both looked over what was left.

Once they had chosen their ornaments and signed them out, they went and sat down to finish their discussion about helping the college kids.

"Could we take a different kid each month and have a spaghetti dinner? Say, five dollars per person, ten dollars for the family? Then ask for extra donations? And all money goes toward one kid that month? I bet we could get plenty of families to bring their favorite spaghetti meals for all to share." After she took a drink of her cooling coffee, she looked up at Brandon for the first time since their hug.

"Like a potluck, only it costs?" Brandon clarified.

"Yeah, it sounds lame." Chloe slumped in her seat and thought about how she could do this and help so many kids.

"Chloe, why so glum? Aren't you enjoying the Christmas festivities?" Mrs. Claus stood next to their table with her arm through Santa's. Both were dressed in their Christmas finest. She had on a long white dress with an intricately designed Nordic overdress, like something one might see in a Norman Rockwell painting, or one of the older movies about Santa and his wife.

She was also wearing her beautiful red cape with white faux-fur trim. It must have been a warm piece of clothing, as she didn't look cold. Her brown leather boots and gloves most likely helped to keep her warm, along with the fuzzy red cap that must have been made from the same material as Santa's suit.

Santa had on his traditional red-and-white suit designed for cold weather. And his large black belt with a gold buckle held his ensemble together nicely, making it look like he really did have a belly full of jelly. Especially when he laughed.

He wore black leather boots and gloves along with the traditional triangle red-and-white hat. The only difference from what a department store Santa might wear was that Santa's looked to be made from a high-quality, faux-white fur with thick red, furry material. This Santa would stay warm as he drove his sleigh around the world and delivered presents to all the good little boys and girls.

Chloe smiled and felt a little bit better just being in the company of their royal Christmas couple. "No, of course not. This is a fantastic event. I'm just trying to figure something out and not having any luck."

Mrs. Claus took a seat next to her. "May I help you figure it out?"

Brandon smiled at the motherly woman. "I'm not sure it's something we can really do. We might have bitten off more than we can chew." He shrugged, not knowing what could be done in the next eight months to help ten students earn enough money to assist with college.

Even if they only tried to raise enough to pay for the first year of room and board for each student, they didn't know how they could raise ninety thousand dollars. And then do it again year after year.

"Ah, I see." Mrs. Claus put a gloved hand to her heart. "You know, sometimes just sharing your burden with someone else can help you see a solution." She arched a brow and looked between the couple.

"Ho, ho, ho. I would listen to my wife. She's one of the wisest women I've ever met." Santa held his black belt as his midsection jiggled with his laugh.

Both Chloe and Brandon gave a quick laugh. Who could not laugh when Santa did? He made everyone so happy with just a simple *ho, ho, ho*. And wink of one eye.

Chloe wasn't exactly sure what Mrs. Claus was trying to say, but it seemed like the jolly woman wanted her to work closer with Brandon. Her heart skipped at the idea of spending more time with Brandon, but her head told her to knock it off. She was only going to set herself up for disappointment, and most likely heartache.

She'd had enough of that, thank you very much.

CHAPTER 13

Two days later when Chloe walked into the coffee shop, she almost turned right around and left. She had done a great job of avoiding Brandon ever since the Christmas tree event. Old feelings she thought best left behind had been plaguing her dreams, and she did not want to deal with them. She knew it was best to ignore her growing feelings for the cute cowboy and focus on Christmas and ensuring that the kids going to college were able to get the money they needed.

While Chloe wished she could afford to pay for even one year of room and board for one student, she knew that was impossible for her, and unfair to the town if she only chose one student to help. Even though she didn't know the other kids.

However, she did know some of the parents from church and other town events. No, she would have to find a way to create some sort of general fund that could be used to provide partial scholarships to kids entering into the University of Montana system.

She wanted to attend the next planning event for the town and see if there was something that could be done. Maybe not for this upcoming graduating class, but possibly for the future. Even if they were able to offer five or six $500 scholarships a year, that would be very helpful.

"Chloe!" a cheery male voice called out.

She sighed and tried to hide her frustration when she pinned on a smile and walked farther into the shop. It was a small town, and Lottie's coffee shop was the only one in town. If you didn't count the coffee counter at the Sip 'n' Go, which she didn't.

"Good morning, Brandon. How're you doing?" What she really wanted to ask was, *What the heck are you doing here this early?* But she couldn't be rude.

"I'm good. Just waiting while Mom is in for an early appointment with her doctor." Brandon tried to hide his grimace over the rim of his coffee mug.

Now Chloe felt bad. "How's your mom doing? Is anything wrong?"

A half smile brought the cowboy's lips up on one side of his gorgeous face and he looked down into his coffee. "Mom's fine. Well…"—he shrugged—"as fine as she can be. I think she's discussing some medication issues. She told me to wait here for her and she'd join me for a coffee and muffin when she was done."

"Speaking of muffins, I heard that Lottie has a new one to try?" Not wanting to keep the discussion on something that was obviously bothering him, Chloe tried to steer the topic to something a bit more palatable…food.

"Did someone mention me?" Lottie's huge smile caused Chloe to smile in return.

"Yes, I heard you had made a new Christmas muffin? I'd love to try it." Chloe turned her attention from the confusing man to her best friend.

Why did Brandon talk to her so much? Why was he

always around now that he was back home? If he wanted to pick up where they'd left off, when he'd abandoned her a year ago, why didn't he say as much? Chloe was just too confused by the cowboy and needed distance.

"Sure thing. But first, I need to ask you a favor." The coffee shop owner put her hands together as though in prayer and put them on her chest. She bit her lower lip and looked between the two people in front of her.

"Sure, what can I do to help? If it involves taste testing, that's no favor. That's a privilege." Brandon grinned.

Lottie laughed and shook her head. "No. Well, I'm sure I can find plenty for you to taste, but I need help tonight with the gingerbread contest. My scheduled help called out sick today."

"Oh, that's too bad. I hope she's not very sick?" Chloe had heard the flu was making the rounds, but one never knew what someone actually had when they called in sick. Some thought the sniffles were enough to skip work, while others would go to work with a hundred-and-two-degree temperature. The latter she wholeheartedly disagreed with.

Lottie sighed. "I hope not. But Dana said she was running a low-grade fever. I told her to stay in bed until she felt better."

"Good idea. You don't need her spreading the flu around any more than we already have it." Brandon shook his head. He rarely got sick, but with his mother having MS, he knew her immune system was down. He would have to make sure she did everything she could to stay healthy. Which included not being around anyone who was sick.

"So, will you two help me out?" Lottie's eyebrows raised, and the hopeful look on her face changed Chloe's no to a yes.

There was no way Chloe would not help her friend. Lottie had been there for her this past year every step of the way.

Shoot, she even brought out her Christmas drinks a little bit early, knowing that Brandon's homecoming would bring her down.

"Of course I will." She patted Lottie's arm and smiled at her friend.

"Count me in." Brandon's smile caused Chloe's stomach to turn.

Chloe just wasn't sure if it was a good thing, or a bad thing.

* * *

As soon as Chloe's work day was completed, she headed straight for the coffee shop. She'd had a difficult time concentrating all day, thinking about that night. On the one hand, she was excited about helping out with the gingerbread competition. But on the other, she wasn't too keen on spending so much time with Brandon. If she could get Lottie to make sure they didn't work together, she might be able to get past the knots in her stomach.

A frown spread across her face when she entered the coffee shop. The entire room had been reorganized for the gingerbread competition already. The tables had been moved in lines, and the chairs taken away to make more room at each table for people to stand and decorate. The decorations had also been removed from the tables. In their place were the basic gingerbread house pieces and various candy decorations to be used to adorn the houses. Along with bags of icing to use as the glue.

Most of the work had already been done. Chloe didn't understand what Lottie needed her for.

"Chloe, just in time." Lottie waved her over to a table

alongside the entrance, where Brandon stood behind a cash register.

"Looks like you've already got it all taken care of. What can I do to help?" The last thing Chloe wanted was to be near Brandon all night long. While they seemed to have a sort of friendship going, her feelings were already getting away from her, and she did not need for her heart to get hurt, again.

If she could get her way, she would be home in comfy sweats watching *It's a Wonderful Life* for the umpteenth time. Or a new Hallmark Christmas movie. Either one would work for her.

"Brandon will need help checking in the contestants and taking the entry fees for those who haven't paid yet." Lottie moved away from the table to give Chloe room to stand next to Brandon.

He waved his hand in an awkward way. "Hey, Chloe."

She nodded in return. "Do you need two people to take tickets and money?" Chloe couldn't imagine it would get so packed that they would need two people doing this. They only had room for what, twenty contestants total? And she knew that at least half of the spots had already been paid for in advance.

Lottie nodded. "With three rounds of gingerbread house-making, it's going to get very busy tonight."

Chloe's eyes bulged. "Three rounds? What, does this go until midnight or something?" Had she known this when she volunteered, she may not have said yes. She still had to get up early for work the next day.

Lottie put her hand on Chloe's shoulder. "No, Chloe. It doesn't take that long. We give each round an hour to make their houses, and everyone is really good at moving away as soon as they're done so we can get the next group in." A warm smile crossed Lottie's face, and Chloe relaxed.

With three rounds, they would be very busy. Especially if they only had an hour for each round. Which meant that she and Brandon wouldn't have any time to talk, let alone time for her to think about his scent as it enveloped her, or remember how much she enjoyed telling him about her day and listening to him talk about his. She shook her head and tried to remove memories of the past.

Chloe needed to think about the here and now. And right now she needed to learn how to operate the register and how they were going to account for everyone who participated.

Two hours later, once everyone had either paid or checked in with their online payment confirmation, Chloe finally breathed a sigh of relief. The third round wouldn't start for another forty-five minutes, but she and Brandon were done with the register and checking everyone in.

The time had gone by very quickly, and with the exception of a few meddling moms, the evening went very nicely. Gracie Brown, who was happily married with four kids, thought Brandon was a fool for breaking up with Chloe when he left, and she was very happy to let her thoughts be known.

When Gracie's bestie, Laura Anderson, walked up, the two began smiling at Brandon and Chloe in a way that caused goosebumps to go down Chloe's arms and spine.

"Say, now that you're back, Brandon"—Laura looked to the cowboy in question and winked—"I think it's high time you picked up where you left off with Chloe. Don't you?" She turned her gaze back on Chloe and took the Manning girl's hands in hers. "I'll bet you agree with me, don't you?"

Chloe was mortified. This was the last thing she needed. It was one thing for her friend to put her and Brandon together during a busy evening where they barely had time to say, "How ya doing?" But for someone to come right out and tell her, in front of Brandon no less, that it was time the two of them got back together, it was all Chloe could do to keep from running away screaming.

Thankfully, Brandon—who could handle a two-thousand-pound bull—was cool as could be. "You know, the next session is about to start. If you two want to sit together, I highly suggest you go and scope out seats before the current contest ends and all the good seats are taken." He gave them each a knowing look that sent the two women away quickly.

"Wow, that was impressive." Chloe had never been so grateful for a save as she was at that moment. She wanted the ladies to leave, or at the very least to change the topic, but she had been completely clueless as to how to make it happen. In her mind, all she could see was herself standing there, mouth agape, and fear running so cold through her veins that it froze her in place.

Brandon shrugged. "It was nothing. You just gotta know how to handle the meddling moms. You'll learn once you've been here long enough."

Before Chloe could say anything else, an entire family walked up and wanted to pay for their spots in the next contest. She was saved again. Saved from having to discuss with Brandon what Laura and Gracie had said. And even saved from having to think too much on what just happened. It was a constant stream after that until they checked in the final gingerbread contestant.

Brandon rubbed the back of his neck. "Uh, tonight was good. Did you get a chance to see some of the completed gingerbread houses?"

When it was just the two of them all alone by the register, Chloe felt a sense of uncertainty flow over her, as well as trepidation. She wasn't sure what they were supposed to do next, and she wasn't sure what she should say to the man who had stood next to her for the past few hours.

The thought of what Gracie and Laura said earlier had crossed her mind for an instant before Brandon had spoken, and now she was given something else to think about. "Not yet. I wanted to wait until they were all done before checking them out. Plus, there really hasn't been time to see them. Did you get a good look at any of them?"

She knew he hadn't left her side, but he was taller than she was. So, it was possible he could see over everyone and everything and get a good look at the completed gingerbread houses along the back wall. Chloe looked up at him, expecting him to be looking toward the entries. Instead, he was looking right at her.

Chloe stood transfixed by his soft gaze. All sound around them ceased, and they stood there looking into each other's eyes. Every instinct she had said to look away, maybe even to run away. But her heart told her to reach out and touch him.

Brandon's eyes began to change to liquid pools of fire. Then his eyes moved down her face and fixed on her lips. She couldn't help it—she licked her lips and noticed a lump in his throat. Did he want to kiss her as much as she wanted him to? Or was it all her imagination?

The air around them was charged, as though a lightning storm was just outside the building. Her breathing was ragged, and she felt herself move infinitesimally closer to him. Or was it him who moved closer to her? She couldn't tell. All she knew was that her body was warmer than it had been moments before.

When his hand alighted upon her upper arm, it was as though that lightning shot right through her arm and zig-zagged its way through her entire body. The hair on her arms had to be standing on end. And if she wasn't mistaken, the rest of her hair was, too. All she knew was the bubble she was in with Brandon, and she didn't want it to burst.

But burst it did. Just a moment before she thought Brandon was going to lean down and kiss her, Cove sauntered up. "Hey, what's up?"

The two of them backed up quickly, and Chloe blinked her eyes a few times before turning her gaze to the intruder. Or was he her savior? Had Brandon kissed her right there in front of the entire town, the rumor mill would have them married by morning. That was the last thing she needed. Wasn't it?

"Um, not much. Looks like the contest is going smoothly." Brandon ran a hand through his perfectly coiffed, messy hair.

How was it that men could get up and roll out of bed without doing anything to their hair and look so sexy? Women had to spend hours on end making their hair look good. Or in her case, halfway decent. Sometimes she wondered if that was just one more part of the curse from God after Eve sinned.

"Did you see the entry from old man Rice? He and his wife did a fantastic job of making it look like something out of a magazine. I bet they win." Cove smiled and looked between the two.

Chloe took every bit of training she'd received from her mom about being a lady, ran it through her head at faster-than-light speed, and pasted a smile on her face. "Yeah, I've heard that my landlord and his wife usually win this event. I can't wait to go and see all the houses."

Every year the style of house was different, but no one knew what it would be until the night of the contest. Lottie baked up the walls and roof pieces in secret a few days before the event and hid them somewhere while they hardened. It was up to the contestants to put them together and then decorate them. Most people planned their décor in advance, in an effort to beat the Rices. But no one knew exactly what the house would look like, so their plans were usually based on the previous year's design. This year, it was a two-story house that looked more like Santa's workshop.

Chloe had no idea how they were able to put it all together and then decorate it so well in the allotted hour. She would still be trying to get the walls to stick to each other when the buzzer went off. There was no way she would even be able to decorate it in that amount of time. While she had always wanted to do one of these competitions, she was grateful she had decided to watch this year instead of trying it. She most likely wouldn't even try next year, either. These townsfolks were more artistic than she realized.

"I'll have to go and find their house. I can't wait to see them all." Even though Chloe wanted to wait for all the houses to be done before looking at them, she also needed to get away from Brandon. He was too close, too warm, and too handsome for her to keep her sanity.

Chloe waved to the two cowboys and walked off.

CHAPTER 14

W *hat was I thinking?* Brandon chastised himself as Chloe walked away. The cowboy had never been happier to see his friend than he was at that moment. He had not planned on kissing Chloe. In fact, he didn't want to until the very moment he began to lean into her. Or was she leaning into him? He was unclear on who was doing the leaning, but they were definitely too close for comfort.

Oblivious to his inner turmoil, Cove patted Brandon on the back. "Dude, that Chloe is one fine lady. Are you going to ask her out again?"

The question took Brandon aback. Did Cove notice the tension between them? Did he see that they'd almost kissed? He hoped Cove didn't notice anything. "Why do you ask? Are you thinking about asking her out?" He wasn't sure why he put that out there. The thought of Chloe and Cove going out actually got his dander up.

Out of the corner of his eye, Brandon watched Chloe walk around the tables with the completed gingerbread houses. He felt drawn to her, just like he did when they'd first met. When she fell, he worried she might be injured, but when he helped her up and held her for a moment too long in his arms that day, his heart had been lassoed by the pretty newcomer.

She had dirt on her cheek that day, and all he wanted to do was reach up and wipe it away, but he knew better than to touch a stranger's face. Especially a pretty woman who was surrounded by an entire family of cowboys. If some strange man had touched his sister's face before even formal introductions, he would have kicked his Wranglers—with him in them—into the next county.

Instead, he'd pulled his arms back too soon and she'd fallen again. Feeling like the cad he was, he helped her up again. But that time he made sure she was steady on her feet before letting go. They had never discussed that day, but he knew she was embarrassed.

Thinking about their first meeting had his heart beating fast and his breathing coming hard.

"Hey, Brandon. Did you hear me?" Cove backhanded him on the chest.

Brandon took a step back and rubbed his chest. "Oh, sorry. I guess I was thinking about something else."

Cove smiled and looked at where his friend was staring. "Don'tcha mean *someone* else?" He chuckled and shook his head. "I don't think I'll be asking that pretty cowgirl out any time soon. But I do think you need to, my friend."

A frown stole over Brandon's face as he turned his attention back to his friend. "Cove, until you get your love life in order why don't you keep your opinions to yourself?"

Sputtering, Cove responded, "I...don...don't know what you're saying."

Brandon smirked. "Oh, I think you do." He looked pointedly at Lottie and nodded his head in her direction.

"So, how's your ma doing?" Even though Cove had changed the subject, Brandon knew he'd gotten to his friend.

"She has her good days and her bad days. I'm just glad I came home. However, I wish I had never left." His gaze went to Chloe and then right back to Cove. "Not because of her, but because if I had been here, then Ma would have gone into the doctor sooner."

"It's not too late, is it?" A worried crease marred Cove's good looks.

"No." Brandon shook his head. "Or, at least I don't think so. But I should have been here for her and not gallivanting across the country, having fun." Even though the work he was doing was to help improve his own family business, he did have a lot of fun combined with the hard work and long hours he put in learning more about raising bulls for the rodeo.

With a hand on his friend's shoulder, Cove began, "Brandon, if your mom is doing good, you shouldn't worry so much. She's in God's hands and you have to trust in Him to heal her, or get her through this."

"I know." Brandon nodded and sighed. "It's just…I feel so out of my league here."

"What do you mean?" Cove furrowed his brows.

Brandon ran a hand over his face. "When I'm on the ranch and working with the animals, I know exactly what needs to be done. It's a schedule that has to be followed. Start out feeding the stock, then go in for breakfast, then back out to check the fence lines, check on any stock that's close to freshening. Move herds to different pastures, etc. The day may have its ups and downs, but I can usually count on most of it being the same."

He looked down at his hands and then fisted them. "But when it comes to taking care of my mom, I just don't know what to do. I feel like a failure. I should have been here to notice the signs. Maybe if we got into the doctor sooner she wouldn't be so tired all the time." All Brandon wanted to do at that point was punch something, like himself. He was such a fool to put the ranch first.

The ranch was important—it was what kept him and his mother fed, clothed, and paid for her doctor's bills. But now he wasn't sure if he resented it just a bit for taking him away from his mother when she needed him the most.

"Dude, you can't blame yourself for where your mom is medically. Even if you had been here, do you really think MS can be stopped? I've done some homework. Even though she's had it for a little while, you still caught it early. Most people don't realize they have it until they've either lost their eyesight or use of their legs. I seriously doubt you would have found out any sooner if you had been home." Cove kept his voice low so as not to attract any attention. So far word hadn't gotten out about Melanie Beck's disease, and those who knew wanted to keep it that way.

"Well, this is exactly why I won't be asking Chloe out. I need to focus on mom. She was supposed to come with me tonight." Brandon looked to his friend. "You know how much she loves the gingerbread contest." He sighed. "But she was too tired to come out tonight. I was going to cancel my participation, but Mom insisted I come."

"She was right. You couldn't cancel on Lottie at the last minute. Besides, I bet your mom had a nice cup of tea and went to bed early. What were you going to do? Hover over her?"

Brandon felt a bit sheepish. That was exactly what he wanted to do. He wanted to be the one to fix her tea, then sit with her until she was ready for bed. Then after she had gone to bed, he had planned on cleaning up the kitchen. Instead, when he left he heard his mother cleaning the dinner dishes and he felt awful for leaving a messy kitchen for her to clean up when she wasn't feeling well.

He knew his mom wanted him gone for the evening. He had no clue what she had planned, other than cleaning and drinking tea, but Melanie Beck had practically kicked him out. Throughout the evening he had checked his phone. She promised she would text him if she felt too bad, or if anything happened. So far, zero text messages. Which he was grateful for.

"You're right. I know you are. But what am I supposed to do?" Brandon rubbed the back of his neck and worried about how he was going to take care of his mom, the ranch, and participate in any more Christmas events this season, not to mention all the other community events throughout the year.

"You're going to live your life. Be there for your mom, but still live your life." Cove put his right hand on his championship belt buckle and stared his friend down. "How do you think your ma will feel if she thinks she's the reason you shut yourself off from the world?"

Brandon's shoulders sagged, and he knew Cove was right. The problem was, how would he manage it all?

CHAPTER 15

The next morning came too early for Chloe. She had been up late with the gingerbread contest and helping Lottie clean up. This morning, she wished she didn't have to go into work. All she wanted to do was cuddle up with a warm blanket, cup of hot cocoa, and a book in her hand while she sat in front of a blazing fire. But that would have to wait for Saturday morning.

Today, she needed to get her act together and get to work.

First stop, Lottie's coffee shop for a peppermint mocha. Chloe figured she deserved a treat to help get her going, so she was also going to get a peppermint scone with cream on top. Or was it more of an icing? Either way, she hadn't tried one yet this year and this was going to be the one time she let herself have something so decadent it would most likely make her teeth hurt.

When the jingle bell above the door to the café went off, Lottie looked up and smiled at her friend. "Oh, Chloe." Her smile vanished and was replaced with lines of worry. "What's wrong?" She noticed the bags under her friend's eyes and the way her lids drooped.

Chloe shook her head. "Nothing, just really, really tired. I think I need an overdose of caffeine and sugar."

"Oh, sweetie. I'm so sorry I kept you up so late." Lottie moved to the pastry cabinet. "Which one do you want? It's on me today."

With a short laugh and shake of her head, Chloe moved to the display of pastries and looked at Lottie instead of the scrumptious desserts waiting for her. "Lottie, I got almost six hours of sleep last night. I'll be fine after my mocha." She yawned, and Lottie copied her actions. "Sorry, I know those things are contagious. How are you up and perky so early in the morning?"

Both girls laughed.

"Don't worry, I've already had about a gallon of caffeine and two of my peppermint scones today." Lottie chuckled.

"I think that's what I want. The peppermint scone, and an extra-large, extra-hot peppermint mocha with an extra shot of espresso." *That should do the trick,* Chloe thought.

Lottie raised her brows. "A little on the wild side today, huh?"

"I've got a conference call at nine, so I figured I better get a bit of a jolt beforehand. The last thing I need is to nod off during one of our monthly"—Chloe looked around and finished in a whisper—"boring calls."

Lottie pursed her lips, trying to hold back a laugh. "You wouldn't be the first one to come in here looking for an extra charge before one of those."

Chloe sighed. "I figured you'd understand."

Lottie handed her friend the peppermint scone and went to make the drink as Chloe needed. When it was complete, she put a few extra peppermint crumbs on top of the whipped cream. "Here, I added two extra shots of espresso. If that doesn't at least get you through your meeting, text me and I'll send another one over right away."

With a sigh and a smile, Chloe felt tears prick the backs of her eyes. Sometimes when she was overly tired, she could be emotional for no good reason. Today looked to be one of those days. She only hoped tears didn't show through a Zoom meeting. "Thank you." She took a sip of the drink and felt the zing of the caffeine all the way to her toes. "I think this is going to work."

As Chloe was leaving the shop, Lottie called out, "Don't forget the Christmas movie on Friday."

She put her cup in the air and nodded, as her mouth was already full of a sweet—and large—bite of the scone. Chloe had the event on her calendar and wouldn't miss it for the world. Even though she had seen the movie a gazillion times, she was looking forward to seeing it again…this time with the entire town.

When Friday came, and Chloe entered the community center, she was pleasantly surprised to see the room full of Christmas decorations and plenty of people had brought their own comfy chairs, in addition to the fold-up community chairs that lined the walls. She had brought her own camp chair that had a drink holder. Along with a bag of snacks.

But she should have known she wouldn't need anything. Lottie had a set-up in the back corner where she sold coffee and pastries in addition to popcorn and candy.

With a chuckle and a shake of her head, Chloe walked over to Lottie and Tessa. "I should have known you'd be selling plenty of goodies to get anyone into a sugar-induced coma."

Lottie smiled. "Let me guess," she tapped a finger to her chin. "You want a peppermint cocoa and popcorn."

"How'd you guess?" Chloe furrowed a brow and wondered if she had it written all over her face, or what?

"I just remember the last time we watched Christmas movies together." The barista went to work on the drink and Tessa put some popcorn into a medium sized bag.

Once Chloe paid for her treats, she looked around for a place to sit.

"We're over on the left side, toward the front. If you want to join us." Lottie pointed to where Cove and Quinn sat in beanbag chairs with blankets over their laps laughing and eating popcorn.

"Quinn sure does love Cove, doesn't she?" Chloe winked and left Lottie staring at her kid and the rodeo star.

Before Chloe made it to her friends, she noticed Brandon and his mom had also taken seats next to Cove in fold-up camp chairs very similar to hers. She hadn't seen Brandon since the gingerbread event, but he hadn't been far from her thoughts all week, or her dreams.

When her heart began pumping extra hard, Chloe wanted nothing more than to run home and hide away. However, she knew she had to do this. Everyone would know something was wrong if she turned tail and left. But it wasn't going to be easy. "Which seat is Lottie's." she asked cheerily when she walked up to Cove and the rest of her friends.

Cove smiled and stood up. "Chloe, it's good to see you again." He motioned to the chair that was Lottie's and she breathed a sigh of relief when she realized that she wouldn't be sitting right next to Brandon, he was on the other side of Cove.

"Thanks. Hi Melanie, Brandon." She smiled and nodded at the Becks before setting her chair up and getting situated.

Quinn looked up at Chloe and beamed. "You're gonna watch the movie with us?"

"Of course, my little chickadee." Chloe reached out and tickled Quinn who in turn giggled. At that moment, Chloe's biological clock ticked for the first time…ever.

Her thoughts turned to Brandon, and her heart ached for the cowboy who sat only a few seats away from her with his mom. It was everything she could do to keep her eyes on the screen once the movie began and not the only man who had made her heart speed as fast as a hummingbird's wings.

Brandon felt eyes upon him and looked to see Chloe watching him. When her cheeks flamed, he smiled and nodded. She really was a beautiful woman. Especially when she blushed. He gulped down that thought and looked back at the movie and tried to focus on the Thanksgiving Day parade from Miracle on 34th Street and how cute little Natalie Wood was as Susan Walker.

While he did try to keep his mind on the movie, he couldn't help but sneak peeks throughout the rest of the night at the only cowgirl who'd ever made his heart sing.

When the movie was over and he was walking his mother out to the truck, Melanie stopped and looked at Chloe. "You know, she's one very special woman. Any man would be lucky to marry her." She arched a brow and moved on toward their truck.

Now his mother? What would be next—their preacher making overt signals that he should abandon his mother and date Chloe? Brandon shook his head and kept his mouth shut.

Sometimes he really had no clue how to answer his mom.

* * *

THE SNOW STARTED EARLY Saturday morning, and Brandon hated leaving his mom home alone. He reasoned with himself that she wasn't truly alone. Two of the ranch hands had promised to check in on her in the morning while he was gone to Bozeman picking up his special delivery of parts for the shed he was going to build when they had their next break in weather.

But with the way the snow had been coming lately, he worried they were in for a nasty year of snow and he wouldn't be able to get the shed built before calving season.

As he continued his drive down the I-90, he prayed. *God, I don't know your plans for my mother, but you said in your Word that you had plans for us. Not to harm us, but to help us. I'm calling on you now to help my mother. I know so little about MS, and it seems the doctors don't know much more than I do.*

Brandon paused and looked around as the snow fell even harder. *Please keep her safe while I'm away today, and bring me back home safely as well. I want to be there for her. Please let me help her. Show me the way, Lord.*

A feeling of peace enveloped his entire being, and he let loose a little smile as he traveled down the highway much slower than the normal eighty miles an hour that he drove when there wasn't snow on the highway. Today he'd have to keep it below sixty, but he knew in his very being that God was looking out for him and his mother.

Melanie had just said goodbye to their ranch hands when a feeling of nausea overwhelmed her. The men who helped out on the ranch had family to get back to before the snow got too bad. The plows tended not to come out to her neck of the woods until after the snow stopped falling, and they were both driving older trucks that didn't do too well in snow.

She knew she needed help, but she didn't know who to call. If she dialed 911, the entire town would know before Brandon got home. And some would surely call him and worry him. The last thing he needed was to worry the entire way home during a snowstorm. No, she would have to call someone else.

Then it hit her: Chloe. While the nice young woman wasn't a doctor, she did know doctors, and she knew enough to let Melanie know if what was going on was serious enough to head to the hospital.

Slowly, she inched her way to her purse, and when she had her phone in her hand she sat down at the kitchen table and dialed.

"Mrs. Beck, so good to hear from you. How are you today?" The sweet voice of Chloe came clearly through the line, and Melanie sighed.

"Well, that's what I'm calling about." Melanie took a breath and waited for the rumbling of her stomach to subside.

"What's wrong?" The change in Chloe's voice told Melanie that the girl had picked up on her discomfort.

"I'm not feeling so well. My stomach is very upset, and I don't know if it's something I just need to wait out or if I should come in to see the doctor." Melanie hated to admit she was weak and didn't know what to do. As a strong, independent woman, she rarely admitted she didn't know what she was doing. Or that she needed help.

"Mrs. Beck…"

Melanie interrupted, "Please, call me Melanie."

"Sorry—I know, Melanie. Tell me what's going on." Chloe was all business now, and listened as the kind woman explained her symptoms.

When Melanie finished, Chloe wanted to sigh. The town's clinic had already closed up because of the storm. That morning the national weather service had issued a storm advisory, and businesses all over her town were closing in anticipation of a very large snowfall.

"How far out is Brandon?" Chloe hoped he would be safe

and be able to make it home before the worst of it hit.

"I can't call him back. He really needs to get out to Bozeman for a supply run."

"Melanie, haven't you heard?"

"Heard what?" Melanie's voice was weak, and she sounded a bit breathless.

Chloe wondered how much she should say. "There's a large storm coming in from the Arctic. If Brandon's too far out, he won't be making it home until tomorrow at the earliest."

"Oh, dear." She paused, and Chloe could have sworn she heard Melanie's stomach make a very loud and scary gurgling noise. "Maybe I should drive into town now?"

"No. If you're feeling sick, I'll come out to you and stay with you." Chloe had been relaxing in sweats on her couch in front of the fireplace just as she had wanted to earlier in the week. But checking on Melanie was more important than cozying up to a fire. "I'll put out my fire and head right over to your ranch. You might want to call Brandon and let him know about the storm. I doubt he's going to want to spend the night away from you, especially if you aren't feeling well."

Chloe stood up and went to her fire to bank it. Then she headed to her room to change clothes and pack an overnight bag, and her first aid kit. Just in case.

"Do you really think it's going to be that bad?" Melanie asked.

"Yes, I do. Are you alright to wait at least thirty minutes? Or should I call for an ambulance to come get you?" Chloe wasn't sure what was going on with Melanie, but she knew that the woman was all alone at the moment, and she was the closest friend the woman had who could help. At least, she didn't think any of the Becks' neighbors knew about her MS, or even knew what to do to help.

"I should be fine…"

Chloe heard the phone drop as Melanie scuffled away. But the sounds coming over the phone were loud enough that Chloe knew exactly what was going on.

Melanie had just upped the dosage on her new medicine, and it didn't seem to be sitting well with her. Chloe stayed on the line as Melanie continued to empty her stomach. She hurried as fast as she could and was in her truck before Melanie got back on the line.

"I'm sorry, I might have caught a bug. Maybe you should stay away?" Melanie's soft, weak voice didn't sound anything like the strong woman Chloe knew.

"Melanie don't worry about me. I'm on my way over now. I suggest you call Brandon right away. If he can, he needs to turn around and head home." Not that Chloe wanted to see Brandon, but she knew the cowboy would be furious if he was stuck away from home while his mother was so sick.

If she were in his shoes, she would want to know so she could do whatever it took to get home to her mom. Especially if her dad wasn't around and none of her brothers or sister, either. Thankfully, the chances that her mother would be all alone were slim to none. Not with their giant family.

They hung up and Chloe called Jillian, the head nurse from her clinic. After they spoke for a little while about Melanie, she felt better. It sounded like Melanie was going to have to change medicines, but would be alright if her stomach settled by morning. With a few orders from Jillian about how best to treat an upset stomach, Chloe was feeling better about the situation.

However, she did pray on the way to the Becks' ranch that it was just a bad reaction to the increased dosage of her medicine and that Melanie would be alright by morning.

CHAPTER 16

W hen she arrived, things were not as bad as Chloe had feared. Of course, the front door was unlocked. Most ranchers left their doors unlocked during the day, so Chloe walked in and called out to Melanie so she wouldn't worry.

"I'm in the kitchen," Melanie called out weakly. And a woof sounded out next to her.

Chloe had been here several times and knew exactly how to get to the kitchen. She turned and walked down a corridor that opened up into a great room set up with the kitchen to the right. "Melanie, what happened?" Even she could hear the worry in her own voice, and she cleared her throat, not wanting to upset Melanie any more than she already was.

Patch, the family dog, whimpered next to Melanie's feet.

A faint smile parted her lips, and she waved for Chloe to take a seat near her. "When I woke up I wasn't feeling well, but that's not unusual. So I said nothing to Brandon when he left for Bozeman."

"Were you able to reach him before he was too far out?" That was the one thing Chloe worried about. He would have to go through a mountain pass on the I-90 before he was out of the Montana forests. And if it was snowing over there anything like what they were experiencing in Frenchtown, the pass would most likely be closed by now. He might be able to go down the mountain, but if he was already in the valley then he wouldn't be allowed back up and therefore wouldn't be able to come home today.

She nodded and reached for her cup of water. "He's on his way back. He was actually stopped getting a cup of coffee. He should be home in an hour or so, depending on the snow."

When her shoulders relaxed, Chloe realized how worried she had been about Brandon not making it back in time. Not that she needed Brandon here, but Melanie would most likely feel better knowing her son was near should anything serious happen.

Chloe took a seat next to Patch and Melanie, and without thinking about it reached down to pet the dog. His fur was soft, and the action of petting dogs always calmed Chloe.

"Have you had any tea yet?" Chloe went to the stove, turned on the burner, and filled up the teapot. She rummaged through the cabinet above the coffee maker, hoping that was where Melanie kept her tea.

"No, just water."

"Hmm, well. If your stomach is upset, you should be drinking tea." She turned around and held up two options. "Which one?"

"The peppermint, I think," Melanie responded.

"Good choice. Not only will it help to settle your stomach, but it will also smell good." Chloe grinned and rummaged through the cabinet full of coffee mugs. She noticed a black mug with a cowboy on it toting a gun in his left hand that said, *The 2nd Amendment is my God-given right.* "Huh, he's a lefty. That's funny."

"That's Brandon's favorite mug. I think you're the only one who's ever gotten the joke." Melanie gave Chloe a week smile.

Leaving Brandon's mug alone, she pulled two mugs down and prepared them both with peppermint tea once the kettle whistled.

After they sat there and took a few drinks of the warm liquid, Chloe asked, "Have you been sick again since you called me?"

Melanie shook her head and took another sip. "I don't know if there's anything left inside me."

The dog at Melanie's feet continued to whimper every so often. Chloe paid closer attention to the dog, wondering if he was sick or injured. But then she considered the bond a dog had with its owner.

With a tilt of her head, Chloe looked the woman up and down, then put the back of her hand to Melanie's forehead. It was warm. She doubted it was from the tea; the patient hadn't drunk enough to warm her body up that much. "Do you have a thermometer?"

Melanie put her mug down. "Yes, I'll go get it."

Chloe put a hand on Melanie's shoulder. "Please, sit. I'll go get it. Just tell me where it is."

A few minutes later, Chloe felt better. Well, maybe *better* wasn't accurate. Relieved? It seemed Mrs. Beck had a temperature of 101.3. It was no wonder the woman felt so sick. "Did you get your flu shot this year?"

She nodded. "I did."

Chloe pursed her lips. "Well, I've heard that this year's shot was a bit outdated. The strains of flu it covered aren't the ones going around. My guess—and mind you, I'm not a doctor or even a nurse—but I'd suspect you have the flu."

Brows furrowed, Melanie looked at Chloe as though she

was speaking gibberish. "I haven't had the flu in over twenty years. That can't be it."

After a couple more sips from her delectable tea, Chloe said, "Well, I would say that your current condition has made you more susceptible to viruses. It's very common. I suggest we call your telehealth team, just to be on the safe side."

After the nurse confirmed that it most likely it was the flu and not a reaction to her MS meds or anything more serious, Melanie winced and sighed.

"Melanie, you did the right thing by calling me. With MS, you never know what it might be." Chloe walked the woman to her room to help her get in bed as the nurse ordered, Patch close on their heels.

"But, you came all the way out here in this snow. Will you even be able to make it home? Or will you be stuck here?" Melanie's eyes darted to the window, which was covered with curtains.

"Don't worry about me. I'm not going anywhere until Brandon gets home." Even if it was only the flu, Chloe wasn't going to leave a sick woman all alone in the middle of a snowstorm. Who knew if Brandon would make it back before the roads closed?

Although, knowing Brandon he would just cut across any open fields and mow down any fences in his way if the roads were closed. He wasn't going to let a little ol' snowstorm stop him from getting back to care for his mom. She was everything to the cowboy, and Chloe knew it.

"Still, I'm sorry to have called you out here for nothing but the flu. I feel like I overreacted." Melanie sat down on the side of her bed. "I mean, really. What grown woman can't handle the flu on her own?"

The dog jumped up on the bed, nestled in next to Melanie, and put his head in her lap. She in turn rubbed a hand down the dog's back, and he quieted. She seemed to relax as well. Tension left her shoulders as she petted her dog.

Chloe tilted her head and considered what to say. On the one hand Melanie had a point, but on the other…? "Melanie, you just changed the dosage on your medicine. It's not uncommon for MS patients to have reactions similar to the flu when that happens. The fact that you haven't been sick since your kids were little only made it appear more likely that you were having a reaction."

Melanie stood back up, and Patch moved over. Then she walked to her dresser and pulled out warm, flannel pajamas with little black bears and paw prints on them. "Thank you. But if you can get out of here, I'd understand. I'm just going to get in bed. And Brandon should be here soon anyway."

She shook her head. "Nope. You're stuck with me." Chloe walked to the window and pulled the curtains back. "Besides, I'm not so sure Brandon is going to make it back any time soon." Outside the window the wind was blowing the snowflakes around, but they were piling up. There were snow drifts at least three feet high already.

Worry lines covered Melanie's face. "Do you think he'll stop somewhere until it's safe to come home?"

"What do you think?" Chloe put a hand on her hip and pursed her lips.

Melanie sighed. "That's what I'm afraid of."

"Woof!" Patch agreed with them both.

Melanie sighed and got into bed with Patch lying on top of the handmade quilt covering her bed.

Two hours later, with Chloe sitting in the kitchen drinking coffee and Melanie fast asleep, the front door banged open and a gust of wind brought snow inside the house.

Chloe jumped up, fearing that the wind had broken the front door. But when she ran into the entryway, she saw a burly man wearing a jacket and covered in snow trying to close the door behind him, and not succeeding. "Brandon? Is that you?"

Chloe had been expecting the cowboy for at least the past thirty minutes. When she tried calling him, her cell wouldn't work. The local towers must have been down, which was usual in a snowstorm.

The man glanced over his shoulder and furrowed his brows. "Chloe?" Snow stuck to the scruff on his face, and he appeared even handsomer than usual. "Can you give me a hand?"

When the shock of seeing Brandon covered in snow wore off, she walked over to the door and shoved her body as hard as she could against it. "Wow, that's some storm out there. How'd you even get inside without getting blown across the county?"

His deep chuckle sent chills through her that had nothing to do with the cold permeating the entryway. "I almost got lost in a snow drift, but I made it." He wiped the snow from his face and flicked the bits onto the ground, then frowned. "Hmm…seems I made quite a mess here."

Chloe looked down. "Don't worry, I'll get a mop and clean it up." The entryway floor was covered in melting snow.

"Don't bother, I'll do it." He walked toward the kitchen and then turned back to Chloe. "Where's my mom?"

"She's fine. She's in bed sleeping right now." Chloe had checked on the woman only fifteen minutes before Brandon arrived, and she had been sleeping fitfully. She wasn't sure if Melanie was having nightmares or just couldn't seem to get comfortable, but she was moving around and getting tangled in her covers. And Patch whimpered when he looked between his master and Chloe.

Chloe had walked in and straightened the covers out for the sick woman and her dog. Then she put a hand on Melanie's forehead. It didn't feel any hotter, but she figured she would have to keep an eye on her patient until that fever broke.

She would never admit it to anyone, but she worried for Melanie. While it most likely was a flu, a high fever and upset stomach could also mean other things for an MS patient. Once the storm was over and the roads opened again, she would insist that Brandon take his mother in to see the doctor. Although, if she were a betting woman she'd bet Brandon would plow the roads himself as soon as it was safe just so he could get his mother in to see the doc.

"Thank you for coming out here and taking care of her. Do you know what's wrong?" The worry in Brandon's voice reminded Chloe that no one had been able to reach him to tell him it was only the flu.

She told him what the nurse had said and what she had done before putting his mom to bed.

"That's good, but I'm going to go and check on her." Brandon left Chloe in the kitchen.

Assuming he would be with his mom for a while, she decided to mop up the mess in the entryway. With the howling winds and snow buffeting the sides of the house, she got to work and in no time had the entryway cleaned and dried. She wasn't about to let it stay wet and have someone slip and fall.

He was still in with his mom when everything was cleaned up, so Chloe went back into the kitchen and began preparing lunch. It was late for lunch, but her stomach had been rumbling and she was past ready to eat. She figured Brandon would be as well, as she doubted he would have stopped to eat along the way home.

As she finished the simple lunch of ham and swiss sandwiches with sliced apples and carrot sticks, she realized she was going to be there for a while. Though they hadn't spoken about the storm, she'd seen enough of it when she helped Brandon close the door that she knew she would be staying the night with the Becks.

Once the lunch was prepared, she took a plate in to Brandon along with a mug of hot coffee. One thing she knew for sure about Brandon was that he loved his coffee.

"Hey, how's she doing?" With a plate in one hand and the coffee mug in another, she used her shoulder to push the door all the way open. Thankfully, it had been left open a crack.

"She's still asleep." He looked up at Chloe, then stood and made his way toward her. "Here, let me help you."

"I wasn't sure if you had eaten lunch, so when I fixed myself something I decided to make you a sandwich as well." Chloe shrugged. No one had told her to make herself at home, but she figured Melanie would have if she were awake.

"Thank you. Did you eat yet?" He held the plate and cup in his hands and looked awkwardly around. The room wasn't set up for eating a meal.

"Not yet. My lunch is waiting for me on the table. I figured you'd want to eat in here while you watched over your mom." In actuality, she hoped he would. Chloe did not need to be spending time alone with Brandon. It would be awkward enough when the time came for her to hit the hay. He probably hadn't thought that far ahead yet.

"Here"—he motioned for her to leave the room—"I'll go and eat with you in the kitchen. There's really not a good place to sit and eat in here." Brandon's chuckle held a hint of nervousness, which only served to make Chloe feel even more awkward.

"Um, alright." What could she say? *No, I don't want you*

eating lunch with me in your own house. He was probably just trying to be polite and keep her company like any gentleman would do.

"So, this storm is fixin' to be mighty strong. I think you'll need to hunker down here with us tonight." Brandon gulped as he followed Chloe to the kitchen. When he had been sitting with his ma, he kept thinking about the pretty girl in the other room and wondering what brought her out here in the middle of a storm. He knew his mom had called her and asked for help, but he couldn't figure out why she'd come.

When Chloe sat down, she smiled shyly up at the cowboy hovering over the table before he took a seat two spots away from her. "Yeah, I figured as much. But it's still hours until bedtime. Maybe we'll get lucky and this storm will end early and they'll get the roads plowed tonight."

He chuckled and thought she must be joking. "Are you serious? They never plow the roads at night 'round these parts unless they have to." He took a bite of his sandwich. "Hm, this is great. How'd you know I like mustard and mayonnaise on my sandwich?"

"Who doesn't?" She turned confused eyes on him, and his heart did a double beat.

Brandon opened his mouth to say something stupid and thought better of it. Instead, he put the sandwich in his mouth and held his thoughts to himself. Only the perfect woman would like her sandwiches the way he did, with the mayo dripping off the edges. He knew it wasn't healthy to have so much mayo, but he didn't indulge too often in sandwiches. And he had been cutting back on the mayo, but this sandwich was heavenly. He had to lick his fingers when a glop of perfect mayo and mustard dripped down on his hand.

"I was thinking about making a hearty soup for dinner.

That way, if your mom wakes up hungry she can at least eat the broth. Do you mind?"

Who was this woman who took such good care of his mom, made him the perfect sandwich, and now hoped he wouldn't mind if she cooked him dinner? If his mom wasn't sick, he'd think he was in a dream.

Brandon shook his head and smiled. "No, I don't mind at all. I think Ma put some beef stew meat in the fridge. And there's plenty of root vegetables in the pantry. I can help chop, if you want?" He hoped he could spend some quality time with this woman, since they were stuck together and all.

Could they be friends and nothing more? He thought it might be possible. Over the years he'd heard urban legends that men and women couldn't be friends, but if both were Christian adults and went into the friendship only wanting to be friends and nothing more, it could happen. Right?

Deep down Brandon knew he was fooling himself, but he didn't care. Every time he was near this woman, his resolve to stay away from her broke. Since they were going to be stuck together for the night, he was going to enjoy the time they had together—in a strictly platonic manner.

CHAPTER 17

Only two hours later, Brandon was kicking himself. They had spent time working on the beef and vegetable stew Chloe wanted to make. He had offered up his cowboy stew recipe, but she wanted to use hers. In the end, it wasn't much different. Well, okay, maybe she'd added a few more vegetables than he would have. And maybe she'd used more spices than he would have, but what was wrong with a simple beef stew? If you had good enough beef along with salt, pepper, and few specialty spices like a Lawry's seasoning packet, what was the difference?

Chloe swore it would taste much better with all of her seasonings. He would give it a try. But boy howdy, it sure did take them longer to make her stew than it did to make his. This one had them both chopping. It also had Chloe tearing up when she had to chop the onions.

Brandon had a much better solution: chopped onions from a spice container. Those dehydrated ones worked just fine, thank you very much.

"Alright, while your stew is simmering I've got to go out and check on the horses and cattle, make sure they're all fed and safe." Brandon wiped his hands on a dishrag and headed toward the back door. He turned around when he felt a presence behind him that he didn't expect.

"What? Did you think I was going to let you take care of the chores while I sat inside all nice and warm and toasty?" She rolled her eyes and began to put on his mom's large red barn coat, designed just for this type of day.

He put his hands up and waved them. "No way, no how, nuh-uh. You are staying inside where it's warm and dry."

"Pft. Please." Chloe waved her hand. "I grew up on a family ranch. I think I can handle helping you with the feeding and checking to make sure all the animals are where they should be."

She tried to nudge past him, but he stood there blocking the door and not moving.

"Brandon." She tilted her head and tried to put her large gloved hands on her hips, but they slid down with all the outer layers, making it difficult to even tell where her hips were supposed to be.

"I need you to stay here and keep an eye on my ma just in case she wakes up while I'm outside. I don't want her to think she's all alone." He pleaded with his eyes for her to agree with him.

"Your mom was just awake half an hour ago. She's not going to wake up again any time soon. And I'm not going to allow you to go out in that weather all by yourself." She pointed to the storm still roiling about all around the ranch. "With both of us doing the chores, they'll get done much faster and we'll both be back in here before your mom even knows we were outside."

He threw his hands in the air. "Fine. Have it your way." He pointed a finger at her. "But I don't want to hear it when you've got frostbite on your toes or fingers." He took a closer look at how she was dressed. "Or your nose." He swiped his finger down the bridge of her nose.

Chloe smiled and swatted at his hand, but was too late and missed it. "Deal. I won't complain as long as you don't."

"Me? What would I have to complain about?" He put his Stetson tightly on his head and turned to open the door after they were both fully decked out in the warmest gear he had in his mud room.

She shoved past him and ran to the barn, zigging with the wind as it blew her to the side. When they were both safely inside and the door closed, she turned and smiled up at him. "That I won." She smirked and headed in the direction of the horses. "I'll check on the horses if you want to start checking the cattle. Do you have any about to freshen?"

Brandon did have a few mommas who were getting close to birthing their calves, but none any time soon. He figured he had at least four more weeks before any of his females would be ready for the calving stalls.

"Nope. None during this storm, at least." He checked that his hat was still on tight and went out the side door, looking for any stray cattle that might be stuck somewhere.

When Chloe had fed the horses and checked that all the water troughs were full, she moved outside to help Brandon. It didn't look like they were going to have to go out and look for any missing cattle. Or, at least she hoped they wouldn't have to. The storm didn't seem as though it would end any time soon. The winds were still screeching and buffeting up against the side of the barn. It was all she could do to stay upright.

"Chloe!" Brandon yelled, and waved back to the barn.

She couldn't hear what he said after he called her name, so she moved closer to him. "What?" She put a hand near her ear to signal she couldn't hear him. When his lips moved and she couldn't hear anything above the roar of the storm, she shook her head.

He moved as quickly as he could back toward her. When he reached her, he pushed her back into the barn. "It's all done outside. The cattle know when to come into the barn. I think they can tell the weather better than those blasted machines can." He chuckled and rubbed his hands up and down his arms. Even with thick winter gloves, his hands were really cold. With the added windchill, he estimated it was easily down around zero, maybe even four or five below. Brandon had no clue how Chloe was doing so well in this weather.

She must have seen the question in his eyes. "You forget, I grew up not too far from here on a family ranch. Days like this it was all hands on deck. Just because I'm a girl didn't mean I got to stay inside."

"I can't believe your dad wanted you out in this weather." Brandon shook his head and whistled.

"Well, he really didn't want us out, but he also knew that with all seven of us working together, the chores would be done quickly and no one would be out long enough to worry about frostbite."

He nodded. "Thank you. Now, let's get back inside where we can get some more hot coffee and sit in front of the fire while your stew is cooking." The sparkle in his eyes when he mentioned food showed how eager he was to get some hot food in his belly.

They both went to the barn door closest to the house. The door wasn't too big, but it would put them outside right in the crosshairs of the wind, which was blowing really hard. It had to be at least forty-mile-an-hour winds out there, maybe more. It was the type of wind that could send powerlines and trees down.

Brandon debated waiting it out in the relative warmth of the barn, or just going for it and trying to get into the house.

The eagerness on Chloe's face to get outside pushed him on. He opened the door and did his best to hold it while they both exited and he stumbled in the wind. He accidentally let go of the door, or the wind whipped it out of his hands—he really wasn't sure which—and when he went back to grab the pounding door, he noticed that Chloe had been knocked over already.

"Figgy pudding!" he yelled out, and let go of the door. When he finally helped her up, he didn't let go of her arm. It took them both working together to get the barn door closed. "Maybe we should have gone out the big door that's on rollers."

Chloe laughed and shook her head. "It's fine. Come on, you big oaf, let's get inside." She entwined her arm with his, and they both ducked their heads and they slowly made their way across the snow-covered yard.

Once they had made it to the back door, the wind wasn't quite so strong. Chloe reached for the back door, and Brandon put his arm around her waist to help push her inside first. Surprisingly, she went inside easily enough. But when he closed the door and took off his snow-covered jacket, he realized she was shivering and her lips had turned blue.

"Oh, Chloe. Why didn't you tell me you were so cold?" He pulled her close to him and opened her jacket so he could share his body warmth with her.

With teeth chattering, she said, "Sssorrry. I was fffine untillll I fffelll."

"Shh, don't talk." He rubbed her back and realized her jacket was wet all the way through. "You must have fallen into more than just a snowbank. Your back is drenched."

She couldn't speak; she only nodded.

He walked her over to the fireplace and peeled her wet jacket away. When he threw it on the hearth so it would dry faster, a sloshing sound emanated from the mess and he pulled Chloe close to him. They stood in front of the fire for a few moments before Brandon realized his mistake.

Her arms wrapped around his body, and she shivered and shook while he rubbed her back. She had her back to the fire and Brandon used his body to warm her front. Any other time or place, this would have been extremely out of line. But with her still shivering, she knew she had zero desire to do anything except warm up.

Brandon, however, felt his pulse increase and he took in a deep breath. He let it out slowly and thought about the cows and the horses. He did *not* want to think about the soft woman he was holding and how she trusted him. *Especially* after he had broken her heart. He knew he had to let go of her before she got the wrong impression. But darn it all if he didn't want to make her his gal.

"Horses."

"What?" Chloe looked up at the stern face of the man holding her and wondered what she had missed while she stood there, teeth chattering.

"Uh, I just wanted to make sure you fed all the horses? And added fresh hay to their stalls?" He knew she did, but he had to do something to get his mind off the beautiful woman in his arms.

She nodded. "They're all taken care of."

"Good, good." He cleared his throat and pulled back a little to look into her face. "You don't look blue anymore. How about I go get you a hot cup of tea? Peppermint?"

Chloe took a step back. "That would be wonderful, thank you."

Her timid smile made his heart beat in overdrive.

"Here." Brandon got a rocking chair and brought it, along with a thick blanket, close to the fire and directed Chloe to sit. He tucked her underneath the blanket, and without another word headed toward the kitchen to fix her tea.

"Stupid, stupid. What was I thinking?" he berated himself once he put the kettle on the stove. Brandon had a plan: come home to take care of his mom and the ranch. That was it. There wasn't time for anything else. But figgy pudding if she didn't feel right in his arms. Chloe Manning was a perfect fit for him. And not just in his arms, but in his life as well. She was a rancher's daughter and knew exactly what to do on a ranch and how to help during a blizzard. She constantly amazed him.

Well, except how to stand up during the onslaught of wind. But to be fair, he'd almost fallen over himself. He actually didn't know of any woman who could have handled herself half so well as Chloe just did. She was freezing cold, literally, and she didn't even complain.

He sighed in tandem with the steam and whistle of the kettle. It was no use; he couldn't keep fighting his feelings for this woman. If she was ready for the challenge of dating someone who was so over his head with responsibilities, then he would go for it.

CHAPTER 18

"Peppermint sticks!" Chloe whispered into her blanket while she waited for Brandon to bring back her tea. She knew he was only trying to help her get warm, but it felt so good, so right, to be in his arms. He had never held her like that before. But then again, she had never been on the verge of hypothermia before, either.

How was she to deal with her growing feelings for the cowboy who kept saving her? She hoped and prayed that the storm would hurry up and pass so she could go home. Staying the night here, while not completely inappropriate, was definitely not smart.

They weren't totally alone, but Melanie was sick. In fact, Chloe hadn't checked on Melanie in a while. She would have to go and check on Brandon's mom after she had her cup of tea just to make sure the woman didn't need anything. Melanie should be getting hungry soon.

Just as she thought about food her stomach gurgled, and she giggled. Food did sound really good at that moment.

"What's so funny?"

The question startled Chloe, and she turned around to see

the cowboy who dominated her thoughts lately carrying a tray with all the tea fixings, including some cookies.

"That looks good." She wasn't about to tell him about her tummy rumblings. If he didn't hear it, then she wasn't going to call it out.

He set the tray on the coffee table and began to fix a cup and plate for Chloe. "I figured you might want something to snack on while we waited for the stew to finish. How much longer do you think it'll be?"

Chloe took the offered food and drink and smiled her thanks. "Not much longer, maybe an hour? I'll need to go and check it soon. Have you looked in on your mom?"

He shook his head. "I thought I'd get you all set up, and then while my tea was steeping I'd poke my head in her room."

"If she's awake, let me know. I think she might want some of the broth. And we should probably take her temperature again soon. I want to make sure it's not going up." She hadn't given Melanie any Tylenol yet. Melanie wanted to wait and let the fever break naturally if possible. If the temperature didn't start to lower on its own, then Chloe would give the woman the medicine whether she liked it or not.

Once Chloe was all settled, Brandon left to check on his mom.

Chloe drank her tea and stared into the fire. The flames had her attention, and she cleared her mind of all confusing thoughts of the handsome cowboy who knew exactly how to take care of her. As she stared into the flames, her eyelids began to droop.

"Chloe, come quickly!" Brandon yelled from the edge of the room.

The noise jolted her awake, and she spilled the tea in her lap. "Oh, peppermint sticks!"

"Don't worry about that. Come and see my mother." Brandon turned around and ran back toward his mom's bedroom.

Dread filled Chloe as she hopped up and put the near empty teacup on the table and moved the blanket out of the way of the fire before running to Melanie's room. All she could think of was how they would get her to a hospital.

Chloe came to a sudden halt when she entered Melanie's room. The sight before her confused her, and she had to blink to make sure she wasn't dreaming.

Melanie was up and dressed in jeans and a warm sweater. Her hair was brushed back into a ponytail, and she looked almost healthy.

"Chloe, thank you so much for taking such great care of me." Melanie looked from her son's confused expression to Chloe. "I feel so much better. My fever is gone."

"Uh, are you sure? Did you take your temp with the thermometer?" Chloe scratched her chin and looked to the bedside table where she had left the thermometer earlier.

Melanie nodded. "Yes, and it's normal. I'd like to take a shower, but with this storm I'm not sure we'll have power for much longer, and I'd hate to be in the shower when the power went out." She chuckled.

Chloe couldn't believe the change in the woman. It had only been a few hours since she was vomiting and running a temperature. She took three steps toward her patient and put the back of her hand on the woman's forehead and then on her cheeks. "Wow, it's a miracle. I've never seen anyone recover from the flu so quickly."

Chloe had prayed for healing, but this was more than she'd expected. Normally a good night's sleep and some beef broth would do the trick. But Melanie had only slept for a few hours, that was it.

"Do you think it was something besides the flu?" Brandon rubbed his temples and smiled.

"I think it was a gift from God," Melanie answered for them. "I'm sure the two of you have done nothing but stress and worry all day. Maybe"—she winked at Chloe—"this is God's way of getting your attention and telling you to trust in *His* ways."

Chloe nodded.

"Maybe," Brandon whispered in awe.

Melanie clapped her hands together. "Well, what have you two been up two while I slept?" She sniffed. "And what is that wonderful aroma?"

Brandon and Chloe both laughed.

"Come on, Ma. Let's head into the living room. I think Chloe might need some more tea." Brandon put an arm around his mother's shoulders and guided her to the living room.

"I need to check on dinner. Be right back." Chloe went to the kitchen, still in a bit of a daze. So far the day had been anything but what she'd envisioned. When she woke up that morning, all she wanted was a lazy day in front of the fireplace with hot cocoa and Christmas movies. But what she got was something so far out there that she wondered if she wasn't home in bed, still dreaming.

The power did go out. Thankfully, it wasn't until after dinner. Instead of the cozy Christmas movies she had envisioned watching, all three of them sat in front of the fireplace drinking hot cocoa that had been heated up over the flames.

"This reminds me of my time with the rodeo." Brandon took a sip of his hot drink and looked off into the distance.

"Really? I don't remember a storm this bad last winter."

Chloe furrowed a brow and thought back, wondering if maybe he'd experienced a blizzard in North Dakota or some other part of the Midwest she didn't pay attention to.

"Not the storm, but the sitting in front of a fire drinking hot cocoa with nothing to watch on TV." He smiled and thought back to the lightning storm that had gone through Iowa last February and hit a power line. "We lost power for two days. All our meals and drinks had to be cooked over a campfire." He chuckled and thought back on those days with fondness.

For the next hour, they all shared stories from their past of various campfires or storms that cut power. In one sense it was calming, and in another it was awe-inspiring to hear about the strength of nature and how it affected mankind.

It always came back to fire. No matter who told the story or what they had to say, it ended with a fire of some sort. Either in a fireplace like what they had then, or a firepit surrounded by cowboys who drank coffee with bits of grounds in the bottom of their cups.

As the evening progressed, Melanie looked better and better. Her coloring improved, and the bags under her eyes that Chloe had noticed earlier were gone. The pioneer woman's transformation was nothing short of miraculous. If she hadn't been there to witness it all, Chloe would have thought it wasn't possible for her to have had a high fever only a few hours earlier.

"Well, I think I'm going to head off to bed. You'd think I wouldn't be tired after sleeping the day away, but I am." She smiled at Chloe, then turned to her son. "Brandon, please help Chloe get set up in the guest room down the hall from my room. Can you get her some towels in case we have power for a shower in the morning?"

Brandon stood. "Yes, ma'am." He turned to walk away and do his mother's bidding.

"Thank you, Melanie. I appreciate it." Chloe smiled.

Melanie took a closer look at Chloe. "Land's sake, why didn't you tell me you needed clean clothes earlier?" The rancher tsk'd and turned toward her room.

Chloe followed her and was confused when Melanie handed her a set of clean sweats and a t-shirt to wear underneath. "What's this?"

"Did you fall in the snow or something earlier?" Melanie pointed out the wrinkles in Chloe's clothes.

Chloe looked down and also noticed the patches of dirt dried onto her shirt. "Oh, yeah. I did fall in a puddle of cold water when I was helping to feed the stock. But I brought clothes for tomorrow, I can change into them."

"You mean there was standing water that wasn't frozen over outside?" Melanie frowned.

"Yeah, I guess so." Chloe wasn't sure why, but a darkness skittered over Melanie's face. She wondered if the woman was getting sick again. Maybe sitting up and talking with them for the past few hours wasn't the best thing for the recovering woman.

"Well, it's too late to do anything about it now, but in the morning Brandon's going to need to check and see if a pipe burst."

Realization dawned on her, and Chloe ran to the bathroom to see if there was still running water. When she turned the knob, nothing came out. Not even a drop of water.

"Ma!" Brandon yelled from down the hall. "We've got a problem."

"But we had plenty of water for the hot cocoa and tea we drank all night." Chloe wasn't the one who had filled the kettle that they kept warm over the fire all night, but surely Brandon had just refilled it from the tap?

Melanie shook her head and sighed. "We have a jug of filtered water that we keep in the kitchen for use with our drinks."

"Oh, no."

"Yup, no showers in the morning." She looked around. "And no flushing toilets, either."

Brandon slapped a hand over his face. "It's all my fault. I should have realized when Chloe was wet after falling in the snow that something was wrong."

Melanie put a hand on his shoulder. "Son, there was nothing you could have done. Not in that storm."

"I could have at least turned off the water main. Now, who knows how bad the leak is and how far back the frozen line goes?" Brandon fisted his hands at his sides and mentally berated himself for not paying more attention.

When the blizzard was over, he'd have to dig up the pipes and fix the leak, but that didn't mean they'd have water. At least not right away.

"Well, I suppose we should gather up some of the clean snow and boil it down, then store it for cooking and drinking. At least enough to last us through this storm. Then when the roads are passable, you can come and stay with me until the water line is fixed." Chloe had space in her small house for the three of them. Maybe it could be fun hosting them for a few days.

Melanie put her hands in the air. "Oh, no. We couldn't impose."

"Nonsense. It's no imposition at all." Chloe tapped her chin with her forefinger. "Besides, don't you have some infusion treatments coming soon?" She had submitted the request to Melanie's insurance and received the approval. This might be a good way to ensure that Melanie stayed close to town in case there was another storm. Sometimes these were back to back, and if Melanie missed her infusions it might cause a problem with the treatment.

Even though Chloe had never wanted to be a nurse—which had nothing to do with not wanting to help patients and everything to do with needles—if she could help Melanie out with this, it would go a long way in helping her to feel as though she was making a difference in someone's life. Something she had not done much of since coming to Frenchtown.

"Ma, I think that's a great idea. You can stay at Melanie's place while I stay out here and get everything working again." Brandon smiled at Chloe, and his eyes softened.

Chloe's heart melted at the way he was looking at her, and she couldn't help but notice how he excluded himself from staying at her place. "Brandon, I have room for you both. You might need to sleep on the sofa, but we can make do."

He shook his head. "Thank you, but no. I think it would be better if I stayed out here. I can heat up water for a daily bath. Not a problem. This way I can spend more time working on the pipes as well as being here for the cattle and horses should there be any issues."

"What about Patch?" Just mentioning the old dog's name brought him trotting in with his beat-up chew toy, an old stuffed sheep that at one time did have a squeak box. Patch had long ago pulled that part out. Turned out he didn't like squeaky toys, but he did like to chew on them. His sheep, however, was more like a baby than a chew toy. He carried it around with him everywhere he went.

"Patch can keep me company as I work here." Brandon ruffled the old dog's head. And he gave a light "woof" in return.

"He's welcome to stay with us." Chloe scratched behind the ears of the old dog and wished she had one of her own.

Patch got up from next to Brandon and plopped down next to Melanie, where he loved to stay, and looked up at her with adoring eyes.

"Are you sure you don't mind? He tends to just lay around and get in people's way instead of acting as a guard dog." Melanie chuckled and leaned down. "Don't you, boy?"

Patch rolled over, and Melanie scratched his belly.

"I'm totally up for having Patch over. He's more than welcome to sleep on the spare bed with you, or on a nice warm rug. Whatever he wants. It will be nice having a dog around again." Mentally, Chloe wondered if she might be able to get her sister, Elizabeth, to find her a dog for Christmas. She had been wanting one, and after spending time today with Patch and having him come to stay with her for the next few days, she was going to miss having a dog around.

"Alright, as soon as the storm lets up, Patch and I will join you in town until Brandon gets the water lines fixed."

CHAPTER 19

The next morning when they all got up, Brandon couldn't believe the storm was still going strong. It had calmed down a little bit. At least, the high winds had abated. But snow was still falling. He doubted they would be going anywhere that day.

When Chloe got up, she headed straight for the kitchen to help make breakfast.

"Any coffee yet?" Groggily, she swiped at her eyes and looked at Brandon, who smirked.

"Yup, we've always got coffee. We may not have water for a shower, but coffee we can manage." He pulled a cup from the cupboard above the coffee maker and poured her a mugful. While the power was still out, he had made campfire coffee.

"Mmmm. Exactly what I needed." Chloe took a whiff of the strong brew before she took a sip. "So"—she looked around—"is your mother up yet?" She spat a few pieces of grounds from her mouth, but didn't say anything about chewing her coffee instead of drinking it. She understood that a fine ground used in coffee makers wasn't exactly what would work in a campfire coffee kettle.

If she had been at home, she could have just popped over to Lottie's and picked up a French press, but they were a little far to go just for a cleaner coffee.

Brandon chuckled. "I swear, she was never sick. She's got plenty of energy this morning. In fact, she's outside checking to see if the chickens laid any eggs."

"Do you think they would in that storm?" Chloe pointed her thumb out the window behind her. She doubted they would have calmed down enough to lay any eggs that morning. Back home when they had storms, their chickens would not lay any eggs. And she didn't blame them. Although, they did have one stout chicken who did lay an egg every day, no matter the weather. But that hen was an exception. In fact, they would regularly get double yolks from that one.

"We have a few who could have. As you know, most won't during a bad storm." He shrugged. "If not, we have the fixins for chocolate chip pancakes and bacon." He waggled his brows.

Chloe laughed. "You and those chocolate chip pancakes."

"You're one to talk. I know for a fact that you go into Lottie's every month for pancake Saturday." Brandon nodded and topped off their coffees.

"True, I do. Okay, so we both have a soft spot for chocolate chip pancakes. But who doesn't?"

"Who doesn't what?" Melanie asked when she closed the door.

"Who doesn't like chocolate chip pancakes?" Brandon asked, and leaned down to help get some of the snow off Patch.

The dog had followed Melanie out to check the hen house. He didn't always do that. But since Melanie had been sick yesterday, he was sticking close to her side. It was almost as though the dog knew Melanie was sick, or at the very least needed his comfort.

Melanie smiled and watched the couple out of the corner of her eye. It was beginning to look as though her plea to Santa, and God, wasn't going unanswered.

* * *

THE SNOW finally stopped dumping on the small ranches surrounding Frenchtown, and the snowplows came through the next day.

"Well, what do you say we get out of here and head back to my place and see if I have power and running water for a shower?" Chloe chuckled and patted Patch on the head.

"I'm ready when you are." Melanie put on her jacket and carried a small duffel bag with the things she might need for a few days. Including the little sheep toy that Patch loved so much.

"Here, don't forget Patch's favorite blanket." Brandon handed a worn but clean dog blanket to Chloe.

"You know, you're more than welcome to come back with us and shower. I probably have food in my fridge that needs to be eaten as well." Chloe had no idea if her power had gone out, but it was cold enough that if it had, the food in her fridge would at least be salvageable. The freezer items, well, she might have to cook up whatever meat she had in there if any had defrosted.

"Thanks, maybe I'll come by later today. But I want to get out there and clear away the snow and see the damage. I'll just get dirty, anyway." He shrugged and opened the front door for the ladies to exit.

As they drove into town, Chloe couldn't stop thinking

about what Brandon had said to her the night before, after his mother went to sleep. Maybe it was a good thing he wasn't going to stay with her while he worked on the pipes.

When Brandon took her hand in his and looked into her eyes, she stopped breathing. Then all of a sudden, she'd sucked in a breath and felt dizzy. She thought she must have died and gone to heaven when he apologized for not trying to make a go of their relationship a year ago.

"Chloe, I was afraid," he'd confessed when they were all alone.

"Afraid of what?" she asked him while the logs in the fire popped and crackled.

"Of my feelings for you." He sighed. "I thought if we tried it long distance I wouldn't be able to focus on my work, and I'd end up leaving early." He squeezed her hand. "To come back to you."

She gasped.

"I didn't want to leave you, but I knew I had to." He licked his lips. "Can you ever forgive me?"

Chloe had watched his tongue dart in and out of his mouth and sighed. They had only kissed a couple times when they were together, but it was enough to make her heart go wild and a bushel of butterflies to run amok in her stomach as she wondered if he was going to kiss her then. Did she even want him to? Of course she did.

She was fooling herself if she thought she was over him.

"Yes." It had come out as a whisper, but they were so close she didn't need to increase her volume.

When she ran over a bump, she came back to the present and realized she needed to pay attention to the road. Just because the snowplows had come through that morning didn't mean it was totally safe to drive back into town on autopilot.

The snow was piled up at least four feet high all along the sides of the road. She couldn't see over them, they were so high. It felt like she was driving through a snow tunnel and not an open road on a Montana highway that was normally covered in hay and dotted with black cattle.

"Do you think the clinic will be open today?" Melanie's question broke through the fog that had enveloped Chloe.

"I don't think so. But when we get to town I'll call and see." Chloe looked over at Melanie and furrowed her brow. "Are you starting to feel bad again?" Worry overtook the feelings of joy and excitement, and she said a quick prayer that Mrs. Beck was going to be alright.

Melanie waved a hand. "I'm fine. I just wanted to check with the doctor that my infusion was still on for Monday. I'm not sure if being sick will make them reschedule."

Chloe didn't know the answer to that, either. Since it was Friday and they'd just had a huge blizzard come through, she wasn't sure of the state of the office. If they still didn't have power, like the Beck ranch, then the clinic wouldn't open to patients.

"At least the cell towers are working again." That morning Chloe had turned her phone back on, after using her emergency power charger, to find that she had two bars. She also had several messages from her folks, which she returned. Everyone was fine, just worried about her since they couldn't reach her.

"True, which makes me think the town has power again, too."

Melanie was right. When they drove into town, the lights were on and the streets were cleaned of any signs of the snowstorm. The general store was open, and the parking lot was full. As was the Sip 'n' Go. Which made sense. She doubted anyone had run out of food after only two days; they were most likely out there to gossip about their neighbors and compare stories.

It never failed to amaze Chloe how one little storm always turned into the storm of the century after the old geezers or meddling moms finished telling their tales. Although, the storm of the past two days was most likely the storm of the decade, at least. She would be curious to hear what everyone had to say about it, and hoped that no one was injured.

When she drove by the clinic, she noted the lights on and several cars parked out front. That was a good sign. It meant Melanie could call and check on her appointment for Monday, and anyone who did need medical attention would be able to get it.

"Oh, that hot shower has done wonders for me." Melanie sighed as she plopped on the sofa next to Chloe.

Chloe had called the clinic and was told to stay home, but to be ready for a crazy-busy week come Monday. She didn't object to another snow day.

"A hot shower does feel good after not having one for a few days, doesn't it? Have you called your doctor yet?" Chloe had thought about asking Jillian about Melanie's condition when she phoned in earlier, but decided she should stay out of it. Mrs. Beck would call and find out for herself.

"Everything is a go. But my doctor is happy I'll be staying in town for a few days. He said to call him directly if I feel sick again." Melanie covered herself up with the throw blanket Chloe handed her.

"Good. What do you say we watch some Hallmark Christmas movies?" Chloe's grin was infectious, and the two spent the rest of day relaxing on the couch watching Christmas romance movies.

When Brandon showed up on her doorstep unannounced, Chloe was shocked.

"What?" Brandon worried that he was no longer welcome for some reason. Maybe he was too dirty and the stench of hard labor was too much for the clean and beautiful woman standing before him in sweats?

"Sorry, please come in." Chloe had to shake herself. A man who worked hard all day and was covered in grime had never looked so handsome before. Maybe it had something to do with the Christmas ranch romance she had just watched. The lead actor had looked similar to Brandon, and she'd fantasized that she was the one being swept up off her feet by a handsome cowboy in dirty jeans with smudges on his face. Not unlike the ones on Brandon's right then.

"How's my mom?" He wiped his boots on the doorstep before stepping inside and taking them off.

"She's fine. I don't think she's sick at all anymore. In fact, we were just about to sit down to dinner. Care to join us?" Chloe closed the door behind Brandon and waved to her small dining room.

"Uh, I'd love to, but how about that shower you promised me? I think my dirt and stench might make your dinner unappetizing for you and my mom." He chuckled and looked down at the mud caked on his jeans and shirt.

Brandon had brought a bag with clean clothes to put on after a long, hot shower. It was still at the front door next to his dirty boots.

"Of course. Let me show you to the guest bathroom and get you some towels." Chloe wouldn't have minded the least bit if he ate dinner with them just as he was. There was something about a man who did hard labor all day and looked like he had worked his tail off. Even now, with all the caked-on dirt, he still smelled of cinnamon and leather. Of course, the other scents of work and dirt were stronger, but she could still smell his own unique scent below it all. And her stomach somersaulted with the memories of last year. As well as his offer to take her to dinner next week, once he had fixed the pipes at home.

CHAPTER 20

I t had been a crazy week. Finally, it was Friday night and Brandon was standing on her doorstep, waiting to take her to dinner. It wasn't anything fancy, just the spaghetti dinner she had put together at the last minute to help raise funds for the college kids.

But he was more handsome than she had ever seen him. Brandon wore black jeans, black boots, a deep-blue button-up shirt, and a bolo tie. He held a black Stetson in his hands and looked at her with wide eyes.

"Wow, you're beautiful." Brandon stood stock-still and took her in.

Chloe was wearing red boots, black jeans, a red button-up cowgirl shirt, and had on more makeup than she usually wore, but it was still done tastefully. She had dressed casually and for comfort and warmth. She hadn't thought she would look beautiful. Pretty, maybe. Well, she hoped with her hair curled and makeup on, he would think she was pretty. But she had not expected him to be practically drooling over her in jeans.

"Thank you, you clean up nicely yourself." She felt a

warmth creep up her neck and into her cheeks and hoped she wasn't blushing.

Brandon was having difficulty getting words to form, so he put his arm out for her, and she took it while she closed her door with her other hand.

When they arrived at the community center, they were both pleasantly surprised by how many vehicles were in the parking lot. The entire town and all the neighboring ranches and farms had been invited, but Chloe wasn't sure how many would come out.

They had put up flyers at all the town's Christmas events and on the town activity website, but not that many folks out in the country looked at the town's website, did they? Chloe wondered if maybe they did. Or at least during Christmas? Either way, she was excited to see everyone come out in support of the town's graduating seniors who were going away to college.

Brandon's wide eyes took in the scene, and he whistled. "Do you think there'll be enough food for everyone?"

She stopped just short of the entrance. "Oh, I hadn't thought of that. When I was here earlier helping to set up, we put up all the tables and set up quite a few crockpots that had been brought in early. But I never imagined we would get so many people coming for a simple spaghetti dinner."

Brandon pulled her forward. "Come on, let's go see. You know how some of these families just love to bring in tons of food for potlucks."

With huge smiles on both of their faces, Brandon led his date into the Frenchtown Community Center and smiled back at everyone who looked their way. The prettiest girl in the county was on his arm, and their effort to help the dozen or so kids going to college looked to be on its way to being a success.

The crockpots and pans of food lined all three walls of tables like a horseshoe. The student who were going to college and needed help were dressed up like little waiters and waitresses. Well, a couple of the boys were big enough to stand tall next to Chloe's brothers, but for the most part the kids looked like kids. And they had on huge smiles and were talking and laughing with the residents of the town and valley.

The students who needed help acted as waiters. They bussed tables, brought drinks, and took care of anything else the diners needed. Other students who needed some more volunteer hours for school manned the food tables and ensured they all stayed stocked and cleaned. When a crockpot was empty, a student would replace it with one that had been sitting by, waiting for a spot to open.

"Should we take a seat close to the serving tables?" Brandon pointed to a table that still had four open seats.

"Sure, that'll be great. This way, we can keep an eye on things and help if needed." They walked to the table, and Chloe set her purse down on her seat. She turned to Brandon. "If you don't mind, I want to take a peek in the kitchen and just make sure everyone is still doing alright."

He arched a brow. "Weren't you just here checking in on them like an hour ago?"

"Yes, but this was my idea, and I feel like I should be in the back helping, not out here enjoying myself." Chloe had planned to help, but when Brandon suggested that they go together on a date, she decided to take a leap of faith. Going on a date with the cowboy who hurt her last year *and* leaving everything up to the kids all night was a huge leap for her. She generally felt that she needed to be in the thick of things when an event was her idea. Not because she wanted any glory, but because she had a vision, and because in this case they were all kids.

Brandon's deep, throaty chuckle sent chills up and down Chloe's spine. "Don't worry so much. They got this. Just take a look around."

She did, and noticed he was right. While the place wasn't sparkling clean like it had been over an hour ago, it was in good shape, and no one seemed to be wanting anything. Did it matter that one table had spaghetti dripping down the side of it and onto the floor next to a toddler's seat? The mother noticed what her child had done and laughed. The rest of the people at her table looked at the little kid like he was an angel.

Just as Chloe was about to head over there and clean up the mess, Mark, one of the teens going to college, headed there with a roll of paper towels and some wet wipes. It looked as though he had it all under control, and Chloe sighed.

"You know, I think you might be right." She nodded and took her seat. "They've got this, and I need to let them handle it all."

"Even the clean-up?" Brandon waggled his brows.

"Well, that's going to be a lot of work, and it all has to be done tonight since tomorrow is the craft show. Everyone will be in here super early to set up." She was lucky the crafters had agreed to wait until Saturday morning for their setup. The only stipulation was that the room had to be spotless, and the tables had to be arranged per their plan. The kids could do that before they all left for the night. Chloe had planned to be here to at least supervise after it was all over.

"Yes, they'll get to do it all. But I'm going to stay until the place is ship-shape. It was my idea to hold it tonight, after all. And I'm the one who signed for the building."

"Fair enough. I'll stay and help as well." He grinned at her when she frowned.

"I'll be fine. You've got to get up before the cows tomorrow morning, so leave this to me." She planned to sleep in before coming to the craft fair.

He chuckled. "You're my date tonight. I can't leave you here. It's my responsibility to take you home."

Just then, Cove and Quinn came up and joined them at the table.

"Hey there, Quinn." Chloe looked around for the little girl's mother, but didn't see her. "Where's your momma?"

"Lottie wasn't feeling well, so I told her to take it easy and I'd take Quinn to the dinner tonight as my date." Cove patted the girl on her shoulder and looked down at her with loving, warm eyes.

If Chloe hadn't known better, she would have sworn Cove was Quinn's daddy, the way the two of them got on. It was obvious they had a special love for each other that only a parent and child held. It didn't matter that they weren't really related; Cove doted on the little girl.

"Oh, I'm sorry to hear this. I hope she'll be alright." Chloe had seen her friend earlier, but she hadn't said anything about being sick. "She's not getting that flu that's going around, is she?"

Cove shook his head. "Nah, I think it's just one of her migraines. She hasn't had one in a long time, but with all the stress lately I'm surprised she hasn't had one sooner."

"Stress?" Chloe furrowed her brow, confused. She hadn't heard anything about stress from Lottie. Well, other than the normal Christmas season stuff, her shop, and the fact that Quinn had been asking a lot of questions lately about her dad. Okay, she realized Lottie had been asking for help and she wasn't picking up on the signs. Some best friend she was.

Right then and there, she decided that instead of heading to the craft fair the next morning, she would go and see her friend and find out if there was anything she could do to help.

"Miss Manning!" Mark, one of the students helping buss the tables, ran to her with frantic eyes.

"What's wrong, Mark?" Chloe put a hand on his arm to help calm him down as she looked around to see if she could figure out what was wrong.

"It's Lisa. She needs your help." Mark gulped and looked guilty.

Chloe stood up and took Mark by the hand. "Come on, you can tell me what's wrong as we head to the kitchen. I take it that's where she and this crisis are?" Without looking back at her table and her date, she went with Mark.

When they got to the kitchen, she realized it really was a crisis. One that would take up most of her evening. The restaurant-quality dishwasher was spewing soap and water all over the place.

"Alright, turn the power off." She pointed to the switch, and Mark headed over there and turned it off.

"Margarite, go find your dad. I think he has some experience with this type of equipment?" Chloe took charge of the mess and directed various kids to start cleaning up the floor and getting the equipment cleaned up so that Mr. Peterson could fix it up.

By the time Margarite was back with her dad, the machine had been cleaned up and the teens were starting to tackle the wet floor. Since Chloe was dressed up, the kids persuaded her to stay clear of the mess. She stood by and helped direct them all. Although, she did inch her way toward a wobbling stack of dirty dishes when the teens weren't looking and straightened them out by scraping off the leftovers and then stacking them up so they wouldn't fall over.

Mr. Peterson looked at the machine and the mess on the floor and sighed. "I told the mayor we needed to do a complete overhaul on this machine three months ago, but would he or any of the council listen to me?" He shook his head. "I'll be right back. I've got my tools outside in my truck. Be sure to clear a space of the water and make it dry over there." He pointed to the area around the breaker box, and what looked to Chloe like the main controls for the old commercial dishwasher.

Mark and Margarite both went over to that area and began cleaning the water and suds from the ground.

Mr. Peterson looked over his shoulder before exiting the kitchen. "Margarite, you know to keep the water away from the power box, right?"

"Of course, Papa. Now go get your tools, and we'll get this mess cleaned up." She shooed her dad out the door and got right to work.

"Should I turn off the breaker for the machine?" Chloe asked.

Margarite shook her head. "Nah, better let my dad do that kind of stuff. We won't touch anything, just clean the floor around it all and wipe it dry so he doesn't slip."

Meanwhile, back in the main room things weren't going so good for Brandon, either.

CHAPTER 21

"Ma, what's wrong?" Brandon had called his mother after receiving a strange text with words that didn't make any sense.

"Huh?" Melanie's voice was distant and quiet.

"Mom, don't move. Stay where you are. I'm calling 911 and heading out right now." Brandon hung up his phone and looked at the confused faces around him. "Cove, can you see to Chloe? She'll need help after the event is over and an escort home."

"Sure, buddy. But what's wrong?" Cove turned worried eyes to his friend.

"It's my mom. Something's wrong. She's pretty incoherent and I don't know why. I gotta go. Can you explain this to Chloe?"

"Of course, take care of your mom. I've got things here for you." The rodeo cowboy patted his friend's shoulder.

"Thanks." Brandon headed out while on the phone to emergency services.

"Uncle Cove? Is Mrs. Beck going to be alright?" Little

Quinn looked up at her adopted uncle with wrinkles between her brows.

Cove knelt down. "Sweetie, Mrs. Beck is going to be just fine. Now you don't go worrying about her. Let's finish our dinner and then see if Miss Chloe needs our help. How about that?"

Quinn smiled and went back to eating her dinner.

But before they finished, Cove's phone rang. When he answered it, all thoughts of helping Chloe flew out the window.

Lottie needed to be taken to the clinic; her migraine had worsened to a point where she could no longer stand. When this happened, a doctor would administer a shot that would make her sleep for a good twelve hours, and when she woke up she would be feeling right as rain.

Three hours later, once the dinner was over and the entire place cleaned, Chloe went looking for Brandon. She had thought about him a few times during the night and wondered why he hadn't come back to check on her. But she was so busy, she figured one of the kids had told him—and probably the entire town—what was happening in the kitchen. Since there were already too many cooks in the kitchen, so to speak, she thought he must have decided to steer clear of the chaos.

However, when she found no sign of him, or his truck outside, she worried. She looked for her purse and found it in a corner of the room with her jacket. There were no missed messaged from him, only one from her sister asking how the event went. A simple text would not even come close to explaining the disaster of this night.

On a brighter note, they did raise over twenty-five hundred dollars thanks to an anonymous large donation of fifteen hundred dollars. And when she added in her savings, now up to one thousand dollars, they had over three thousand five hundred for the college kids to split. That was not a shabby night.

"Miss Manning, do you need a ride home?" Mr. Peterson asked when he and his family were about to exit the room. They were the last of the partygoers.

Chloe had the keys to the building and would lock up once everyone was outside. "Actually, yes. I think I do. My date seems to have left me." She felt the heat on her cheeks and hated that her embarrassment of a date had done this to her.

Mrs. Peterson tilted her head. "Sorry, Chloe. I saw Brandon heading out earlier in the night. It looked like he was in a hurry. Cove and Quinn weren't here long after him before they hightailed it out as well."

Chloe bit her lower lip. "Hm, I wonder if something might have happened at his ranch?"

Mrs. Peterson patted her upper arm. "Don't worry, that man is head over heels for you. I'm sure whatever happened was an emergency, and he'll be calling you soon to apologize."

Not convinced, but also not wanting to spur any gossip, Chloe pasted on a smile. "I'm sure you're right." She looked around the room. "Why don't you give me a few minutes to lock up and I'll meet you out front?" She was grateful for the ride home. Even though it was completely safe for her to walk home alone late at night, she was exhausted and wanting nothing more than to get home and get in bed.

Which she did. But sleep did not come easily. She worried about Brandon and Cove. No one had said what was wrong, and even though she checked her phone for messages every two minutes, none came. She did try sending Brandon a text, but she received no response. Chloe wasn't sure when she fell asleep, but it was very late.

After a fitful night of sleep, she woke with a headache and wondered how anyone could manage migraines on a regular basis. Her head ached, but it was nothing like what Lottie had described a migraine to be like.

She checked her phone and noticed that a message had come in from Brandon while she slept. The timestamp said it came in at 4:13 a.m. that morning.

CHAPTER 22

Brandon worried the entire way home. Hearing the way his mom sounded, his mind had created too many different scary scenarios. Her MS treatments must not have worked that week. She had had three days of IV infusion of steroids. The doctor had said to keep an eye on her while she was receiving the treatment, but she had seemed fine. Nothing worse than an injection-site redness. But who wouldn't have a little bit of swelling with an IV in their hand for two hours a day, three days in a row?

It was a good thing the speed limit outside of town was eighty miles an hour, because he was speeding like a madman. All but one local cop was at the spaghetti dinner that night. He guessed the one man on duty was most likely at the office keeping an eye on things while everyone else went for dinner. Their town was like that. They took turns supporting dinner events as much as possible. And then someone would bring back dinner to the one lone cop manning the station.

When Brandon pulled into his ranch, he drove right up to the steps of the house and slammed on his brakes, barely missing the post holding up the covered patio. While he did turn off the truck and put it in Park, he didn't bother with taking out his keys or even closing the door.

He ran up the steps and into the house. "Ma! Where are you?" He had beaten the ambulance to the house—no surprise, since he was most likely doing closer to one hundred than the speed limit. With no response, he headed to the kitchen.

"Ma?" He looked around, expecting to find her sitting at the table drinking tea, or maybe decaf coffee, but she wasn't there. Then he ran to the living room, thinking she might have fallen asleep on her chair watching TV. When he didn't find her there, he ran to her bedroom.

Melanie Beck was laid out peacefully on top of the covers with her hands clasped over her stomach. Almost as though someone had posed her like a sleeping doll.

Fear shot through him like a bolt of lightning. "*No!*" he screamed as he ran to her side. Fearing the worst, he listened for her breathing with his ear directly over her face.

"Brandon?" A slight sound coming from beneath him, and then a slight pressure to his chest had him standing bolt upright.

"Mom? Are you alright? What happened?"

"I don't feel so well." She sounded more like a wounded bird than the strong ranching woman he had always known her to be.

He knelt on the floor next to her bed. "I'm here, and an ambulance is on its way." Before he could ask her what was wrong, he heard the voices of the paramedics coming in.

"Mrs. Beck?" called one female paramedic. Brandon would know that voice anywhere. They grew up together and were in the same classes until the day they graduated high school.

"Back here, June."

A tall woman with a bag over her shoulder and a hard case in one hand came in and looked between Brandon and his mom. "What happened?"

"I'm not sure. I just got home myself. When my mom called earlier she sounded strange and confused, like maybe she was having a stroke?" He looked down at his mother. "Ma, can you tell June what happened?"

"I feel funny. My entire body is zinging and my head's all wobbly. I laid down and think I fell asleep?" Melanie rubbed her eyes.

"Are you on any medication?" the other paramedic asked as he wrote down everything on his tablet.

"Yes, she's got MS and is taking a daily pill for it, and earlier this week she did a three-day steroid infusion treatment." Brandon gulped, fear still controlling him and adrenaline running through his system.

June took a deep breath. "I think she might be having a reaction to the steroids. It's common. Didn't the doctor tell you to keep an eye on her this week?"

"Yes, but when she had nothing more than a slight rash at the injection site, I thought she was fine. She's had a lot of energy and today she said she felt like a million bucks, but then she cancelled on the spaghetti dinner at the last minute saying she was tired." Brandon mentally kicked himself for leaving his mother alone, again. He would never make that mistake again.

It was his job as the son to care for his mom. He wasn't supposed to let anything get in the way of caring for the one person in this world who loved him without condition. The woman who nursed him back to health when he was sick as a kid. The woman who bandaged up all his scrapes and told him to take it like a man, and then when no one else was around kissed his scrapes, or his cheeks, and said everything would be alright. Then served him her famous chicken noodle soup. And then everything was alright.

It was his turn to give her the love and attention she needed. His mother was sick and needed someone to bandage her scrapes, kiss her booboos, and make her chicken noodle soup. While he had no clue how to make that soup, he would do his best to learn, for his mom.

June's partner, Mike, took Melanie's vitals and wrote them down while June went out to get the gurney. They'd left it in the ambulance in their hurry to get inside.

When June re-entered the room, she brought it next to the bed. "Mrs. Beck, I want to take you into the clinic for a work-up. While I think I know what the problem is, you need to be seen by a doctor to make sure it's just a reaction to the steroids and not your MS flaring up."

"But I'm starting to feel better. I don't want to go to the clinic," Melanie complained.

"Ma, listen to June. She knows what she's talking about. Let's go in and see what the doc has to say." He pleaded with his eyes in addition to his words.

She did give in, and the paramedics loaded her up and Brandon followed in his truck. By the time the doctor had run tests and finished looking her over, it was almost three in the morning. Melanie was going to be fine. It was a reaction to all the steroids in her body. Usually this type of reaction happened the day of a treatment, but it wasn't unheard of to have it happen two days later.

Melanie fell asleep in the truck as Brandon drove them home. After he helped her inside and put her to bed in her sweats—he doubted she would care about sleeping in sweats instead of jammies—he texted Chloe.

Sorry I left you alone. I hope Cove took good care of you. Mom is going to be fine. We need to talk. - Brandon

Then he went to bed and slept through his alarm. When he finally woke up, as the sun was peeking through his blinds, he jerked up and realized he had missed the regular feeding of the animals. They were going to be antsy. He just hoped the more unruly ones didn't try to bite him.

But before he went outside, he went to his mother's room and poked his head in. She was still sleeping in her sweats. Brandon hoped she would sleep until noon, or even later. His mom needed extra sleep right now, and he intended to make sure she got it.

Closing the door behind him, he went into the kitchen and set up the coffee maker so he would have some as soon as he was done feeding the animals. He had a feeling it was going to be a three-pot-coffee kind of day.

Later, after all the animals had been fed and he'd barely missed getting nipped by one of the feistier horses who insisted on getting his morning meal at the exact same time every day, he went into the kitchen and sat down with three cups of coffee before he started making his breakfast.

He had done it again. Brandon had promised himself he wouldn't hurt Chloe, but he knew he had. Even though it was only a sorta-kinda date, he had left her there without a word in front of the entire town.

"Ugh!" He put his head in his hand as he realized the sort of gossip that would be going around today.

"What's the matter, son?" Melanie walked into the kitchen and yawned when she sat at the table and took Brandon's mug from him. She took two sips and pushed it back his way.

"Here, let me." He got up to get her mug and brought it back to the table and poured her a cup of hot coffee.

"What's wrong?" she asked again.

"Nothing, just a crazy morning. You know, we might want to think about replacing our Mr. Ed. He just about took a chunk out of my arm today because I was a few hours late in feeding him." Brandon chuckled and shook his head. He knew they wouldn't get rid of the horse that his father loved to use for plowing the fields.

Melanie shook her head and joined her son in laughter. "You know, your dad would say it's your own fault for not getting up on time."

He sobered up quickly. The loss of his father five years earlier still got to him. Brandon wasn't sure he would ever get over losing his father. The man had meant the world to him. When he was little, he thought of his dad as Superman. But when he got sick and didn't make it, that was when he finally realized that no one could outlive their time.

God took who he wanted, when He wanted. While we will never understand here on Earth why God sometimes takes the best of people, Brandon knew that one day he would be in heaven and have all the answers. Until that time, he had to trust in God to make the right decisions. Even if he didn't like them, or agree.

"And he'd be right. I slept through my alarm today. The cattle have access to the grass, but the horses in the barn don't. I'll be more careful moving forward. And I'll bring Mr. Ed an apple later today to make peace with him." Brandon took a long drink of his coffee, then topped it off with more hot liquid.

"Good." Melanie gave a tight smile that didn't reach her eyes. She still missed the love of her life every day. While she looked forward to seeing her Stan again, she knew that God still had more work for her to do on this plane of existence.

Brandon cleared his throat and tried not to dwell on the

fact that both he and his mother were missing his dad right then. "How are you feeling today? Up for some breakfast?"

Melanie set her cup of coffee down. "Actually, I'm feeling pretty good. I still have some residual bees under my skin, but it's almost gone. How about I help with breakfast?"

"Nope, I've got it. You just sit there and drink your coffee. The doctor said you needed plenty of rest for a few days, and I intend to make sure you get it." He got up to prepare a simple breakfast of steak-and-cheese omelets with toast and his mom's homemade huckleberry jam.

Later that day, while his mom was inside watching Hallmark movies—or at least, that was what she said she was going to do—Brandon was out in the barn with Mr. Ed, trying to make up to the old horse. They used to use him for chores around the ranch, but he was too old. The horse had put out to pasture just before he left for the rodeo. Most likely, Mr. Ed was so grumpy because he had nothing to do. Animals weren't too different from humans. Maybe if he just gave the horse some work, on occasion, he wouldn't be so petulant.

"What do you say we head out with some tools and get working on that old leaky shed?" Brandon handed his apple to Mr. Ed, then brought the horse out to gear him up to pull a small cart with some tools in it.

The horse whinnied and seemed to stand taller.

"Huh, you want to work, don't you boy?" Brandon chuckled. His dad did always say that Mr. Ed was the truest of work horses. He would have to find small ways to use the horse here and there. There was no way Mr. Ed could pull a plow again, or a wagon, but he could pull the small work cart at times. It would give the horse something to do and show the others in the barn that he wasn't past his prime.

While they were working on the leaky roof of one of the outbuildings, Brandon looked up and noticed that more storm clouds were coming in. They had just barely made it through one storm and here came another one. He would be stuck inside the next day, maybe even two. Which made him think about Chloe. He hadn't yet had a chance to call her, and her only response to his text was that she hoped his mom would be alright. Had he hurt her by leaving her alone the way he did? Well, she wasn't really alone. The entire town was there. Maybe that was the problem?

He would have to talk to her, and over the phone would be cruel. If the storm passed quickly, maybe he could see her after church the next day and they could talk. He would have to figure out a way to let her down gently. He really hoped she would forgive him for doing this.

CHAPTER 23

The storm did come in, but it wasn't as bad as Brandon and half the town had feared. It only brought three new inches of snow. The city had the main roads plowed before church.

"Ma, do you feel like going to church today?" Brandon knew his mother hated to miss church, and she had missed a few meetings lately. But with her being in the clinic Friday night, he just wasn't sure how she was feeling about going out.

"I say we should go. I'm feeling pretty good today, and don't want to miss out on the lunch after services today." She had prepared one of her favorite dishes—crockpot chicken noodle soup. It was simmering in the pot right then, and could easily be unplugged and then plugged back in at the church. It would be ready just as services ended if she got the timing right, which she always did.

* * *

CHLOE BARELY MADE it on time to church that morning. She wanted to make fresh bread for the lunch after services, and it took her longer than she expected. It didn't help matters that she continually looked at her phone, hoping to have a message from Brandon. She should have known better.

She doubted he knew about the town gossip yet; he'd most likely stayed home with his mom yesterday, and she would be shocked if they showed up for services today. But somehow the entire town found out about him abandoning her to go help his momma. Word was out about her MS. She didn't say a word, but when she was in the coffee shop yesterday, that was all anyone could talk about. Well, that and the fact that Brandon dumped her, again. The pitying looks were enough to keep her indoors after that.

Today was a new day, and she hoped that the gossip mill would take a break for at least church services. She needed to feel surrounded by the Spirit and her friends, without all the whispers that usually accompanied gossip.

"Lottie, how are you today?" Chloe walked over to her best friend after the service and hugged her.

"So much better. Migraine's all gone, and I slept so much yesterday that I'm feeling a bit antsy today." She led Chloe over to the side room, where they hosted their indoor lunches during the winter. Baptists loved their potlucks and were not about to let something as trivial as a blizzard stop them from meeting and sharing a meal once a month.

Thankfully the last snowstorm wasn't a blizzard, but they had happened on potluck Sundays before. Those who could make it, did. Those who couldn't get out of their property prayed for the safety of the rest of the congregation.

This week, it looked as though just about everyone would be in attendance. She had heard that the flu was making its rounds, but people who lived on ranches and farms were made of sturdier stock than those who lived in town and rarely let something like the flu get them down for long, if at all.

"Have you heard from Brandon?" Lottie whispered after looking around to make sure no one was eavesdropping on them.

Chloe's face fell, and she shook her head. "Not since that one text early Saturday morning."

"Do you think his mom is alright?" Lottie had known that Melanie had MS for a while, and she had kept her mouth shut. But she hadn't heard anything yesterday other than what Chloe told her.

"From what I heard, she's going to be fine. The French-town rumor mill is nothing if not up on the latest gossip. Once it was out about her having MS, the usuals worked overtime to find out what happened Friday night." Chloe winced and looked around to make sure no one overheard her. "I think it was just a bad reaction, that's all. I bet she's at the snowman-building contest Tuesday night."

"Well, as long as the weather holds out, you mean," Lottie added.

Chloe chuckled. "Yes, the snow has really been coming in lately, hasn't it? I didn't think we'd get this much before Christmas."

"Quinn's all excited about having a white Christmas and has been out with Cove every day for the past week with her sled." The proud momma smiled and looked over at her daughter, laughing with Cove.

"Is that a sparkle in your eyes?" Chloe pointed to her friend's face, and a huge cheese-eating grin spread across her features. *Finally, something good going on.*

With both hands over her cheeks, Lottie answered, "I don't know what you're talking about."

"Oh, there it is! Spill, my friend." Chloe laughed and hoped that things were progressing nicely with Cove. They all deserved happiness, especially Quinn. And Chloe knew that without a doubt, the little girl loved that rodeo cowboy just like he was her daddy.

Before Lottie could protest, Mrs. Rice walked up and began speaking to the girls. "Did you see Brandon and his mom come in late to services today?"

A feeling of dread coursed through Chloe's entire being. Not that she would begrudge them the opportunity to attend church, but today was going to be all about gossip if they were there. Chloe wondered, not for the first time, if she should skip the luncheon.

Lottie looked around with wide eyes. "No, I didn't see them. Where are they?" She smiled when she found them sitting at a table in the far corner with food already set before them. And a table full of the worst of the gossiping moms.

"Why can't they just leave Brandon and his mom alone?" Chloe groaned. She knew they would be hitting up both of the Becks, trying to find out what was going on with Brandon and her, as well as Melanie's illness. It was none of their business.

"They mean well." Mrs. Rice patted Chloe's arm and gave her a pitying look.

Lottie rolled her eyes. "I doubt that." She took Chloe's hand and pulled her toward the tables. "Come on, let's get some lunch and go sit with my little girl. She always cheers you up."

Chloe smiled and nodded her head. "How could she not? She's the cutest thing around and always has a hug and a smile for me."

Uncomfortable did not even come close to how Chloe felt during lunch. All eyes kept going between Brandon and her.

She caught snippets of whispers in the air here and there, and cringed whenever the word "dumped" was bandied about.

"I don't know how much longer I can do this, Lottie." The tension in the room could be cut with a knife, and Chloe only wanted to leave. But she knew that running away would be seen as a sign of weakness, and the sharks would close in. She was not going to stir the waters and get their attention if she could help it.

"Smile," Lottie said between her bites of food, and smiled. "Don't let them see you bleed. They'll pounce on you at the first droplet of blood."

Cove leaned down and whispered into Quinn's ear so low that Chloe couldn't hear him. But she didn't need to. The moment he was done, Quinn began talking about her upcoming nativity play, and Chloe's attention was diverted from everything else going on.

"Aunt Chloe, you should see the donkey they brought in for me to ride!" Quinn gushed about the real animals they were going to use that year, and everyone at her table was entranced by the little girl's enthusiasm. "I get to ride her on the stage and everything!" She widened her arms as though she wanted to encompass the world with the breadth of the stage.

"That is fantastic! I can't wait to see your performance. Will you be using a real baby for Jesus?" Chloe knew they were only going to use a doll, but she wanted to see how Quinn would react.

The little girl deflated like a balloon. "No, Miss Ginger said we couldn't use a real baby, it had to be a doll."

"Why's that?" Cove asked.

Quinn picked up her breadstick and started tearing off pieces. "Because she's afraid the baby would cry during the whole thing." She sat up straight and looked the adults in the eyes. "But I think it's because she's afraid I'll drop the baby." Quinn turned to her mom. "But Momma, you know I wouldn't ever hurt a baby, right? I hold all the babies when they come into the shop and I've never dropped one." Her lower lip protruded in a tiny pout.

"Ah honey"—Lottie put a hand on her daughter's arm —"I know you wouldn't drop a baby. But I think Miss Ginger is right. We can't know for sure if the baby would behave during the entire play. You wouldn't want a crying baby interrupting your lines, would you?"

The little girl quirked her lips and thought about it a moment. "I guess you're right. That wouldn't be much fun for anyone. And it might upset my donkey." She nodded as though the issue were settled and moved on to other topics.

Chloe did all she could to keep from busting up laughing. Of course Quinn would be worried about upsetting the donkey she would ride in on. But Chloe don't think she realized that she wouldn't be riding it again once she was at the inn. Better to keep that little bit to herself, she mused. Quinn would figure it out soon. They still had one week of practice left before they did two dress rehearsals. She did not want to be the one to deflate the little girl's excitement. Especially since that was exactly what Chloe needed right at that moment.

Of course, she sat in such a way that she could see Brandon and his mom out of the corner of her eye. And she never once let them out of her sight. Try as she might, she couldn't stop thinking about Brandon and how he'd abandoned her at the spaghetti dinner without even a word. All he had to do was come back to the kitchen and tell her he was leaving, or better yet, send a friend to tell her. Then she wouldn't have worried.

Well, she probably would have worried about Melanie,

but she wouldn't have worried about why she was left all alone in front of the entire town.

"Uncle Cove?" Quinn pulled on Cove's sleeve.

"Yes, dear?"

"Did we forget to tell Miss Chloe about Brandon during the spaghetti dinner?" The little girl's ears had perked up when she heard one of the gossiping moms walk by and say what a shame it was that Brandon had abandoned Chloe.

Chloe heard it, but had chosen to ignore them. That is, until Quinn watched them walk away and then asked her Uncle Cove about it.

Cove's eyes widened. "*Oh*, Chloe. I'm so sorry. I completely forgot to tell you."

She narrowed her eyes. "Tell me what?"

The cowboy rubbed the stubble on his chin and looked between Lottie and Chloe. "Brandon got a call from his mom that had him very worried. So he asked me to let you know what was going on and to take you home that night." He blew out a deep breath.

"But Lottie called you requesting your help before you could tell me." Chloe nodded, and a lightbulb went off over her head. She had hoped he wouldn't have completely forgotten about her. But since they hadn't had a chance to speak, and Brandon never said anything to her about Cove taking her home… Well, she'd just jumped to the worst-case scenario.

Chloe chuckled and hoped that was what Brandon wanted to talk to her about, just to make sure all went well with getting home that night. Maybe things weren't as bad as she feared.

CHAPTER 24

Brandon's leg bounced up and down under the table as he and his mom dealt with the ladies at his table asking him all sorts of embarrassing questions. He had no idea the gossip was this bad. He feared what Chloe was going through, since the ladies at his table were already discussing his breakup with Chloe. He hadn't even had a chance to talk with her yet.

Wait, could we even be broken up if we weren't officially together in the first place? He shook his head and looked to his mom, who was frowning.

"Ladies, I hope you aren't talking off Melanie and Brandon's ears today. They could probably use a bit of a break, don't you think?" Mrs. Claus eyed each lady at his table, and if it wouldn't have caused a giant hullabaloo, Brandon would have jumped up and kissed her cheek right then and there.

Kate Denning, the leader of the pack, turned pink and she stuttered, "Mrs. Claus, so good to see you." She put her hands in her lap and twisted the paper napkin until it was nothing more than scraps.

"Kate, how's your kids? I saw them running outside a few

minutes ago, but they haven't returned yet." Mrs. Claus arched an eyebrow while smiling sweetly. No one could say she was rude, but when she arched that brow it was as though everyone knew they might end up on the naughty list. Even adults didn't want to be on Santa's bad-kid list.

"Really? My Kurt was supposed to be watching them." She looked around nervously and stood up. "I better go see if I can help." She took off, and when she did the other gossiping moms stood up and left to look in on their families as well.

"Thank you." Melanie sighed and leaned back in her chair.

Brandon smiled and stood. "Would you like to join us?" He pulled a seat out for Mrs. Claus.

"Thank you, but I need to get going. I just thought I'd stop over and say hi. And ask how you're doing, Melanie." She smiled sweetly at them both.

"Thank you, I'm feeling much better. It was just a bad reaction to the infusion, which the doctor said isn't uncommon."

"Good, good." Mrs. Claus looked to Brandon. "I think Chloe might enjoy coffee one afternoon this week." She winked at Brandon and didn't wait for a response before she left to join her husband.

Brandon chuckled. "I think she's got the wrong impression."

"Does she?" His mom tilted her head and looked at her son, waiting for his excuse.

"Well, yes. Chloe and I are just friends. We weren't officially anything, and we won't be, either." Brandon took a bite of the chicken noodle soup his mother had made and followed it up with a large chunk of homemade bread. He didn't know who made it, but it was perfect with his mom's soup.

"Does she know that?" Melanie nodded toward Chloe's table.

Brandon wasn't sure, but it looked as though Chloe had been watching them. When he looked her way, her hair swooshed as though she'd quickly turned her head. An ache began deep down, and he squashed it before anything could take root. He had already decided that his mom was going to be his top priority. He couldn't let a pretty blonde turn his head. Not again.

However, he did need to have a conversation with her and apologize for running out the way he did. And make sure she understood they were never going to be anything more than friends. No matter what his gut or his heart had to say. Maybe he should call her up later and arrange to have coffee Monday evening. The sooner they spoke, the sooner he could get past his infatuation with the pretty cowgirl and get his focus back where it belonged.

Later that evening after getting his mom settled at home, he did call her. "Chloe, hi there. It's Brandon."

Chloe's heart pitter-pattered when she heard his voice. "Hi, Brandon. How's your mom doing?"

"Much better, thanks." Silence ensued on both ends of the line as Chloe waited to hear what he had to say.

She had hoped he would call, and now that he had, she had a bad feeling. He'd waved and smiled at her before he left with his mom that afternoon, but he had never once come over and spoken to her. If things were alright between them, he would have. Even Lottie had questioned the cold-shoulder treatment.

He cleared this throat. "Uh, listen. I was wondering if

you'd like to meet me for coffee tomorrow afternoon some time?"

This was it. Chloe knew what he was going to say. He had acted the same exact way when he called her up to meet and discuss his leaving last year. While she doubted he was going anywhere any time soon, she did get the sneaking suspicion that he was going to break things off before they even had a chance to begin again. Her heart sank, and she began to mentally berate herself for trusting him. She knew better. There was a reason Brandon Beck was still single. He didn't have the ability to commit to anyone. She just knew it.

"I have to work. Why don't you just say your piece over the phone and we can just move on?" Chloe was getting frustrated and it came out over the phone, but she didn't care. He wasn't going to get any more of her time. Nor was he going to get another chance to publicly humiliate her in front of the entire town. *What sort of man breaks up with a girl in front of everyone?*

Brandon winced when he heard her harsh tone. He deserved it. She probably knew exactly why he wanted to meet up. While it would be easier to do it over the phone and not while looking at her beautiful face, his pa had raised him to look a woman in the eye when delivering bad news. He said it was the respectful thing to do.

"Maybe I can come over to your house after work?" He thought about it and realized breaking up was not something you did in a very public place where people could overhear. Especially in their town.

"I don't think that's necessary. If you're going to say we can't see each other anymore, then just say it so we can move on." She was done with him. And she was done setting herself up for more disappointment. She had it right before—

now was the time to focus on her career, not men. All men did was get your hopes up, only to dash them.

It might be cynical of her, but that was how it seemed to go for her. She wasn't as lucky as her twin sister Elizabeth, who was now married to her high school sweetheart. Sure, they'd had a rocky go of things and it did take them an extra ten years to get where they were today, but her sister was still blessed. Chloe, not so much.

"I'm sorry. I really am, Chloe. But my mom needs me right now. Friday night just proved how selfish I was being by leaving her all alone and going out with you." Brandon did sound remorseful.

And the bit about him being selfish by being with her was tearing up her heart. Now she felt selfish and rotten. How could she begrudge him this time with his mom? His dad was gone, his sister was several hours away with a family and ranch of her own. Melanie needed Brandon right now.

She sighed. "I understand. I really do hope your mom gets better and all of these treatments and medications begin to sit right with her, and she can get back to her normal routine." Chloe really did wish all of that for Melanie. And not just so she could have another go with Brandon. No, that ship had sailed.

What do they say? If you love something, let it go, and if it comes back it was meant to be? Or something along those lines? Chloe knew what she had to do, even if he never did come back to her. And she knew then and there he would not.

Their time, short as it was, had passed.

"Thank you, Chloe." His hoarse voice gave her the impression he was dealing with some emotion, but she didn't know what it was, nor did she want to know.

It was time to move on. Really move on, and not hope and pray that he would come back to her. She knew it wouldn't be easy, but it was the right thing to do. Melanie needed her son more than Chloe needed him.

"You're welcome." She paused, not sure if she should say any more. "I wish you the best. Really, I do. And if there's anything I can do to help your mom, please let me know."

"Thanks. I wish you all the best, too."

She hung up and had herself a good cry. She reasoned that by doing it then and there, she could get it out of her system and be ready the next day to get on with things. It was still Christmas, and she had a lot going on. Plus, she knew Lottie would have a peppermint mocha and hopefully a new scone for her to try.

THE NEXT MORNING, Chloe had to put some extra concealer on to hide the fact that she had cried—a lot—the night before. But her bags would be gone once she got going. And surprisingly, she felt a lot better after some time in prayer giving it all to God. She always prayed, but last night she felt a true burden lift when she made the conscious decision to let go and let God, as her pastor back home had once said.

By giving her burdens to the Lord, He could carry them on His shoulders, and she would no longer have the heavy load weighing her down. This was something she should have done when Brandon left last year. Chloe thought she had given it to God, but she realized that every time she gave it to Him, she stole it back when thoughts of Brandon flitted through her mind.

And when he returned home a few weeks ago, she had not only stolen her burden back from God, but she had been selfish about the entire situation. Of course, Melanie needed her son right then. She would probably need him for a few more months, if not longer. She had no business getting in the way. Had they not gone to the spaghetti dinner together as a date, he would have been home with his mom when she began feeling off.

Chloe was just grateful that it wasn't something more serious, and the time it took for Brandon to get home, get her in the ambulance, and to the hospital hadn't hurt her. She never would have forgiven herself if it had been something more serious. And she believed that Brandon would never have forgiven himself, either.

No, this was the right outcome. They could be social friends. A step above acquaintances. Maybe one day they could be actual friends, but Chloe wasn't sure that was possible right now. She needed to stay clear of him and let God keep the burden on His shoulders. She would do her job and forget about Brandon Beck and the way the ends of his hair curled above his collar when he was in need of a haircut.

"Nope, not going there, God. You can keep this one," she said out loud as she walked down the street to Lottie's coffee shop.

With a deep sigh, she pulled the door open and walked in, pasting a huge smile on her face. Lottie would know the moment she saw her that something was wrong, but no one else would.

"Good Morning, Chloe?" Lottie started out with a smile, and then it turned to confusion as she stared at her friend.

"Today's a day for your largest peppermint mocha, and whatever new treat you have for me to try." With that statement she walked to the counter with head held high and waited for her turn to pay.

Lottie made her the drink and brought it out with a peppermint scone in a little bag. "No charge. My treat." She nodded toward the back table and led her friend to an area with some privacy.

They sat down, and Chloe took a drink of the best mocha she'd ever had. "Mmmm, is there extra peppermint in here? Or is that the whipped cream I'm tasting?" She licked her lips and pulled in a tasty bit of Christmas cream on her top lip.

Lottie chuckled. "That, my friend, is double caffeine and extra topping." She waggled her hand in front of Chloe's face. "You might be able to fool others, but I can see it."

Not wanting anyone else to hear, Chloe looked around. Once she was certain no one was eavesdropping, she said, "I had a rough night. *He* called."

Lottie did not need to ask who *he* was. She knew. "Was it what you thought?" They had speculated Sunday afternoon about what Brandon might say if he ever called her again.

Chloe nodded. "Yeah, it was exactly what I thought."

The barista put a hand on her best friend's. "I'm sorry. I thought for sure this time you two would end up together for good."

"So did I, if I'm being completely honest." Chloe sighed. "But you know what?"

"What?"

"It's not meant to be. I cried a lot last night, but I also prayed. I gave it all over to God and I feel so much lighter for it."

Tears formed in Lottie's eyes, and Chloe hurried to assure her friend.

"Now really isn't the time for *him* to be with anyone. You know what he has to focus on, and so do I. It was selfish of me to think I could take his time away from Melanie right now. Until she's stabilized, she needs him too much." Even though Chloe wasn't a nurse or a doctor, she understood better than most people how much time and attention Melanie was going to need with all her doctor's appointments. And if she needed more treatments, then Brandon would need to spend even more time with his mom.

From everything Chloe had learned the past few weeks about MS, she knew that until Melanie's symptoms were under control, she should not be at home alone. At least not for any prolonged period of time. If Brandon had another sibling who lived at home it might have been different, but he didn't. No, she was going to do the right thing and back off.

"Are you sure? I mean, isn't there something that can be done to help her?"

"Prayer. That's all any of us can do right now. It's all in God's hands now, and we have to accept that." It had always been in God's hands. It was just that Chloe hadn't realized that until last night.

Lottie nodded. "But still, it has to be tough. I'm sorry this happened now, and at Christmas, too."

Chloe snorted. "Yeah, my favorite time of the year has been a bit difficult this year. But you know what? I'm going to enjoy the rest of this month. Christmas isn't about me, it's about the birth of my Lord and Savior, Jesus Christ. And I think I might have forgotten that for a moment."

"We all do at times. But we can still enjoy the season with our family and friends. I think God wants us to be happy." Lottie also had a kid who knew who God was, but still loved how much fun the season was. And she enjoyed participating in everything with Quinn, too. She was most especially looking forward to the nativity this year with Quinn playing Mary.

"True, true. So, for the rest of the month"—Chloe clapped her hands together—"I say we focus on the events and our family and friends. And forget about the what ifs and what might have been. Let's just enjoy the here and now."

With a huge grin, Lottie leaned over and hugged her best friend. "Sounds good to me. Does that mean you'll be at the snowman-building contest tomorrow night?"

"With bells on." They both laughed, and Chloe stood up. "Alright, I gotta get into the office. Thank you for my special treat today. It's very much appreciated."

"You're welcome. Will I see you at lunch today?" When Chloe had rough nights, she usually stopped in at the coffee shop for a pick-me-up. If that was the case, then Lottie would have something special for her.

"Yes, I think I'll need some extra caffeine today. And I'm not going to feel guilty about it, either." With all the Christmas events still to come, Chloe knew she would get in more steps than usual and therefore would most likely work off any extra calories she received from her afternoon pick-me-up. Besides, she'd packed a healthy salad for that day.

With this great start to her week, Chloe was confident she would stay on track and not steal back the burden she gave to God last night.

CHAPTER 25

"Brandon, what are you doing here still? Shouldn't you be heading into town for the snowman-building contest?" Melanie shook her head at her pigheaded son. He had told her he wouldn't be seeing Chloe anymore, but she hadn't understood.

"Ma, we spoke about this Sunday on the way home from church. I'm not interested in a girlfriend right now. I have too many things to think about and don't need a woman messing it all up." He leaned over and bussed a quick kiss on his mom's cheek. "What do you say we watch a Christmas movie tonight? Just you and me?"

"I think I want to go and see the snowman contest. Let's get warm and head into town. I'll even put a pot of decaf on so we have something hot to drink tonight." She was not about to let her son make such a huge mistake just so he could babysit her. Melanie may have bad days, but right now she was feeling like a million bucks. Ever since the strange side effects of the infusion wore off, she'd only needed about seven hours of sleep a night. She had even spent a few hours the past two days outside in the barn helping with chores.

And still, she had energy. "Take that, MS!"

Brandon had been halfway down the hall smiling at his mother when he heard her murmuring. "What's that?" he asked when he turned back toward her.

She waved a hand in the air. "Oh, nothing. Go get some warm clothes on while I set the coffee up. I don't want to miss this event. It always was one of my favorites when you and your sister were younger." She chuckled, remembering the year when Brandon and his sister Bayley entered together. It was the first and last year they teamed up for any of the Christmas events. By the time it was all said and done, they had used more snow in snowball fights then they did on their Frosty.

Melanie would not trade those memories for anything. It didn't matter to her that they were disqualified for throwing snowballs at the judges, it only mattered that she and her husband Stan were there to see it all. She even had it on an old VHS tape somewhere. Maybe later that week she could get Brandon to head up to the attic and find the old family tapes.

By the time they both had on warmer clothes and coffee in travel mugs, she had a huge smile on her face.

"What's got you smiling so wide?" Brandon was happy that his mom was doing so well. The past two days seemed like normal again. His mom had been up early making a full breakfast when he came in from feeding the animals both mornings this week, and earlier that day she had been whistling. He couldn't remember the last time he had walked in on her whistling. He didn't think she had done it since his dad died five years earlier.

"Nothing, just very happy to be here right now."

Brandon looked over to his ma sitting next to him in the truck and caught a glimpse of the glint in her eyes she got when she was up to no good. "What are you up to, Ma?" He hoped and prayed it had nothing to do with him.

She patted his arm. "Don't you go frettin'. All's fine. I'm just happy we're getting out and about. And that the weather has decided to stay in check tonight. We got all that snow last week, and most of it is still here. This is going to be perfect for the contest."

He didn't want to argue with his mom, but he knew there was more to it. He would just have to wait and see what she did at the event that night.

Turned out, Brandon didn't have to wait long. As soon as they arrived, she made a beeline to the sign-up booth. She made it just in time to sign them up for the adult contest.

The town had two phases. One for kids, and one for adults. The kids were putting the finishing touches on their masterpieces when Melanie sauntered toward Chloe.

"Chloe, it's good to see you out tonight. Will you be in the adult contest?" Melanie's voice was cheerful, and Chloe had no idea what the woman was up to.

"Actually, I'm just watching tonight. Are you entered?" She smiled at Melanie and crossed her fingers that Brandon would stay away. She knew he was there; she had noticed him the moment his truck pulled up. How could she not? He was the best-looking cowboy in the state of Montana.

Melanie nodded. "Yup, and I'm looking forward to it, too." She massaged her lower back and winced.

"What's wrong? Should I get Brandon?" That was the last thing Chloe wanted to do, but if Melanie was in trouble, she would do whatever it took.

"No, no." She waved off Chloe and winced again. "I think I just need to sit down. I probably overdid it today when I helped with the chores. You know how it goes. The body gets aches and pains once it passes a certain age.

Nothing to worry about." Melanie winced again and slowly made her way to a chair in front of the snowman-building area.

"Can I get you anything? A hot cocoa, or coffee?" Chloe was starting to worry for the woman and wanted to help, she just didn't know what to do. If this was the normal kind of aches and pain older women got, then there probably wasn't anything she could do.

Her father got them once in a while, especially when it was cold like this. Caleb Manning rarely complained about anything, but once in a while his arthritis would kick in and he would have to stop working and take a hot shower. Just to warm his bones up, he would say. It was rare, but lately it had been happening more often. Maybe Melanie had the same issues and only needed to warm up.

The older woman chuckled and then winced and put a hand to her hip. "No, no. I'm fine." She held up her mug. "I've got my decaf coffee here and it's still nice and hot. I'm sure I just need to sit for a few minutes, and once the adult snowman contest begins I'll be ready to go."

Chloe nodded, then looked out to see where Quinn was. She had entered with a friend from school. Their snowman, or probably snowgirl, looked pretty good. Quinn had accessorized her as though she were a faerie and not a snowperson. There was a set of sparkly wings on her back that miraculously matched the pair Quinn had on over her puffy jacket. Then there was a tiara on the snowgirl's head, and a wand in her makeshift stick hand. And it appeared she also had on one of those Disney princess dress-up gowns. The kids had gone all out on this one.

"Time!" the judge called.

Chloe watched as a few of the kids stopped what they were doing, but two teams finished up putting a hat or gloves on their snowman before stepping back. She chuckled when she saw all the entries. Disney was the theme for the night.

One of the boy teams had dressed their little snowman up as Oogie Boogie, complete with green snow and worms. The boys took a stick and picked off one worm and chased one of the other girls around with it, saying that Oogie Boogie was going to get them.

"Ah, the simpler times," Brandon said as he walked up to his mom and Chloe.

"Hi." Chloe's face warmed and she made to walk away.

Brandon put a hand on her arm. "Wait. I just wanted to say I was sorry and that I hoped we could still be friends."

"Uh-huh. Sure thing." Chloe knew she needed to get out of there right away. She looked around for an excuse to leave when she noticed the look of pain crossing Melanie's face.

"Ma, are you alright? Should we go home or to the ER?" Brandon knelt next to his mom. "I knew we shouldn't go out tonight. It's too cold for you, isn't it?"

Mrs. Claus walked up with a Christmas blanket and smiled at them all. "Melanie, do you need a blanket?"

The look of relief that crossed Melanie's face was a total change from the look of pain she'd had only moments before. "Yes, thank you. I should have thought to bring one myself."

Mrs. Claus laid it over Melanie's lap, and the rancher smiled up at Santa's wife.

"That's much better."

"Why don't you keep it and bring it back to me later?" Mrs. Claus winked at Melanie and walked away when the woman nodded.

"I'll go and take our names off the list." Brandon stood up and turned to head toward the booth.

"Brandon, don't." Melanie put a hand out to stop her son. "I love this event. And I know you do, too. I remember every year that you entered as a kid. Why don't you partner with Chloe tonight? I'd love to watch the two of you work on a snowman together."

Chloe shook her head. "Oh, no. I don't think that would be a good idea."

Brandon agreed with her and shook his head, too.

"Please? For me?" Melanie put her clasped hands up to her chest and looked up at the two with pleading eyes.

Feeling guilty, Brandon turned to Chloe. "Don't feel like you have to. It's fine. I can get someone else to help me make the snowman."

Chloe gulped and looked around. She decided that if one of Brandon's friends was standing alone, she'd ask him to help. But the only one she could identify in all the giant winter clothes was Cove, and he was with Lottie. They looked like they were getting ready to work together, and Quinn was jumping up and down next to them.

The little girl must have won first place while she and the Becks were talking, because there was a trophy in her hand. A quick scan of the faerie snowgirl confirmed her suspicion— she had a blue ribbon on her belly.

"Ah, are you sure you don't feel up to it?" Chloe asked, and wanted to kick herself. Of course Melanie didn't feel up to it. She had seen her wince in pain multiple times. With a deep breath and a quick prayer for forgiveness, she changed her mind. "Sorry, I'll be happy to help Brandon make you a snowman to be proud of."

"Uh, I don't know if she'll be proud of it, but she will enjoy looking at it." Brandon chuckled and remembered all the snowmen he had built over the years and decided this was not one of his best skills.

CHAPTER 26

"Does your mom do most of the work when you guys build these?" Chloe had no idea why Melanie wanted her son to enter the competition so badly unless it was to make her laugh, which she was doing plenty of, thank you very much.

He chuckled. "Actually, I'm horrible at this. I don't think I've even come close to winning before." Brandon was working on rolling the larger bottom piece without much luck. It looked more like Frosty's bottom snowball had gone through a press instead of being rolled up.

Brandon looked appreciatively at Chloe's perfectly round middle-section snowball and whistled. "You've done this before." It wasn't a question, but a statement.

She nodded. "And won several times with my twin sister, Elizabeth."

"I'm sorry to say, but I think the only ribbon we're getting today is last place." Brandon grinned and threw a small snowball at Chloe's back when she began making the head piece for their snowman.

"Hey! What was that for?" Chloe turned around and narrowed her eyes at Brandon.

"It wasn't me, honest." He tried to cross his fingers in his big gloves behind his back, but it wasn't easy.

"Yeah, sure Pinocchio." She pointed at his nose.

When Brandon crossed his eyes, she brought her hand out from behind her back and threw some loose snow at his face.

"Hey now, at least I didn't hit your face with my snow." He swiped at the few wet pieces sliding down his face.

"I don't think you have anything to worry about." Chloe chuckled and got back to work on the head of her snowman. She really didn't want to come in last place, or get disqualified for not even finishing. Which was looking to be their lot. Everyone else had their snowman put together and were accessorizing it.

Their snowman? Well, it looked like a truck ran it over. She shook her head and got back to work. Once she was done with the head, she went over to help Brandon get his bottom piece finished. All they had to do was get the three pieces together and then at least put up a face on the thing. Then they would qualify. If they couldn't do even that much, they would be disqualified and not even a last-place ribbon would be in their future.

Once they worked together, the form of the snowman began to take shape. It certainly wasn't going to win any awards, but it was better than a flat-tire snowman, which was what Brandon seemed to be going for.

"Didn't anyone ever tell you that snowmen have three *round* pieces? Not flat?" Chloe chuckled and moved the head around to ensure it would stay in place.

She wasn't surprised when another snowball hit her back. But what did surprise her was that Brandon stood on the other side of the snowman, facing her. So it couldn't have been him. When she turned around, she smiled and leaned down to make a snowball and fight back.

Cove and Lottie had basically finished their snowman. It wouldn't win, but they did do enough to qualify and now they were embattled in a snowball fight that seemed to have spilled over to Chloe.

Before Chloe could retaliate, a large ball of packed snow flew over her head and whacked Cove in his shoulder.

"Hey! You two need to get back to work on your snowman!" Cove retaliated and hit Brandon's snowman, instead of Brandon.

Sadly, the force of the impact acted like a Mack truck, and the entire snowman fell over. Parts of the bottom "ball" began to crack and fall apart. Chloe hated calling that piece a ball, since it never really was a ball. It was an oblong thing that looked better than a donut or pancake, but it was no surprise that the poor snowman wasn't going to make it.

Instead of being upset or even trying again, Chloe took snow from the frozen lumps around her and began making multiple snowballs and placing them at Brandon's feet.

Brandon, without a word, realized what she was doing and picked them up. He easily threw them at Lottie and Cove's snowman. At first it didn't seem like anything would happen, just lumps of packed snow clinging to the body of their snowman. But after a while, things began to change.

Lottie and Cove both noticed what Brandon was doing and stopped lobbing snowballs at each other and turned their attentions to Brandon and Chloe. But it was too late—Chloe had built up quite a reserve of hard-packed ammunition, and before long the rodeo star and coffee shop owner were not in much better shape than their poor snowman.

Some time along the way, time had been called on the contest. Most of the spectators were laughing and enjoying the show the two couples were giving instead of watching the snowman contest.

Melanie was sitting in her chair with Mrs. Claus, and they were laughing so hard that warm coffee came out of Melanie's nose, which only served to make the pair laugh harder.

The Cove/Lottie snowman, which hadn't yet been named, fell over when both Chloe and Brandon aimed for the head of the snowy man with a corn-cob pipe and a button nose. The eyes, however, weren't made out of coal—they had been made out of multiple whole coffee beans.

"Ready, set, go!" Brandon called, and they both threw their balls at the snowman's head for a second time, causing it to lob off the body and roll away.

"Yes!" Brandon cried, and held up his arms in triumph.

"We did it!" Chloe held her arms up as well and was surprised when she felt warmth all around her.

"We make a great team," Brandon whispered in her ear before letting her go.

She cleared her throat and took a step back from the man who had recently broken her heart for the second time in a year. She was not going to let him get a third try. Besides, she had given him to God, and jingle bells, she was *not* going to take it back!

The warmth in his eyes dimmed a bit when it dawned on him what he'd done. Brandon had just been going with the moment and letting himself have fun for the first time in a while. Since returning home, he had been so focused on his mom and the ranch, then a little bit on Chloe, he hadn't really had time for fun and shenanigans liked he used to. This had been a great stress-reliever until he went and messed it up by hugging the one woman he wanted but couldn't have.

He was about to apologize for hugging her when he was interrupted.

"Hey, what was that all about?" Cove ran over and slapped a hand on Brandon's back. "We had qualified for the contest."

"But you never would have won." Brandon smiled and slapped a hand on his friend's back in greeting.

"Sorry, Lottie. Your snowman was cute. But, sometimes these things happen." Chloe shrugged and batted her eyelashes.

"I see how it is. Don't worry, we'll get you back. Won't we, Cove?" Lottie put her hands on her hips and smirked.

"Oh, you know it! It's on, man." Cove chuckled and wrapped an arm around Lottie's shoulders. "Come on, let's see who ended up winning. I'll bet there were some really great snowmen tonight."

And there were. The winning team actually had a snow-bride and snow-groom. The woman wore a veil and held a bouquet while the man wore a black coat and red rose boutonniere.

Tears pricked the backs of Chloe's eyes. She prayed that God would keep the burden she had given him and not let her take it back. If a husband wasn't in the cards for her, she would have to accept that and move on. And who knew, maybe the man for her just hadn't come to town yet.

"You two were hilarious. Thank you so much for the laughs." Melanie looked much better than she had before. She stood tall in her red snow boots, matching puffy jacket, and jeans. She did have the blanket wrapped around her shoulders, so she must still be a little bit cold. Chloe noticed that Mrs. Claus had brought over a mug of something, and she usually had cocoa on her. Maybe the hot cocoa helped?

"How are ya feeling, Ma?" Brandon walked to her side and fixed worried eyes on her.

"Don't worry about me. I feel right as rain now that I have the blanket and hot cocoa." She held up the mug and took a long drink.

"Would you two care for some?" Mrs. Claus made her way to the little group and held up a carafe and two paper hot cups.

"Sure, I love your hot cocoa." Chloe reached for one cup and held it as Mrs. Claus poured. "Thank you."

Brandon also got a cup, and the four of them drank in silence for a few moments.

"You know, you two make a very cute couple," Mrs. Claus said over her shoulder as she walked away.

"She's right." Melanie winked at them and took off, leaving the two of them gaping at the older women in surprise.

"I...ah..." Brandon cleared this throat. "I'm really sorry. That was not very appropriate of my mother."

"Or of Mrs. Claus," Chloe added. "I think I need to go. This was fun, thanks."

"No, thank you. It was exactly what I needed after the stress the past month." Brandon was about to apologize for the hug, but thought better of it. He took a drink of his cocoa instead.

"Have a great night." Chloe waved and walked toward Lottie.

"Hey girl, what's up with you and Brandon? I thought he wasn't interested?" Lottie waggled her brows.

Chloe slapped her arm. "Shhh, we don't need any more gossip right now. And that was just a favor to his mom, nothing more."

"Uh-huh. Just like that hug at the end was a favor?" The barista gave her a pointed look and a half smile.

It seemed the entire town was out to get them together. Chloe had no idea what to do.

Instead of sticking around, she decided to head home. The contests were over, and the winners announced, so there really wasn't much left to see or do that night. Besides, she needed to spend time in prayer to make sure God kept his burden away from her. She was weak and wanted it back. She wanted Brandon back.

On the way home from the contest, Brandon thought his mom would sleep, or at least doze, but she seemed full of energy and wanted to talk the entire way home.

However, what she wanted to talk about was a subject he most certainly did not want to discuss with his mother.

"I don't see why you and Chloe aren't together. It's very obvious to me, and the entire town, that the two of you are perfect together."

"Ma, you know I don't have time for a girlfriend." It wasn't that he didn't want Chloe, it was that he couldn't make the time for her, and Brandon wasn't sure how to get that across to his mom without making her feel bad.

"Brandon, that's hogwash and you know it." She turned in her seat to look at him. "You aren't doing this because of me, are you?"

His hands gripped the steering wheel, and his foot became like a lead weight on the gas pedal. The sooner he got home and away from his mom, the safer he would be. "I'm just not ready for a girlfriend."

"Brandon Beck, don't you dare lie to me!" She put a finger in the air and pointed it at him. "You need a wife. I'll be fine."

"But you weren't fine last Friday night when I was out with Chloe, were you?" He turned angry eyes on his mom. While he wasn't mad at her, he was quite angry with himself. Even now.

Frustration filled the cab of the truck, and Melanie took a deep, cleansing breath before saying anything she might regret. "Son, you can't put your life on hold for me. You know as well as I do that when it's my time, it will be my time and nothing you or I do will stop it."

"I know, but that doesn't mean I can't make your life as comfortable as possible while you're still here." God and Brandon had had many conversations over the past month about his mom and her illness. While the good Lord hadn't given him any sort of timeline, he did know that his mom wouldn't be around forever.

"You listen up, and you listen good. I won't be repeating myself again," she started.

"Ma, I'm a grown man now. You can't go treating me like I'm your little boy again." His chuckle helped to cut the tension in the cab.

"It doesn't matter how old you are, you're still my little boy. And you will listen to your mother." The tone of her voice would brook no opposition.

Brandon wiggled in his seat like he did as a little boy when his mom took that tone with him. "Yes, Ma."

"That girl still cares deeply for you. Goodness knows you don't deserve her after what you've done, but you need to get your head out of your derriere and go for it." She hmphed and crossed her arms over her chest.

"But what happens next time I'm out with Chloe and you need me?" He would never forgive himself if something happened to his mom while he was out having fun. In fact, the fear of last Friday happening again would most likely keep him from enjoying any outing he might take without his mom.

"If you're going to act this way, then I'm going to head up to see your sister for a few months." She threw her hands in the air. "I just don't know what happened to you. But you need to trust in God, not yourself."

That hit him hard. So hard his chest hurt. Brandon thought he was trusting in God and doing what he was supposed to do—take care of his family first. But what if he was wrong? He didn't have peace the past few days. But he thought it had just been because he'd hurt Chloe. Was God speaking to him, and he was too self-involved to hear His still small voice?

CHAPTER 27

C ome Friday, Brandon was dragging.

Every night when he went to bed that week, he heard his mother's voice telling him he needed a wife and Chloe was the girl for him. Looking back over his life, his mom had been right concerning just about everything she'd insisted on, the way she had that night after the snowman contest.

Brandon had spent hours each night on his knees in prayer. One would think that doing so much soul-searching and spending so much time with the Lord would be invigorating, but it was not. Which meant he was on the wrong path.

He knew from experience that when he did things God's way, he would have peace and get rest. Because he was fighting this, he would get no rest until he succumbed to God's will, not his own.

That night was the town's Christmas nativity play. The entire town would be in attendance, and that included the Beck family. He had hoped to be able to speak with Chloe earlier in the day when he was in town getting supplies, but the woman ignored him. Brandon couldn't blame her; he had given her mixed signals, and she was doing what she needed to protect her heart.

"Alright, Lord. I'm willing to give this another try, but please don't let me fail my ma. My pa would tan my hide, even at my age, if I did. And I don't want to let her down, either." When tears pricked at the backs of his eyes, he pulled out the handkerchief he kept in his pocket and wiped them.

He told himself it was just allergies.

Later that day, when he and his mother were driving into town for the play, his mom asked him about Chloe. "So, have you figured it all out yet?"

He furrowed his brow. "What do you mean?"

They hadn't spoken again of Chloe since their ride home Tuesday night. Melanie wanted to give him time to come to terms with everything and decide on his own to make the right choice.

"That girl—I know you haven't been able to get her out of your mind all week. What have you decided?" Melanie had seen her son on his knees in prayer several times during the week, and she had prayed that he would hear God's Word and do the right thing.

For Christmas's sake, she wanted grandbabies before her MS progressed too much to enjoy them. And Chloe would make the perfect daughter-in-law. Even Mrs. Claus agreed with her on Tuesday night.

"Sadly, I doubt Chloe will give me the time of day anymore." Not that he'd tried very hard earlier in the day, but he knew she had seen him, and still she avoided his gaze and ignored his wave.

"What did you do?" Melanie practically growled.

He held up one hand and kept the other on the steering wheel. "Ma, I didn't do any. Not really."

"Not really? What does that mean?" She crossed her arms over her chest and gave him the evil eye.

How his mother could make him squirm in his seat just from one look still amazed him. He was a thirty-two-year-old man. This was just plain wrong. "Ma, I already told her that I couldn't date her, that I had to…" He trailed off when he realized what he was about to say. Blaming this on his mother's condition would only make her feel bad. Or, it might get him a slap upside his head. Either option wasn't worth it.

"That you had to take care of your sick ma? Mmhm, I see how it is." Melanie backhanded his shoulder and pulled her hand back. "Ow, you've really bulked out since you were a scrawny teen." She chuckled.

"Ma, what did I do?" He knew he deserved that light tap on his shoulder. He had been treating his mom as though she were an invalid, and it wasn't fair to her. She was much stronger than he gave her credit for.

"You need to remember who takes care of whom around here. If you can't get that through that thick skull of yours, then I'll be heading out to your sister's place after Christmas."

"But Ma, I need you here." And he did. She did a lot of work around the ranch. If she couldn't keep up with her regular duties after Christmas, he would hire help for her. But Brandon knew that no matter how bad his mom felt, she would *never* just lay around doing nothing. And every time his mom went to visit Bayley, she never let Melanie help around the house. She might get to run the kids around after school for practice or other events, but that was all his sister would allow. She was a very hands-on mother and keeper of their house.

Brandon honestly didn't know how mothers took care of so much and then ran their ranch to boot. His dad used to say that he believed *he* ran the ranch, but in actuality he knew that his wife was the one who kept it all moving in unison. A ranch was nothing without the mother and wife keeping everyone going.

Even today, Brandon wasn't sure he believed what his father had told him, but he did know that without his mom, the ranch would never be the same. He didn't want her leaving him.

"What happens if Chloe and I do marry? What role will you take?" Brandon had thought of this before. The wife of the man who ran the ranch was the official queen of the ranch. Then he thought back to history and wondered how the dowager mothers of the old English nobility handled it.

"I'll move into one of the smaller rooms, and you and Chloe will take the master suite, as you should. In the beginning it might be a bit uncomfortable, but she and I will work it all out. I really like her, and am ready for her to come in and take over." Melanie smiled. "Besides, once you start having babies I'll be needed like crazy."

"Oh, Ma! Please, no talking about babies. It's way too soon for that." He shivered, but secretly he hoped they would have a whole passel of kids. He had always wanted more brothers and sisters. And their ranch was big enough to accommodate a large brood.

Melanie laughed. "Just you wait."

Brandon had no words for his mother. He loved her, but sometimes she just was too much to handle. Maybe having a wife around would help? He was getting ahead of himself.

"But *how* do I get her to talk to me again?" he asked.

"Hm, yes. You did do a number on her image here in town. The snowball fight the other night has gone a long way in helping people to rethink things, but what you need is a big gesture."

He wrinkled his nose. "A big gesture? Like lots of flowers?" Brandon did *not* go for those types of things. At this time of year, only flowers from a florist were available. He liked wildflowers, and figured that Chloe was more of a wildflower kind of gal, too.

Melanie shook her head. "No, she's more *An Officer and A Gentleman* kind of gal."

"What? I'm not in the military. How's that going to help me?" *Really,* he thought, *how in the world will I impress Chloe if she prefers military men?*

"No, silly." She shook her head. "Didn't you ever pay attention to the movies I watched while you were growing up?"

"Unless they had horses or explosions, I wasn't the least bit interested." Growing up, they didn't have cable TV. They received a few channels over a tall antenna that his dad had put up on the roof before he was even born, but even still, they mostly watched movies on VHS and then DVD. His mom had a subscription with Blockbuster, and they received movies on a weekly basis until the company went out of business.

But they never spent much time watching anything other than news, or the local Montana station that played older movies and cartoons. Cartoons were his thing until he was twelve. And even then he still snuck in a few Saturday-morning cartoons, after his chores of course.

"Well, a big, grand gesture in front of the town will help."

"But what does *An Officer and A Gentleman* have to do with it?" He scratched his head and thought about the military movies he'd seen. There was one where a pilot sang to women in bars. But no one would want to hear his singing voice. Even the showerhead cringed when he sang there.

"Well, at the end of the movie Richard Gere had to make

up with the woman of his dreams, Debra Winger, and he came into the factory where she worked and picked her up and carried her out in his arms. And of course, there were a few kisses in there." Melanie put a hand to her heart and sighed. "It was one of the most romantic movie scenes ever."

Huh, he could pick up Chloe very easily. But would she appreciate it? Or would she hit him? There was only one way to find out. It would definitely tell the town that she was his, and he was hers.

Brandon thought about it a moment, and then worried that Chloe wouldn't like such a public display of affection. In fact, she would most likely punch him in the gut if he tried something like that. No, he would have to do something that was more up Chloe's alley.

When they made it to the play, he still didn't know what he was going to do. But he followed his mom inside and was surprised to see that they were sitting directly behind Chloe, Lottie, and Cove.

Brandon gave his mother a terse look, but took his seat anyway. *Great,* he thought. Now he would be focused on the beautiful blonde in front of him instead of the kids on stage. He always loved the nativity play, and this year he doubted he would see much of it.

During the play, he kept smelling peppermint and chocolate. Normally that scent wouldn't entice him, but it was mixed with something else and it reminded him of Christmas and spring all wrapped up together in one pretty present. It was Chloe. He knew her favorite drink was a peppermint mocha, so he guessed she was drinking one then, or maybe she had right before the play began.

He kept watching her, waiting to see if she drank anything, but she didn't put anything other than a water bottle up to her lips. How he wanted to pick her up right then and there and carry her out, like the scene in the movie. But he knew he couldn't do that. No, he had to find something else. Something that would be all his.

When his attention was caught by the play, he smiled. An idea was forming, and he hoped it wouldn't come off as lame.

Quinn Keith caught his attention again when she picked up the baby during the manger scene, and then proceeded to drop it. The look on the little girl's eyes was priceless. If he hadn't known better, he would have thought she dropped a real baby. The little girl was mortified and eked out an almost-scream before remembering she had no lines at that point. So, she did what any professional stage actor would do: she leaned down and picked up the baby doll. When her face came back up, she was back in character and moving on with the play.

The entire audience had gasped, and Lottie put a hand to her throat. But when Quinn recovered so quickly, the house all breathed a sigh of relief in unison and everyone relaxed back in their chairs and watched the rest of the story of baby Jesus's birth play out.

When the play ended, the entire audience stood up and applauded. After the kids had taken their third bow, they began to leave the stage. That was Brandon's chance to get his own prop and get to working on winning Chloe back.

Melanie turned to her son to ask him how he liked the performance, but all she saw was his back leaving their row. She watched him walk toward the stage and head into the back of the house.

Lottie turned around. "What's he up to?" She pointed over her shoulder at Brandon.

With a shrug, Melanie responded, "Who knows."

"Why don't you join us for refreshments while we wait for the kids to change their costumes?" Cove asked Melanie.

"Yes, I have to go back and help Quinn, but Cove and Chloe know the best spot for dessert." Lottie winked at Melanie and put a hand on Cove's arm before she turned and left to find her daughter.

"Chloe, was that your first nativity here in Frenchtown?" Melanie asked as she followed the young lady to a spot that featured flaky pastries and creamy hot cocoa.

"Yes, it was. I see why the entire town comes out each year for it. I just loved it. And when Quinn dropped the baby?" Chloe put a hand to her chest and gasped.

"I know, right?" Cove chuckled, then handed her a cup of hot cocoa.

Chloe took a sip. "Mmm, is that peppermint cream on top?"

Chloe looked up in surprise as Cove chuckled.

"Yup, with Christmas less than a week away, everything is going to have peppermint in it now." He pointed to the pastries, and both women licked their lips.

"I really shouldn't," Melanie protested.

Chloe bit her lip. While Melanie might be right, it was also a special occasion. However, since she wasn't a medical professional, she decided not to argue with her. "Well, if you aren't, then I'm going to take your share." She reached down and took two of the peppermint-chunk éclairs that were calling out to her.

"Hold up." Melanie put up a hand. "I never said I wouldn't, just that I shouldn't." She grinned and took one of the pastries off Chloe's plate.

"Ahh, nutcracker! And here I was hoping I'd get an overload of Christmas sugar tonight." Chloe smiled good-naturedly at the woman next to her. She knew she didn't need two of those calorie-busting desserts, but little drummer boy if she didn't want more.

"Ladies, ladies. No need to fight over them. You'll see these in the case for the rest of the week at Lottie's. This is her specialty this week." Cove picked one up and ate almost half of it in one bite. "Mmmm, okay," he said around a mouthful of peppermint cream and flaky pastry, "I think I'll be making several stops at the coffee shop this week."

Mrs. Claus walked up and smiled conspiratorially at Melanie, then looked to Cove. "Aren't you in there every day already?"

He nodded. "Yup, but I might have to make some special afternoon trips for this yummy bad boy." He looked at Mrs. Claus. "Will this put me on Santa's naughty list?"

Everyone laughed.

The room quieted, and Chloe felt the hair on the back of her neck stand on end. She felt as though the entire room was looking at her. Slowly, ever so slowly so as not to attract any more attention, she turned around when she noticed Melanie's wide eyes focused on something behind her.

"What the…figgy pudding?" Chloe exclaimed.

Standing in front of her was Brandon…with a donkey, of all things.

CHAPTER 28

"Brandon, what are you doing?" Chloe took two steps back, away from the flaring nostrils that seemed intent on her plate. Donkeys did not scare Chloe, but no one, not even a cute animal, was going to take her peppermint-chunk éclair. Especially since there were dark chocolate chips still waiting for her taste buds to explore.

"Chloe." He stopped, not knowing what to say. Instead, he moved forward and took her face softly in his work-worn hands. He stared intently into her eyes and slowly leaned down to kiss her, giving her plenty of time to push him back.

When she didn't move, he closed in and lightly touched her lips with his.

A collective sigh could be heard in the room, but Brandon had tuned them out. Instead, he kissed her again, this time with more intent.

Chloe couldn't believe it. Her mind went blank for a moment, and then fireworks went off all around her. She dropped her plate, not caring in the least bit for the tasty treat, and wrapped her arms around Brandon's neck when he kissed her again.

When they finally broke from their kiss, Chloe noticed that her entire plate had been licked clean and the donkey was smiling giant, white teeth. She took a double-take when she noticed some cream on his whiskers. The laugh that bubbled up from her core caught the animal off guard, and he began to bray.

Everyone in the room joined in the laughter, and Brandon leaned down to get the reins. "Well, that didn't go as I planned."

"Oh really? And what was your plan?" Chloe asked.

"Well"—he scratched his head—"I thought I'd kiss you, then you pick up and put you on the donkey, and we would ride into the sunset and be happy forever after."

Chloe put a hand on his cheek and caressed the edge of his smile. "You know, we could still ride off into the sunset."

He grinned, picked her up, and put her on the saddle of the donkey.

Chloe squealed, and the donkey brayed again.

The entire room burst out into applause, and Cove yelled out, "It's about time!"

Brandon looked at his friend. "What about you? Isn't it about time you did something, too?" When he looked at Lottie, her cheeks were flaming red already.

The new couple went outside with Chloe on the back of the donkey and Brandon leading it by the reins. When the door closed and they could no longer hear anyone's laughter or clapping, Chloe looked down at Brandon. "Please tell me you aren't going to dump me again."

With his heart beating a mile a minute, Brandon put everything he had into his eyes when he looked at her. "I'm not running away again. This time I'm running *toward* your heart. And I plan on winning it, and giving you mine."

"But what about your mom and the ranch?" Chloe knew

how important his mother was to him, and she understood it, too. Plus, the ranch. Well, she grew up on a generational ranch herself, so she understood that a family's land was in their blood, in their DNA, and they wouldn't let it go without giving it everything they had.

While she didn't want to play third chair in his western choir, she did understand where he was at that point in his life. God had helped her get to that point, and she wasn't going to let that work go to waste.

He moved them toward the town's stables down at the end of Main Street, where the donkey stayed.

"Chloe, I spoke with my mom. Or rather, she spoke to me." He chuckled. "When God puts a good woman in a man's life, it's his responsibility and honor to accept her love. And dag-gummit"—he pounded his chest with his fist—"I'm going to cowboy up and accept God's gift."

She wasn't sure if she was being wooed or told she was a task on his list. When her brow furrowed, Brandon went on.

"Oh, figgy pudding! I'm explaining this all wrong." He took his Stetson off and swiped it against his leg. "Woman, I care a great deal for you, and want to spend time getting to know you."

Chloe bit her lip. "What happens next time we're out on a date and you get a distressing call from your mom?"

"I'll be sure to talk to you first. Then we can decide if you'll go with me, or stay. But I won't rely on someone to take care of you in my place."

When they were just outside the town's livery stable, Brandon stopped them on the side of the snowy road. "What do you say?"

Chloe got down off the donkey and stood toe to toe with the man who towered over her. "I want to give this a real try this time, but if you pull back from me again, we're through for good. Got it?"

His smile reached his eyes. "Yes, ma'am." When he leaned down to kiss the girl, the donkey brayed, and both of them laughed.

"Alright, alright. I guess it's time for your oats, after your fantastic performance." Chloe took the donkey by the reins and walked into the stables, holding Brandon's hand for the first time in a year.

EPILOGUE

A few days after the Christmas nativity, Chloe went home to spend Christmas with her family for the last time without a husband. By the next fall, they had a beautiful wedding surrounded by both of their families.

And Melanie was there every step of the way, healthy as a horse. It would be many years before she experienced any more difficulties with her MS. The medicine regulated her condition, and her diet helped keep her strong and full of energy.

Only two Christmases after they were married, Brandon and Chloe began their family.

"Push one more time and you've got it," the doctor said to a tired and frazzled new mother.

When the baby was out, the doctor smiled and said to the excited couple, "It's a girl. Do you have a name for her?"

"We do," they said in unison.

"Noelle." Chloe smiled up into her husband's face as he squeezed her hand in return. Although, thankfully not as tightly as she had only moments before. With all thoughts of pain and birthing wiped away, she waited to see her newborn gift from God.

"She's beautiful," Chloe breathed as the nurse put the newborn babe in her arms once she was cleaned and ready to see her parents.

"Just like her momma." Brandon leaned over and kissed Chloe's forehead, and then Noelle's.

"Are you upset it wasn't a boy?" They had known the sex of the baby, but Chloe thought the entire time that Brandon was secretly hoping the test was wrong and they would have a boy.

"Are you kidding? This little beauty has already captured my heart." He lightly touched a finger to her cheeks, and she made a gurgling sound.

"I think she knows who her daddy is already." Chloe looked between her daughter and her husband and knew she was going to love being a momma.

"Six more, right?" Brandon confirmed with a wink.

The nurse laughed, and the doctor chortled. "I think you might want to wait a few weeks, or months, before trying to build your family. Spend some time with little Noelle and enjoy her before bringing her a brother or sister." The doctor patted Brandon on the back good-naturedly.

"Thanks, Doc. I mean it." He put a hand out for the delivery doctor and shook it vigorously. "I think we'll be seeing you again next Christmas."

"Ah." Chloe raised a hand. "Don't I get a say in this, too?"

"Of course you do. It was your idea to have lots of kids, remember?" Brandon knew they both wanted a passel of kids, and he did not want to wait any longer than need be to grow his wonderful family.

The nurse walked up to the little family. "Your mothers are out in the hall and want to know if they can come in."

"Sure, let them in." Chloe arched a brow. "Be on your best behavior." She cuddled the baby closer to her chest before waggling a finger in Brandon's direction. "And no talk of increasing our family. The doctor is right—we need to spend some time bonding with Noelle first."

"Anything you want." Brandon looked to the babe in her mother's arms. "Does that mean I can start bonding with my baby girl now?"

Chloe smiled. "Yes, you can." She held Noelle out for daddy, who took her gently and held her close to his chest.

There next three kids would be boys. All boys who, while they loved and adored their big sister, were *all boys*! Chloe was very happy when another girl finally showed up, and at Christmas, too.

"There's just something special about having a Christmas baby, isn't there?" she asked her husband who still, even after five kids, got teary-eyed and happier than any man deserved to be when he was in the delivery room and held his child for the first time.

"Still game for a full football team of kids?" Brandon gave his wife a cheeky grin and took his newest little girl in his arms to cuddle. She began to cry and make sucking motions with her mouth.

"I think little Christmas Eve Beck is not going to be happy with that lot." Chloe laughed and reached for her newest little babe.

"Hey, Chrissie is going to love playing football." Brandon watched and felt dejected when the baby kept crying. "How about basketball?"

She kept crying.

"Baseball?" Brandon thought surely the favorite American pastime would get his little girl.

But it didn't.

"I think she wants to be a princess." Chloe held out her hands, and the moment she was transferred to her mother's arms she quieted down. With a smirk, she said, "What were you saying about our little Eve?"

Brandon climbed into the bed with his wife and little baby, wrapping them both up in his arms. "I think our little Chrissie can be whoever she wants to be."

Chloe lay there, more than content to fall asleep in her husband's arms. As she began to doze, she thanked God for all her blessings. Even for the disappointments from the beginning of their relationship. Had he not left her, they may not have ended up together with such a wonderful family.

Second chances can sometimes be better than first ones.

Or was it a third chance, in this case?

THE END

RANCH HAND SLOW COOKER BEEF STEW

This is a simple stew designed for the busy ranch hand who doesn't have a lot of time in the morning to prepare meals. And it makes for great leftovers, so be sure to make a giant pot and have plenty of Tupperware to store this stew for lunches and dinners. You can also freeze some if you've made more than you can eat in a week.

I almost always buy my onions already chopped as well as the beef stew meat. Then I buy a small bag of petite peeled carrots and don't both to chop them, they work great as they are, or you can cut them in half.

Ingredients:

2.5 lbs chopped stew beef (more for a heartier stew)*

32 oz beef broth*

5 – 6 Russet Potatoes chopped into small bite-sized cubes (clean potatoes and keep skins on for more nutrients)

2 - 14 oz cans of sweet corn (water included)

1.5 cups petite peeled carrots

½ cup chopped onions

¼ c flour (I prefer almond flour)

2T pink Himalayan seasalt

3T Lawry's pepper seasoned salt (or a black pepper)

2T garlic powder

2 bay leaves (whole)

1 oz Hidden Valley Ranch Seasoning

*Vegetarian option would be to substitute beans for beef. 3-4 cans of your favorite beans. And use a vegetable broth instead of beef broth.

Instructions:

Use a 5qt slow cooker, or larger

Put the stew meat into the bottom of the slow cooker and pour the flour over the meat. Mix until the meat is covered with the flour.

Then just dump the rest of the ingredients into the pot (minus the bay leaves). Be sure to use the water included in the can of corn. The liquid should be to about the top of all of the ingredients. If the ingredients go too far above the liquid line, then include a little bit more beef broth. Don't completely cover the stew with liquid, just get it to about the same line.

Add the two bay leaves on top of the stew.

Cook on low for about 8 – 9 hours (or 4-5 hours on high), stirring occasionally if you're home. Check that the potatoes are the right tenderness. Remove the bay leaves. Then serve hot with either crackers, or your favorite rolls and enjoy!

Brandon would make this while he was working and then come back to his little house, or trailer, and sit in front of the TV watching a rodeo, or a western. And he would make up cornbread from a box. For him, this was a perfect meal that was easy to store and reheat whenever he needed a hot meal. In fact, he would chop the potatoes the night before and store them in his fridge so all he had to do was dump everything into the crock pot in the morning before he left for working on the ranch, or during a rodeo.

AUTHOR'S NOTES

Thank you so much for reading my newest Christmas series! This year has been really tough for everyone, and authors all across the globe have had a tough time finishing their work in a timely manner. I was no exception. I struggled with this book and trying to make it light-hearted and something that would take readers' minds off what's going on this year. My editor, Shavonne, worked with me to help me get back on track with the story. But the ones who really helped me to finish on time, were my Scotland Sprint Sisters! A special thank you to Amie and Audrey for allowing me to join them in sprinting. And I don't mean running (*shudders at the thought of running*). Writing sprints are what helped me to finish this book in a timely manner, and also get the second one done.

At the end of September, I was chatting with Amie and she told me how she was sprinting with Audrey and they were really getting a lot of words in. I asked if I could join them and of course they said yes. The three of us met in Scotland at a writer's conference back in 2019. We've stayed in touch since then, and I'm going to be forever grateful to them. I now can't imagine a workday without our sprint sessions. It isn't always the three of us. Sometimes it's just two of us working together, but no matter how many of us show up, we always get so much more done than if we were going it alone.

So, a huge thank you to Amie and Audrey! I look forward to killing our word count in 2021! Pun totally intended. Which is a little hint of what's to come for me next year. First, I will be finishing up the Triple J Ranch series. I have 3 more books to write. Then I'll be doing something a bit different for me. I don't want to say anything just in case it doesn't work out, but keep an eye out for more information about my next series, after I finish up Triple J.

And for those who haven't heard about the Triple J Ranch series, it's all about the Manning family. Chloe has a twin sister, Elizabeth, who stars in Second Chance Ranch. Then her 5 brothers take over for the rest of the books in the series.

And if you want more Christmas, then be sure to read Her Christmas Rodeo Cowboy! Keep reading for a sneak peek of the second book in the Big Sky Christmas Series.

For those of you who love social media, here are the various ways to follow or contact me:

BookBub: https://www.bookbub.com/authors/jenna-hendricks

Instagram: https://www.instagram.com/j.l.hendricks/

Twitter: https://twitter.com/TinkFan25

Facebook: https://www.facebook.com/people/JL-Hendricks/100011419945971

Website: https://jennahendricks.com

After Lottie's husband died riding a bull on national television, she swore she'd never be with a rodeo star again.

Now, seven years later, her promise is going to come back and bite her in the figgy pudding. If only her daughter, Quinn, didn't love a certain cowboy so much.

Cove promised his best friend he would look after his wife and daughter after he died, but he didn't think that Sam meant for Cove to fall in love with Lottie.

When 8-year-old Quinn asks Santa for a Daddy, no one is ready for what comes next.

Can a rodeo star help the widow of a bull rider love again?

Don't miss out on the second Christmas story of the heart-warming Christmas Cowboy romance series, Big Sky Christmas. Where the romance is clean, and Christmas takes center stage!

E ven after all these years, Cove Hamilton never forgot Lottie Summers. Well, now she went by Lottie Keith.

Before Cove could get up the nerve to ask out the prettiest girl in junior high, his best friend, Sam Keith, did. When she said yes, it broke Cove's heart.

His heart broke again when his best friend and rodeo buddy died during a show. He was gored by the bull he was riding and left behind his wife and baby girl.

With Sam's dying breath he said, "Take care of them. I know you've loved Lottie our whole lives." He coughed up blood.

"No, Sam. You're going to make it." Not caring that tears ran down his cheeks, Cove held his best friend's hand and prayed that God wouldn't take him.

"It's alright, you're what they need, now." Sam didn't say anything else. He left this plane of existence on the way to the hospital and Lottie never got to say goodbye to the man she'd loved since she was only thirteen years old.

Cove stood outside of the Frenchtown Roasting Company and wiped the lone tear from his cheek. He hadn't thought about Sam's final words in many years. His best friend died seven years ago, but it still hurt to think about that final day.

He had kept his promise to Sam and whenever he was in town he checked in on Lottie and Quinn, Sam's little girl. Only she wasn't so little anymore. She had turned eight a couple of months back and he sent her several gifts and a long letter apologizing for not being there on her special day. It was the first one he had missed. He hated doing it, but he thought he had to compete and win that rodeo.

While Cove also rode bulls, he hadn't had the level of success Sam did, until his best friend was gone. Part of him felt guilty for taking his buddy's place in the rodeo line-up, his sponsors, and even the love of his daughter. But he knew that Sam would have wanted it that way. They'd had several conversations about what to do if one of them died. Bull riding was one of the most dangerous sports out there, and they both knew what they had signed up for.

Over the years, Cove had won many belt buckles and saddles, and even two finals in Vegas. Every time he won, he wished Sam was there with him to celebrate. When he came home for visits, Quinn was always the one who wanted to see the buckles or saddles, and celebrated with him. Lottie...she wanted nothing to do with rodeo cowboys.

Now, Cove wished he would have come home for Quinn's birthday. It didn't matter that he had won that rodeo. His season was now over. He hadn't won another one after that and continued to drop in the rankings until he was cut from the finals.

Looking in the window of Frenchtown Roasting Company, his heart soared when he saw Quinn sitting in the back with the new girl in town. Cove hadn't seen Lottie yet, but he knew she was in there. She was never far from her little girl.

A huge smile spread across his face when he watched Lottie walk in from the back and smile at a customer.

He was home.

* * *

WHEN HE FINALLY GOT UP THE nerve to walk inside, he was assailed by the sights, sounds, and scents of Christmas. Cove knew how much Lottie loved Christmas. She had always gone overboard, even when they were kids. In fact, Lottie wore ugly Christmas sweaters before they became a thing. She just thought they were cute and whimsical, or something like that. He was pretty sure that was what caught Sam's attention in the eighth grade.

That Christmas was when Sam had started telling Cove what a pretty girl Lottie was, instead of complaining that she always interrupted their time fishing. Or wanted to get a game of boys versus girls together for softball instead of letting the boys play baseball. Sam had always thought, up until that year, that girls should be cheerleaders, not players. But after that Christmas, Sam was usually the first to join her softball games.

When his senses went into Christmas overdrive, he felt a thud against his legs and looked down to find Quinn hugging him. "Princess Quinnie. I've missed you."

"I've missed you, Uncle Cove." She hugged him harder.

He wasn't exactly her uncle. Since he wasn't related to Sam, he wasn't related to Quinn. But, he had been there when she was born and for almost all of her major milestones in life. And he loved it when she called him *Uncle*.

"What did you bring me this time?" The little girl pulled back and smiled adoringly up into the face of the cowboy whom she had wrapped around her little finger.

Cove smiled at Quinn. "What makes you think I brought you anything?" He raised a brow.

With a dramatic eye roll and tossing of her arms, Quinn responded, "Because you alllllways bring me gifts." Then she narrowed her eyes and put her little hands on her tiny hips. "Now, you didn't forget, did you Uncle Cove?"

Lottie stifled a laugh.

Cove chuckled. "Precocious little queenie, aren't you?" He patted Quinn's cheek.

The little princess backed up. "I'm not preco..co..toos." She tossed her blonde locks behind her back. "I'm pretty."

With a smile the size of Montana, Cove said, "Of course you are."

Quinn clapped her hands and beamed. "So?"

"Oh, you want a present, don't you?" Cove looked stern and put a hand on his heart. "I'm sorry, but I think the only presents I brought you aren't ready for you to open yet."

The little girl frowned. "What's that mean?"

"It means," Lottie pointed a finger at her daughter, "That you shouldn't be asking anyone for gifts, even Uncle Cove. It's not a *gift* when you demand it."

Quinn's little bottom lip protruded, and she blinked rapidly.

"Oh, be still my beating heart." Cove looked to Lottie. "Your little girl is going to have every male, no matter their age, from here to Timbucktoo wrapped around her little finger within the next year, two years tops."

Lottie sighed. "I know." She shook her head and smiled proudly. "I don't know what I'm going to do once she turns sixteen."

"Sixteen? I think you're gonna need to carry around a shotgun when she turns twelve. Those little boys aren't gonna know what hit 'em the second they *notice* her."

"Now don't go borrowing trouble. She's just barely eight years old. I have a long time to go before we need to worry about boys." Lottie pursed her lips and clucked her tongue.

Cove put his hands in the air. "Hey, now. I just think you might want to start thinking about getting yourself a man soon. Someone who will love Quinn like a daughter and help shoo away those pesky boys. That's all."

"Now I know you've gone crazy. Did a bull dump you on your head, Cove Hamilton? How many times do I gotta tell you, I'm not ever marrying again." Lottie turned around and headed to the back room grumbling to herself about not needing a man, nor wanting one.

"What did I say?" Cove turned confused eyes to Quinn and shrugged his shoulders.

"I think Momma needs a man." Quinn sounded way to grown up for Cove's heart and he gulped.

"We might want to keep that between us," Cove whispered.

"Oh, I don't know. I think that might be a request for Santa to help fill." The jolly ol' man whom the entire town referred to as Santa Claus during the Christmas season smiled at Quinn and shook hands with Cove. "Cove, it's good to have you home again. How long are you here for?"

Santa's wife, affectionately known as Mrs. Claus, but who is really Jessica Lampton, smiled and leaned down to hug Quinn. "Have you asked Santa for a husband for your Mommy?"

The little girl's eyes widened and she squealed. "Not yet." She turned to Christopher Lampton, AKA Santa Claus and asked, "Santa, when can I tell you what I want for Christmas? I already know." She clapped her hands and bounced on the balls of her feet.

"Ho, ho, ho. I think now is as good a time as any. Why don't you come join me at a table and sit on my lap?" Santa led little Quinn over to a clean table and sat down in a chair.

He put her on his lap and she leaned in to whisper in his ear. "I want a daddy and a baby brother for Christmas."

Not surprised by the first item, but shocked by the second, Santa leaned back in his chair and thought for a moment. "Do you know long it takes to make a baby?"

With wide eyes, Quinn nodded. "Mm hm. Mrs. Anderson at school had a baby boy last year and she said it took nine months to cook it up in her oven."

Santa chuckled. "Yes, but she also has a husband, doesn't she? Do you think that a Mommy should have the Daddy before she *cooks* up a baby?"

Again, the girl nodded enthusiastically. "Of course. It's better if there is a daddy. Can I get a daddy this Christmas? Then next Christmas a baby brother?"

Santa looked to Cove and then down to Quinn. "Do you have someone in mind to be your new Daddy?"

Little hands went up to cover the cute lilting sounds of Quinn's laugh. "I do."

"I see. And do you think he wants to be your Daddy?" Santa thought he might, but before he meddled in the affairs of another man's heart, he needed to make sure, first.

Her enthusiastic nod had Santa laughing heartily. "I'll see what I can do. I might need the help of Mrs. Claus on this one."

"I can help, too, Santa." Her earnest eyes melted his heart and he hugged little Quinn.

"I bet you can."

DON'T MISS out on Cove and Lottie's story! Will Quinn get her Christmas wish?

Her Christmas Rodeo Cowboy

CPSIA information can be obtained
at www.ICGtesting.com
Printed in the USA
LVHW111452300622
722464LV00001B/38

9 781952 634086